The
Measured
Man

Also by Howard Owen:

Littlejohn
Fat Lightning
Answers to Lucky

The Measured Man

a novel

HOWARD OWEN

HarperCollins*Publishers*

HarperCollins books may be purchased for educational, business, or sales promotional use. For information please write: Special Markets Department, HarperCollins Publishers, Inc., 10 East 53rd Street, New York, NY 10022.

FIRST EDITION

Designed by Ruth Lee

ISBN 0-06-018654-2

97 98 99 00 01 ❖/RRD 10 9 8 7 6 5 4 3 2

To Karen,
who makes it all possible
and worthwhile

I refuse to accept the idea that the "isness" of man's present nature makes him morally incapable of reaching up for the "oughtness" that forever confronts him.

— Dr. Martin Luther King, Jr.

It is dawn.

Imagine you can rise like the sun and be suspended above the blanket of smoke. Looking west across still-smoldering Cottondale onto the ridge that forms the west bank of the Rich River, you might first conclude that life on River Road is unchanged.

Eventually, you see the naked man.

He is lying two-thirds of the way up a large, newly cut lawn, face down before one of the largest houses along the skyline. His right arm is reaching upward, and his legs are bent, the left higher than the right. He looks as if he has been climbing. Or swimming.

He is not far above the smoky cloud. The sun's first rays make his body look as white as marble. But for his twisted shape, he might be a fallen statue from some rich man's garden.

And then, graced with the ears of God, you hear, far below, a voice thundering through the smoke, carrying across the river and awakening people on the hill, frightening them, bringing them cautiously onto their back porches to stare uncomprehending down into the acrid cloud.

Finally, some of them can make out the words, booming, demanding over and over: "Give me your son! Give me your son!"

They shiver in the morning breeze, go back inside, and deadbolt their doors.

1

THE FOURTH PITCH LANDS WITH A DULL THUD ON HOME PLATE, SAME AS THE FIRST THREE. THE UMPIRE MOTIONS THE BATTER TO first base, starting a chain reaction that ends with a beer-bellied left fielder trotting in from third base and stomping home plate to signify the winning run.

Walker Fann stands transfixed for a moment, frozen in the expectant pose slow-pitch softball pitchers assume while waiting to see where the high-arcing ball will come down, his toes lifted slightly as if to boost the pitch into the elusive strike zone. Then he turns and marches purpose-fully toward the visiting team's bench, a distant curse ring-ing out behind him from the general direction and distance of center field. As he crosses the foul line, he flings his glove as far as he can, then stomps over to the chain-link fence, which he kicks vigorously enough to leave it bowed out semipermanently, a reminder for the rest of the playoffs of the night Walker Fann lost his temper and his glove. He takes the equipment bag and hurls it, scattering bats all over the infield, keeping one of the wooden ones, which he beats into splinters against a metal support post.

People who have known Walker since he was a boy look on in rapt wonder. Others nod their heads as if this is just what they knew would happen eventually.

Bobby Hill, Sycamore Baptist's captain, pats him on the back nervously, tells him to take it easy. Glen Murphy, the first baseman and his friend since elementary school, comes over.

"Easy, J.W.," he murmurs, reviving the shorthand nickname hardly anyone uses or even remembers anymore, a remnant of the year Walker and Joe Willie Namath both quarterbacked their teams as far as they could go, albeit at different levels. "It ain't nothing but softball."

Using the old name seems to help. As quickly as the tirade started, it's over. Walker, leaning into the fence as if he wishes to push it over, looks up at his friend, grimaces, and shakes his head.

"Did I really say 'shit' right in front of Reverend Graham?" he softly asks.

"About ten times." Glen nods, grinning. Then he leans closer, so only Walker can hear him. "You ought to broaden your vocabulary. My kid can cuss better than that.

"You ought to do that more often," he adds, winking as he walks away.

Walker Fann sits down on the old wooden bench for a moment. Two more teammates mumble something as they walk past. It's the last game of the night, so Walker can take his time.

Slow-pitch softball is a simple game, a child's game, something that precedes and follows baseball. And pitching is the easiest thing of all. All you have to do, Walker reflects, is just get the damn ball over the damn plate.

Before the seventh inning tonight, Walker hadn't given up a base on balls for five games. Then, for no apparent reason, he lost it. He walked the first batter on five pitches, the ball feeling as slippery as glass. One pitch he lost control of completely; it landed a good six feet in front of the batter as a child laughed somewhere near the concession stand.

He knelt and rubbed some of the dry dirt around the pitcher's mound on the ball, but it didn't help. He walked the next batter, then lost the one after that when he overthrew the third baseman after fielding an easy grounder.

He tried to tell himself it was just slow-pitch, that a former three-sport starter for St. Andrews High, a former all-conference quarterback and second baseman, was better than this, even at forty-two. He tried thinking of real darkness, just for the perspective.

But nothing worked, and Sycamore Baptist was eliminated from the St. Andrews Division I playoffs, in the second round, three days past Labor Day.

"If I coulda just had one more at-bat . . ." he hears the kid center fielder, Oakley, say, then stop when he sees Walker there.

A parks department employee turns out the mercury-vapor lights, and in the near-darkness Walker believes he can feel the first breath of fall moving the damp night air.

He shakes his head and turns to leave, alone. He's glad Big Walker and the kids didn't see this.

Then he remembers the glove.

It's a first baseman's mitt, left-handed of course, and Walker's had it since he was fifteen. It's as brown as pine bark and sometimes comes untied at the pocket, but Walker knows every centimeter of it, knows exactly how far to stretch his hand to stop a line drive, precisely the movement that will snag a hot grounder the instant it comes up from the hard clay infield with the solid leather pop of fulfillment. There is no stiffness to it; he's packed it away every fall since the Johnson administration, rubbed it with linseed oil, held it up to his children as an example of Responsibility until they almost despise the sight of it. He admits to himself that what once was unquestioned love has turned into something between tradition and chore. Even as he tells himself that he's through with young men's games, though, he feels a pang at the thought of losing a worthless piece of dishrag-malleable leather.

He remembers seeing it barely clear the fence behind the visiting team's bench. As he walks out to retrieve it in the night, guided by the nearest parking-lot street light, just as he glimpses it in the tall grass the city seldom cuts, a shadow crosses his line of sight. The bicycle and its occupant are already past him, the old glove scooped up at full speed, before Walker can even blink.

He yells at the receding figure as it speeds toward the river. Already, he knows how hopeless his protest is, that by the time the boy realizes the glove's worthlessness to anyone but Walker Fann he'll be six blocks away.

And then, while Walker stands alone, hands by his side, defeated, justice arrives unexpectedly. Suddenly, a blinding blue light illuminates the lot, and a city police car, parked a hundred yards away, moves quickly in the direction of the bicyclist, who is staggered for a second and now moves in a weaving pattern, as if to make himself a more difficult target.

Walker can see the car turn right down Lee Street and assumes that the thief is too rattled to cut through somebody's yard. He can see the blue light come to a halt just across First Street, where Lee turns to dirt and dead-ends on the bank of the Rich River. He hears yelling and runs toward it.

When he gets to the car, there are already several people outside on the street, and Patrolman J. D. West is just getting a foothold at the top of the bank that drops six feet down to the river. He is half-dragging, half-helping a boy of perhaps thirteen years. On the street next to the car is a red Schwinn bicycle, thrown down in haste as the boy apparently tried to escape into the darkness by the water.

The boy struggles to get away, and someone in the crowd calls out, "Whatsa matter, officer? You all ain't got enough murders to solve? Got to find something you can catch?"

The general laughter is hard-edged. Patrolman West is white; the boy is black, as is the crowd.

"Let's get in the car," he tells both the boy and Walker. He puts the boy in the backseat, locked in behind a mesh screen. He and Walker get in the front, he locks the doors, and they speed away. "No sense in asking for trouble," he says to Walker.

They go four blocks back toward the center of town along First Street, paralleling the river. The patrolman pulls into a parking lot at the edge of Neely Industries.

The old mill buildings are only half full these days even during peak hours. Now, with the only other visible cars belonging to night watchmen, they appear to Walker as an ominous monolith with scant, barred windows, surrounded by razor wire, casting its shadow at them in the full moonlight. When Walker was young and the mill was still in its prime, it was a scary place to him, always either swallowing or disgorging throngs of tough, rude, dangerous-seeming men and women, mostly black. Big Walker wanted to send his son to work in the mill the summer he was sixteen "to see how the other half lives," but Dottie wouldn't allow it.

Patrolman West sits with the engine idling. He turns to look at the backseat.

"Now, then, Superfly," he says to the boy, "want to tell me what of this gentleman's you were hauling ass with?"

Walker looks back, too. The boy looks too thin beneath his floppy, too-large pants and shirt. He has a smooth brown face, heavy-lidded eyes, ears that lie flat against his head and his tightly cropped hair. Below the level of conscious thought, Walker recognizes something. The boy's lip is poked out, and he won't look at either of them. He doesn't look as if he's going to cry, or beg. Something about him, maybe it's the too-bushy eyebrows or the cynical twist of his mouth, makes him appear to be more a rather short, thin man than a child.

"He's got my glove," Walker tells the patrolman, then realizes that, unless the boy has been able to stuff it in some unseen orifice, he doesn't actually have the glove at all, at least not now.

"Is that what I heard splash?" Patrolman West asks the boy. The boy doesn't answer, but Walker's fairly certain that his prized ancient glove, talisman of happier, or more gullible, days, is either somewhere in the depths of the Rich River or floating rapidly toward the sound and the ocean in the fast-running current.

"Why did you throw the glove away?" Walker asks the boy. "Did you think I was going to have 'em throw your butt in jail for taking a glove?"

The boy just sits there. He's crossed his arms and has assumed a pose of indifference, his eyes looking out the left side window.

"He took it because it was there," the patrolman says, exasperated at spending so much time on so little. He would like to catch a murderer, he thinks to himself, but the last time somebody took a dirt nap on that block he just came from, some crack dealer who was out of his neighborhood, nobody saw anything. It was three in the afternoon on a Saturday in June, people all over the place outside, and nobody saw a damn thing.

"They'd steal the trees if they could figure out a way to dig 'em up."

The boy blinks and faces forward again. He mumbles something that neither Walker nor the patrolman can understand.

"Say what?" Patrolman West asks.

"I said," the boy replies, "it weren't nothin' but some old raggedy-ass baseball glove. I wouldn't of give you a dollar for it."

Walker shakes his head. He wonders how people can just trash other people's stuff, not even care. Who raises these kids?

He is silent for a few seconds.

"I tell you what," he says to the policeman. "What can I press charges for? That glove isn't much, but I don't like this little SOB's attitude."

Damn, Patrolman West thinks to himself, paperwork.

"Well," he says finally, "we can charge him with theft, of course. Might want to wait till in the morning, though. I'm not sure anybody would come get him tonight."

Screw him, Walker's thinking.

"I want to press charges right damn now," says Walker. "Let him spend the night in jail. That's the least he can do for stealing something I've had since I was his age."

The boy mumbles something again.

"What?" Walker says. "Speak up, boy."

The eyes flash right at him, not afraid of anything, surely not him, Walker understands.

"I said," the boy repeats, emphasizing the second word as if he's talking to someone who's hard of hearing, "it looks like you had it since your granddaddy was my age. And I ain't no boy." He points a finger at Walker, who wonders how long it will be before he has some more effective way of getting white folks' attention.

"That's it." Walker turns toward the patrolman. "I'll be pressing charges tonight. Now. First this little bastard steals from me, and now he acts like he's put out that he's got to answer for it."

Patrolman West sighs and slowly backs up and turns around.

Walker's part of the paperwork down at the station doesn't take more than forty-five minutes. Rather than go home, he calls from the station and tells Dottie not to worry, that he'll be there in a while. Then he drives back south along the river.

He turns onto the dirt street and stops where the red bicycle was. It isn't there. Probably stolen, Walker thinks. Serves him right.

He brings the emergency flashlight, scrambles down the bank, and sinks to his ankles in the mud.

The Rich River, fueled by rain in the foothills, is moving fast. Walker realizes that, despite the fact that he's probably three miles' drive from home, he can see Big Walker's home atop the hill across the river, not much farther away than the length of a football field. He can see the floodlight, even the curtains in Ginger's room.

The glove, of course, is nowhere to be seen. Walker had hoped it might have somehow fallen short of the water.

He scans the river's surface, seeing nothing but the endless surge of it.

Standing there, suddenly chilly, somehow soaked halfway to his knees, he thinks about how relentless, how merciless water is.

Back at the car, he fights the urge to just sleep right there, sitting up in the driver's seat. He is very tired.

2

THERE IS A CERTAIN ASYMMETRY TO BIG WALKER AND DOTTIE'S TABLE.

They sit at each end. She's nearest the stove and refrigerator to provide seconds and refills; he's closest to the small kitchen television.

Mac and Ginger sit on the side next to the china cabinet. He, right-handed, is on the right, she, left-handed, on the left, but they still bump and gibe each other.

Walker has the other side of the table to himself, plenty of elbow room. The fifth wheel.

The kids are usually looking past him, at their grandfather's TV, and he sometimes has to raise his voice to get their attention. Walker would rather his father kept the idiot box out of their main eating area; he feels that everyone would talk to each other more if they had to. But Big Walker wouldn't hear of it, he knows.

They seldom eat in the spacious dining room next door, with its drop-leaf table that can seat fourteen. Walker wonders how many meals he's eaten here since Big Walker moved them here in 1957.

This morning, Walker arrives last, and the sudden hush, broken only by the background noise from the TV, tells him that, as usual in St. Andrews, his actions have not gone unnoticed.

"Whoah, Dad," Mac says, finally. "I hear you really lost it last night."

Walker looks at his son. Mac will probably be handsome someday. Walker had acne, too, had it worse than his son does, and he can remember being fourteen and awkward as a colt. Mac has Walker's dark brown hair and greenish eyes, has the strong chin and good cheekbones that you can see in family photographs all the way back to old Hector McNeill Fann, who started the *Standard* in 1885. When he learns how to smile and not smirk, Walker thinks, he'll be O.K., but he wishes it would happen soon.

"Scott Hill called last night. His dad said you busted up all the bats, you were so mad," the boy continues.

"Now, Mac," Dottie says, "leave your father alone." She rises to get more orange juice out of the refrigerator. "You got enough eggs there, honey?"

Both the children break into snickering.

"You hush that," Dottie says. "He's my boy, and I'll call him 'honey' if I like."

Walker realizes that he is blushing, and he wishes his children would hurry and mature. The last year hasn't been easy on them, of course, but he sometimes finds himself admitting you can love someone and not always like them very much.

Even Ginger, sweet little Ginger, has been no prize in a box of Cracker Jacks, as Big Walker would say. At twelve, she seems to have gained twenty pounds in the last year. The beautiful red hair and green eyes, the cherubic face, are counterbalanced by a pudginess that he's never seen in his family before this generation, and with every pound she seems to become more sullen. But it isn't all her fault, he knows; hell, if he'd had an unlimited supply of Dottie's pork-and-potato cuisine, plus all the snacks he wanted, he'd probably have been overweight, too. They were stricter—much stricter—with him when he was his children's age.

What keeps Dottie and Big Walker fairly thin is all the work they do.

Dottie cleans and cans and gardens the same way she did when Walker was a boy. He believes she'd die without what she calls her chores.

And Big Walker: he works out an hour a day, still puts in a full eight hours most days at the *Standard*, even when Walker wishes he wouldn't.

Walker himself has always taken pride in his physical fitness, still finishes the 10K race the paper sponsors every year, although even he has gained five pounds since the last one.

What he can't understand is how little exercise means to his children. Mac plays soccer and plays at basketball, but neither he nor his friends ever seem to work up much of a sweat. Walker wonders if the coaches are riding them hard enough. Hell, he thinks, they probably can't. The little buggers'd quit on 'em if they did the stuff that Coach Kell used to do to us. It seems to carry over to schoolwork, too: do just enough to get by.

Walker knows he can't blame it all on teachers and coaches and grandparents, though. Mac and Ginger have been spoiled, the last year, by him as well as the rest. But what can you do?

Walker sees it everywhere, now, not just in his family. He'll run into some friend at the lake or the beach, some friend who was lean and mean, just like him, thirty years ago, and the friend's kids will be little chunkers, snacking away on a slice of pizza or some french fries, fatter than his or her momma and daddy dared to get before they were in their thirties.

Walker, late because he wanted to put in another fifteen minutes on the Stairmaster, yearns to tell both his children to shape up, literally and figuratively, but he knows from experience to let it ride.

"Don't worry about what I do," Walker says to Mac, taking a sip of his orange juice and fixing him with what he hopes is a flinty stare. "If you'd have done what I did last night, you might have lost your temper, too." Walker shakes his head.

"Walker the walker," Ginger says, looking up from a large plate of Dottie's fried apples, and he knows that the family has been completely filled in on how he lost the game.

"Yeah," he turns and stares at his daughter until she looks away, "Walker the walker. Can't do it anymore in the clutch. That's it for me, though. This is my last year of softball."

"To be sure not," Big Walker says. "Why, you're still a young man," which breaks Mac and Ginger up again.

"I should've quit before now. If you're too old to do anything but pitch, you ought to quit anyhow."

Big Walker makes a snorting sound but is soon distracted by an interview on *The Today Show*. He shushes everyone as a well-fed politician looks into the camera and talks earnestly about "winning back our streets."

"Amen to that," Big Walker says after a few seconds of enforced silence. "That man knows what he's talking about."

"Maybe we ought to do another editorial about it," Walker mutters.

The St. Andrews Standard, which serves three counties, is passably unbiased in its newsroom, although the people who write letters to the editor constantly accuse the paper of being liberal if not downright Communist. Its editorial pages, though, produced one floor up, are relentlessly right-wing. Walker can think of three articles in the last week that have bashed the standing Democratic president and called for Republican change.

Big Walker's editorial writers, a self-satisfied group far above the rabble of the newsroom, have more or less fallen in love with the concept of white male anger, an anger that Walker himself finds puzzling. He is irritated when he encounters it at the country club or in board meetings.

"If you don't hang on to what's yours with both hands," Big Walker admonished him once when he expressed his distaste for a peer of his father's who was irate over having to pay taxes at all, "somebody will take the whole thing away from you. Show 'em you're weak, and you're done for. You can't have half of it and give the other half away. Give 'em half and they'll take the rest."

The "they" of Big Walker's cigar-after-dinner ruminations with his old cohorts were amorphous, but it was safe to assume that "they" were most of the rest of the world outside the Sycamore Country Club. The club was where Big Walker usually tested the waters of public opinion.

Big Walker, who is chairman of the board, usually lets Walker run the newsroom. Big Walker, though, gets his way on the next floor up. Walker himself sometimes writes editorials. Early in his tenure, shortly after his father had made him publisher at thirty-five, Walker got into trouble for suggesting editorially that government was sometimes needed to "make us do right." Big Walker told him in no uncertain terms, as soon as he read it, that *The St. Andrews Standard* was not in the business of approving of "big government." When Walker argued with him, his father silenced him by holding up his big right hand like a traffic cop.

"Son," he said, "you're the fourth generation of Fanns that's run this paper. Someday, it'll all be yours to do with whatever the hell you like. But until they plant me, I'm going to run this paper the way my daddy and granddaddy did. I hope you'll have the decency not to change it after I'm gone, but you don't have any choice while I'm still breathing."

From then on, Walker contributed only the occasional editorial that he could stomach, leaving what he considered to be the more mean-spirited ones for Ry Tucker, who'd been drinking with and writing editorials for Big Walker since the late 1950s. In the seven years Walker has been publisher, though, he has come to see, more and more, the wisdom of looking out for those who, in turn, look out for him.

"Those bastards at *The New York Times* or *The Washington Post*, or even *The Charlotte Observer*, they can play Mr. High-and-Mighty Big Shot and spit on the folks that made 'em what they are," Big Walker told his son two years ago, over bourbon at the club. "Most of us, though, we have to look out for each other."

Walker, who saw Rich Valley Mall and Neely Industries continue to advertise heavily in the *Standard* when they could have taken all their money to the bigger state papers or TV, wearily agreed, something he has found himself doing more and more of as the years go by.

Walker has spent almost all his life on the hill. They moved from a two-story Victorian two blocks from the Old Market the year before he started school. The seven years Big Walker and Dottie lived in Cottondale were also the only ones Big Walker had lived out of sight of the Sycamore Country Club golf course. His father, the first Walker McNeill Fann, had wanted the newlyweds to experience at least a little bit of "suffering" before he got them a sweet deal on the Tudor they still occupy, with its view of the river—whose brown water Walker can see through the trees, one hundred feet below—and Cottondale. Big Walker still owns the old Victorian, now a dubious rental property.

Walker never thought he suffered living in the bottom. He remembers playing games all day with the sons and daughters of millhands, along with a few other country-club children whose parents were also playing at pulling themselves up by their bootstraps.

One day after they'd moved, though, when Walker was seven, he went downtown with Big Walker, and they went a block out of the way to see the old place. As they approached it, Walker saw a couple of his old playmates. He begged his father to stop, but Big Walker refused.

"That's all behind you now," he told his young son. "You've got plenty of friends up there on the hill." Walker's little friends had seen him and were waving, but they stopped waving when the car speeded up. Walker saw them for the last time as friends out the back window; they'd forgotten him and were back playing again before the car was out of sight.

The last time Walker saw the old house, just before the last tenants abruptly left, the wood was peeling badly and there were two half-naked black children playing on and around a tire swing in the side yard. It looked like the same tire swing Big Walker had put up for him, the one he wouldn't let him take with them when they moved.

"You used to live here?" Ginger asked, looking at the little boy staring straight at her and picking his nose a few feet away. "Gross." But she made him drive by there several more times, and she seemed, until the last silent year, to see this different, adjacent world as something bordering on the exotic.

*   *   *

It's almost eight o'clock, time for Mac and Ginger to leave for school, when the doorbell rings.

When Walker opens the front door, expecting one of his children's friends, he is face to face instead with a black man, about his height, some pounds lighter. The man is wearing glasses, a New York Yankees baseball cap, a light-blue shirt with vertical stripes, and gray Levi's. Even though he appears so angry that he can hardly keep his feet on the ground, he seems somehow beaten down. At first Walker thought he was several years older, but now he isn't sure.

It takes him a few seconds to make the connection. By the time he does, Raymond Justus has already spit out a couple of sentences.

"How the shit can you put a thirteen-year-old boy in jail? What kind of a man would have my son arrested over a got-damn baseball glove?"

"R.J.?"

While the visitor continues to hector him from the threshold of Big Walker's front door, Walker tries to remember the last time he saw his old receiver. Surely not more than twice in the last five years, and then just once to talk, an awkward moment at a men's store in the mall, R.J. not saying much. That damn troublemaking Dexter Cates, Rasheed Aziz, whatever, was with him, trying to get Walker's goat with his mean, teasing "Mistuh Fann, suh," like they hadn't all been Saints together, all on the same team, like Rasheed was a field hand now instead of a lawyer.

He's heard through the years about R.J. going up North, after all that trouble, then coming back down to Cottondale again, with a wife and family, something about the wife leaving him. But it was always second- or third-hand. None of the forty or so African-American students in St. Andrews

High's graduating class of 1970 came back for the twentieth reunion. Thinking back to their high school days, Walker doesn't blame them.

But here's Raymond Justus, right in his face, and Walker knows what that little nagging reminder tugging at the corner of his brain was last night, trying to tell him something while the boy in the patrol car's backseat gave the two white men up front his best five-hundred-yard stare. He should have picked up on it at the station when the boy gave his name, Carneal Justus. But he wasn't paying attention, and there are many Justuses in Cottondale.

What the boy's stoicism had almost brought back to Walker's consciousness then, and did bring back now, was R.J., taking a mean-spirited tongue-lashing from a junior varsity coach for some small misstep that would barely have earned a white player a sharp word. The white players, still in the extreme majority, smirked and hooted, hoping to run this luminous splinter of speed off the team. But Raymond Justus didn't crack; he just seemed to have his eyes fixed on the Soda Shop across the street, not offended, not cowed, only acknowledging the coach's existence when he screamed a question at him.

"I'm sorry, R.J.; if I'd had any idea it was your son . . . "

"Who gives a shit whose son it was? Just another black boy that needs to be taught a lesson, right?"

Big Walker has come to the door, and when his son glances back, he sees the rest of the family there, right behind him, wide-eyed.

"Do you know he spent most of the night there?" R.J. asks him after nodding slightly at the rest of the Fanns. "If Boyce Evers hadn't got work as a jailer and hadn't seen him, I don't know that he wouldn't still be there."

"I thought they'd call . . ." Walker starts.

"Call? Hell, they like to teach us a lesson, like to start us out early. You know they had him in a cell with two grown men. He was just crouched down in the corner when I came and got him."

Walker tries to explain about the glove, about all it meant to him, about how if he'd just known whose son it was . . .

R.J. waves him off.

"I don't want to hear nothin' about it, man. You throw a boy like that in jail, like he's a damn murderer or something. It's a good thing he didn't steal your watch, or they'd been strapping him in the chair by now."

Walker feels sick with shame, and with the lifelong aversion he's had to confrontation, to unpleasantness. Big Walker, though, comes charging forward, over the initial shock of some uppity black man coming right to his front door at eight o'clock on a Friday morning to take him and his family to task.

"I tell you what," he says, "I don't know who you are, but I'll give you one minute to get off my property, or you're going to find out what that jail's like, too."

"I been there," R.J. tells the old man, sizing him up and smiling with no warmth.

Raymond Justus stares the whole family down, then turns slowly and starts walking back down the brick walkway to the red secondhand Buick looking so out of place on the grassy shoulder, alongside the sharp-cornered hedges of River Road.

"R.J., wait . . ." Walker begins halfheartedly, taking a tentative step forward.

The black man turns.

"No," he says. "It's done. All done. I've already beat Carneal within an inch of his sorry life. And I've done something else. He's coming over here tomorrow morning to work for you. I know there's grass to mow or bushes to trim or something. Maybe he could give that jockey a new paint job."

R.J. points to the white lawn jockey, which Walker forced Big Walker to have painted over from the original black ten years ago.

"No, R.J., that's not necessary. It's bad enough . . . "

Raymond Justus shakes his head.

"Uh-uh. You're a sorry human being, Walker Fann, for having a thirteen-year-old boy thrown in jail, but the Justuses make up for their sins. He'll be here tomorrow to work it off. I figure if that glove was important enough to have him thrown in jail for it must be worth at least a week-end of yard work. I want him to account for every cent of anguish he's caused your poor, aggrieved white butt."

Damn you, Walker's thinking. R.J. always had a way of making you feel lower than whale shit. But he used to do it with a quiet dignity. The rage is something Walker hasn't seen before.

"I'll drop the charges right now . . ." Walker starts. Raymond Justus's departing shoulders rise in an exaggerated shrug. In a moment, he's gone, the smell of the old car's exhaust the only reminder of his visit.

Mac Fann looks up at his father.

"You had his son put in jail for stealing that old glove?" His look is as accusatory as R.J.'s was.

"I can't believe this," Ginger says. With her hands on her hips like that, Walker just wants to tell her to lose some weight.

He's never been good at apologies; Mattie used to chide him about that. He figures the one he just had thrown back in his face by Carneal Justus's father, his old teammate, is about enough for one morning. He's already lost his temper once in the last twelve hours, and he's afraid if he doesn't leave soon he'll do it again. Besides, he's late for work.

Walker turns and stomps back into the house, picks up his briefcase, puts on his coat, and heads back out again. Big Walker and the children are arguing; they're already late for school. Dottie is, as always, trying to play the peacemaker, smiling and close to crying at the same time. She'll eventually end all the bickering by bursting into tears.

Walker goes out to the gray Lexus, cranks it, turns on NPR and is sliding out the driveway before they're really aware he's gone.

Eight-fifteen, he thinks to himself, and the day's already spoiled. Raymond Justus. Damn.

3

MY FIRST MEMORY OF WALKER FANN IS THE DAY HE THREW UP ON MY SHOES.

It was the first day of school in second grade. I guess we had different teachers the first year. Anyhow, he sat behind me at the Myrtle Hodges Elementary School, which was named after, of course, Myrtle Hodges, who had taught grade school around Cottondale and St. Andrews for about a thousand years.

He told me years later that he wasn't very happy to be seated where he was. He wanted to be beside Glen Murphy or Eddie Kraigh or some of his little buddies, but the teacher decided we'd be seated alphabetically, front to back in the first row, back to front in the second, and so on, and that put "Gray" right in front of "Fann."

So he comes clomping over there. I'm Miss Priss, all starched and pigtailed within an inch of my life. Momma never let me go out of the house back then unless she'd, as she said, "dressed me properly."

I swear, there were times I couldn't remember my parents' birthdays, when I grew up, but I'd always remember, always, Walker Fann's little face the way it was when we first laid eyes on each other that morning. I thought he was the handsomest thing my little seven-year-old self had ever seen. He admitted to me later that his only memory of me, before he got sick, was that they'd put him between two "damn girls."

Walker has always had kind of a nervous stomach; it was a problem at more than one big function over the years. I think that was one of the main reasons he never wanted to go anywhere that he might have to eat squid or snail or kidney or "something weird" like that. He always told people that he just didn't want to go anywhere where he couldn't play golf but my theory was always: nervous stomach.

Anyhow, we've been in class for maybe an hour when the teacher gets involved with passing out our little second-grade books, and I take the opportunity to turn around and introduce myself to this good-looking boy behind me. (Janie Watts, Rebecca Winslow, and I had already made a pact among ourselves that we'd all have boyfriends before the week was over. We all had older sisters, and that can kind of mess up your perspective on boys.)

Well, when I turned around, I could see that Walker looked a little strange, like he just wanted to be left alone. But what do you know in second grade? I pressed on.

"How do you do," I said, just like Momma taught me to talk to grownups. "My name is Matilda Gray." And I extended my hand.

But he didn't shake it. He just mumbled his name, which I already knew but wouldn't have caught otherwise. It seemed to me that he wasn't being very friendly, but you know how, at that age, you aren't old enough to know to be shy? And I could hear Janie snickering all the way across the room (I didn't get to sit by my friends either), and I was bound and determined not to be shut out by my first boy.

Well, what are you going to do? I finally remembered that I had my lunch with me, which Momma had fixed and packed for me inside my little lunch box. It couldn't have been ten o'clock yet, but food was the only icebreaker I could think of.

So I reached down and pulled up my lunch box and opened it. Momma had made me two sausage biscuits, so I took one out, hoping nobody would notice me. I turned around and offered one of them to my new friend, stuck it right under his nose, actually.

Well, Walker told me, again years later, that he was always kind of uptight the first day of school, worrying about what teacher he'd get and if he'd be able to do everything right—Walker always had to have everything perfect. Of course, being seven years old and having never, to my knowledge, laid eyes on Walker Fann before, I didn't know that.

When he got a whiff of that cold, greasy pork, he got this really funny look on his face. His eyes bulged way out, and he got up like he wanted to go somewhere in a very large hurry. But before he'd even gotten away from his desk—and mine—he lost whatever he'd had for breakfast. Mostly he lost it on the floor, but a goodly part of it he lost on my brand-new velveteen shoes, the ones I'd picked right off the shelf at Daddy's store two days earlier.

I just about puked myself from the smell and general

grossness of it all. Walker ran out of the room of course, the teacher right behind him. The one split second when our eyes met, though, before he ran, I've never seen anybody so ashamed-looking in all my life. I felt so sorry for him.

Of course, they had to clean me up, too, and they wound up sending me home just like they did Walker, although I wasn't sick, and it made me mad to miss a day of school. I hadn't missed one the year before and didn't plan to ever miss one again (they told me later, when they found out what, other than being vomited on, was bothering me so, that I still got credit because I'd been there at the start of the day). I did have to throw those shoes away, though.

But that kind of did it for me and Walker Fann for a while, although he did sit behind me the rest of the year. Both of us got teased so much by the other children that it kind of ruined us for each other. Eventually, I got a second-grade crush on another poor, unsuspecting little boy, and Walker just blended in with the surroundings.

Our houses weren't half a mile apart. We'd have met before we did, but Momma and Daddy were Methodists and the Fanns were what Daddy unkindly called High Baptists, meaning that they sometimes had delusions of grandeur but didn't have the nerve to become Episcopalians.

Daddy owned the big department store downtown. Feldman-Gray was half a block from the Old Market before Momma sold it and they moved to the mall, and most of St. Andrews came down there to buy their clothes at one time. How Daddy got into it was he started work for Mr. Abraham Feldman during the Depression, when Daddy was just a teenager, and Mr. Feldman took a shine to him. Daddy's family were farmers, although pretty well-off ones for around here, and Daddy was just trying to get ahead any way he could, I guess.

Mr. Feldman was not universally loved. For one thing, he allowed, even encouraged, black customers. He even had a couple of black sales clerks. You know all the hell that was raised all over the South over segregated drinking fountains (and everything else). Well, Daddy said Mr. Feldman told his black clerks, and any white customers that would listen, that any human being with breath could use the one water fountain in Feldman's, next to the men's section.

Daddy said that people would get mad at Mr. Feldman and take their trade to Roberts's Big Store, a block down, but most of them would come back, because Feldman's had better prices and better help.

There were a couple of places where black people could buy their clothes, other than Feldman's, but the choice apparently wasn't much, and I don't guess the black businessmen who owned them were too thrilled about Mr. Feldman's liberal nature. And maybe he was just trying to make a dollar any way he could, but he certainly didn't make life easy for himself. Being Jewish around a place like Cottondale (which was what the whole town was called until 1949), you didn't have much margin for error anyhow. Daddy said that the Klan once burned a cross in Mr. Feldman's yard.

Anyhow, Mr. Feldman lost his only child, Neil, in World War II; he got run over by one of our own tanks. After the war, Daddy came back—Daddy was already just about running things when he left at twenty-two in 1943, to hear him tell it—and Mr. Feldman pretty much adopted him.

Mr. Feldman had a very sad life. He buried his only son and then his wife passed away, killed by a hit-and-run driver in 1949. Momma said that Daddy would sometimes spend the night at the big old house Mr. Feldman now had all to himself not far from the store, just to keep him company. And Daddy was definitely running the store on a day-to-day basis now.

When Mr. Feldman found out he had cancer of the colon in 1952 and didn't have much longer to live, he put Daddy into his will, left him the store, lock, stock, and barrel. The only stipulation of any consequence was that he had to keep the Feldman name on it as long as there was a store.

Mr. Feldman died not long after I was born, and Feldman's became Feldman-Gray. Not long after that, we moved up on the hill, over on what they now call a cul-de-sac, right by the golf course.

Over the years, Walker and I would be in the same class, go to our first boy-girl parties at the club (although not together), run into each other at the swimming pool. The so-called upper crust of St. Andrews was a pretty incestuous little group, and it was inevitable, ruined velveteen shoes and all, that Walker and I would eventually be thrown together, although the second regurgitation incident probably ought to have done us in.

It was April of our sophomore year. Rebecca Winslow, who had now shortened her name to Becca and was a case, I'll tell you, was dating Rudy Blake, one of Walker's buddies. They got me and Walker to go along for a double date, although I think that the main reason was so Walker would drive and they'd have all the room in the world, in the back of Walker's daddy's Lincoln, to get to third base, if not home plate itself.

I don't know how many dates Walker had been on before then, but I'd guess not many. He and I had just turned sixteen, just got our drivers' licenses. Girls that age, they're so much more experienced, from dating older boys and all. We went to the Miracle Drive-In, out on Route 30, which was where just about everybody at St. Andrews High went back then to make out and raise hell.

So we parked in a very cozy little spot, a lot closer to the back fence than the screen. And they've got those little speakers, the ones like you used to hook up to your car? They're showing *Bonnie and Clyde*, followed by *Blow-Up*. I tell you, those double features at the drive-in could be rough. I've known girls that went all the way just because they didn't have the stamina to say "no" for five hours.

The first feature, *Bonnie and Clyde*, was pretty tame stuff, and a pretty good movie. Becca and Rudy were making out a little in the backseat, and Walker and I were just, up to that point, watching the movie.

Then, at intermission, Rudy got Walker to go with him, all winks and snickers like they had something up their sleeves.

"Probably gone to buy rubbers," Becca said, laughing, and I kind of hoped she was kidding.

When they got back, it was pretty obvious that they'd somehow managed, in addition to popcorn and Cokes, to get their hands on some bourbon. Back then, Walker told me later, there was an old black bootlegger that would hang around the drive-in, selling liquor and beer to under-age kids. Daddy drank a little bit in the afternoon or after dinner, and I knew that smell, had even tasted a little, which turned out to be a little more than Walker had.

The boys got back in, and they started passing that fifth around, us drinking from the bottle, pretending we could actually stomach it. And, of course, the boys got a little bolder.

Me, I'd been to second base, up the blouse but not down the pants, with a boy who was then a senior. But it was pretty obvious to both Walker and me that Becca and Rudy had been farther, were in fact going farther right there in the backseat. That second feature, *Blow-Up*, was supposed to be pretty hot. Becca had told me that it even had full frontal nudity, although we were long gone by the time that happened. I never did actually see all of that movie until two years ago.

Walker and I kissed, not even using our tongues, not at first anyhow. We felt obligated to do something, either leave the car or at least give a pale imitation of the lust that was threatening to stain the backseat of Walker's daddy's car.

Since Becca and Rudy were already lying down, it was just Walker and me and that fifth of Ten High up front. We'd make out a little, then take a swig of the bourbon, then make out some more. I even let Walker play with my boobs a little.

The first indication I had that something wasn't right was when Walker seemed to lose interest in second base.

He sat up straighter, and I was starting to think I was damaged goods or something. I had this birthmark right above my right breast, and I wondered if Walker had seen it and gotten turned off. I was terribly self-conscious about that birthmark back then. Everybody would tell me what a beauty I was, but I'd look in the mirror, and that dark area that Walker would always swear he hardly even noticed just screamed out at me.

But it wasn't me. It was the bourbon, of which Walker Fann the Third apparently hadn't drunk much prior to that night. Add that to the fact that he was probably more nervous than I was, and you get the picture.

This time, at least, he turned completely away from me. If it hadn't been for the speaker, he'd probably have been O.K. God, what a mess. Puke was all over the speaker, running down the window, inside and out, seeping into the crack where the window rolls down. It was on the carpet, everywhere.

Walker eventually got the speaker put back and he staggered out to try to get himself cleaned up. Rudy and Becca thought it was the funniest thing they'd ever seen, and I was sure it would be all over school Monday morning. Selfish rat that I was, I was more concerned about the reflected embarrassment that would fall on me than anything that might happen to Walker.

But Walker looked so pathetic, and it was pretty obvious that nobody else in that car was going to offer him any solace. So I walked with him, although a step or two away, up to the concession stand, and waited for him outside the men's room while he tried to clean himself up.

When he came out, he thanked me, I said, You're welcome, and we went back to the car, where even Rudy and Becca had been roused from their grubbing by the smell. They were standing outside, looking sorely pissed. When another couple they knew drove by, on the way either home or somewhere even more secluded, they caught a ride with them.

Walker drove me home, with the windows down. He didn't say a word, and I figured that was pretty much the end of it for Walker and me. Considering his propensity for throwing up in my presence, I felt strangely sad. Some part of me looked on Walker as my first beau, I guess.

The next morning, Momma and Daddy and I were having breakfast. It was just the three of us by then, with Kyle and Debbie both in school at Chapel Hill. We were out on the patio; you could see golfers go by every five minutes or so. Daddy was so cheap that he'd sneak out on the course—we lived halfway up the fourteenth fairway— and play two or three holes for free late in the afternoon.

I was just about to get up and help Momma with the dishes when Walker Fann suddenly appeared at the sliding glass door.

"Well," Daddy said, rising from the table, "you must have made quite an impression last night, Little One." Which is what he called me right up to the day he died.

I went outside, and Walker asked me to sit in the little gazebo Daddy'd had built out by Momma's rose garden. I wasn't sure what he wanted, but I wasn't unhappy that he'd come around.

"I just wanted to tell you," he said, looking out toward the golf course, "that I'm sorry. I never should have drunk that bourbon. It made me stupid."

I started to tell him that it was O.K., that at least he missed my shoes this time, but he broke in, like he might lose his nerve if he stopped.

"I just wanted to tell you one thing. I think you're the prettiest girl in St. Andrews. I hope you'll give me another chance."

Walker Fann, at sixteen, was a handsome boy who would have been a lady-killer if he'd been more confident. I think being an adored only child, and then going to first grade and suddenly not being special anymore, at least not that special, worked on him in some kind of permanent way. And it must have been overwhelming at times, being Big Walker's boy. Big Walker was into power. He wasn't so much a journalist as he was a mover and shaker, a Force. Walker, who didn't rebel outwardly, seemed determined at times to be whatever his daddy wasn't.

Up to that point, I'd dated a few real jerks, and I like to think that I saw something substantial in Walker, something that would stand me well for as long as we had together. But hell, it was probably just looks. Walker had that square jaw that he would pass on to Mac. God, it hurts me to think of them, of all three of them, for that matter. His hair was dark brown and his eyes were a three-dimensional green, pools to drown yourself in. He wasn't the finished product, though; he was a skinny boy still trying to grow into his shoes and his destiny.

In a lot of towns, Walker (and I) would have been sent to some private school, but the only private school in St. Andrews was a fundamentalist segregation academy. And as Daddy told Momma, knowing Bible verses won't help you much on the SATs. Plus Big Walker thought it would be treason not to send his son to the public high school, even if it was integrated. And nobody in our town sent their children off to boarding school. We never thought twice about sending Mac and Ginger to the public schools, even though there's a pretty good private one in town now.

So Walker and I started going out, first occasionally and then exclusively. Just to make me mad, Daddy would say that if Walker had been a stock I had bought him cheap. When we first started dating, Walker was the second-string quarterback on the football team and one of the guys on the end of the bench in basketball and baseball. But he was a late bloomer, gaining three inches in height between his sophomore and junior years and filling out considerably.

He became the first-string quarterback on the football team the next fall, although everybody black in town and some white thought Raymond Justus would be the one. And then the team won the state championship our senior year, in 1969. Walker was the quarterback and a starter on the basketball and baseball teams, and I was the head cheerleader. It's funny, though; even in high school, I knew the quarterback was supposed to be the leader, the one that grabbed people by the jersey and told them to straighten up and fly right. But Walker never was like that. Sometimes, I think the other boys did what Walker said just because they knew he'd be disappointed if they didn't. People liked Walker; still do, I guess.

I know one day our junior year, during the season, I was supposed to meet him after the last class. He had Coach Kell for typing class, and as I came up to the door, I could hear Coach Kell's voice.

"Hell and goddamn, son," he said. "You got to get meaner. You got to get mad at people. You don't want folks to think you're a pussy, do you?"

"No, sir," I heard Walker answer, polite and even like he usually was.

"Today at practice," Coach Kell said, "I want you to chew out the first son of a bitch that drops a pass. Get on their ass, son."

There was a silence. I'd stopped breathing. They called him Coach Hell behind his back, and everybody up to the principal was half afraid of him, it seemed like.

Finally, I heard Walker's voice again.

"No, sir."

I couldn't believe it, and the coach couldn't, either.

"Don't you tell me 'No, sir,'" Coach Kell said. He didn't yell. It was scarier, like he was using all his energy not to yell. "Don't you tell me you ain't going to do something."

"It isn't right to yell at people when they're doing the best they can."

"Doing the best they can?! I don't want 'em doing the best they can. I want 'em doing better."

But Walker didn't back down an inch, in that quiet way he had, and I figured that my boyfriend would be sitting on the bench on Friday night. But there was this long silence, and then a sigh, and then Coach Kell went stomping out of the room. I ducked into the girls' bathroom and then came out when I was sure he was gone.

I was so proud of Walker for standing up to the coach, and told him so, but I was sure it was going to cost him.

In those days, though, Walker couldn't lose for winning—with a little help from me. I told Becca Winslow and another cheerleader what I'd heard, even though Walker told me not to, and it took about two seconds for the story to get back to the football team. Pretty soon, it became common knowledge that Walker had stood up for the whole team. After that, they'd have died rather than let Walker down, even if he was younger than some of them.

Even the black kids, who almost boycotted in August when they heard Walker and not Raymond Justus was the starting quarterback, appreciated him for that.

Part of it, though, was that Walker was not going to get on people's case. He hated that. He was always the good guy. Coach Kell got to be the heavy. The people under him at the newspaper got to be the heavies. Hell, I got to be the heavy.

It isn't that I'm complaining. Walker was wonderful, then and later, right up to the end.

Sometimes, though, too much of a blessing can be a little bit of a curse.

4

WALKER INSISTS ON GOING TO WORK BY HIMSELF MOST DAYS, IN HIS OWN CAR, THE GRAY LEXUS MATTIE PICKED OUT TWO years ago. This hurts Big Walker's feelings, but God knows he sees enough of his father every day without sharing a ride with him. Being under one roof first at home and then at the office, Walker cherishes these few minutes of privacy.

Today, despite the fact that he's running late, he turns left instead of right out of the driveway, south on River Road.

His former home, the contemporary just eight doors down from Big Walker and Dottie's, looks the same as it did the last time he went this way, two months ago. He resists putting it up for sale, but he's sure he will never go inside it again. He doesn't even know, a year later, how he managed the courage to spend two days there packing, before he told Big Walker to just hire somebody to pick up everything and they'd sort it out later. Mac and Ginger have gone through and reclaimed most of their possessions, but there are still boxes and boxes inside Big Walker's garage, unopened.

Walker isn't sure why he went this way today. Maybe it was seeing R.J. again, or the impossibility of anything, even the sight of that mailbox with "Walker, Mattie, Mac, and Ginger" on it, making this day much worse. R.J.'s kid. Damn, damn, damn.

Walker stops the car. The Bradford pears are growing; the hedge needs trimming. It's time to get one of the Myers boys to mow the yard again. In the winter, you can see Cottondale down below in the gap between the trees, because of the downward slope from River Road to the house, but now the sycamores and oaks form a wall of green. Only from the back porch was there an unobstructed view of the river during the summer.

Walker rests his head on the steering wheel for a few seconds, then slowly pulls away.

River Road is actually a large semicircle. The road runs two and a half miles south, along the river, then does a slow, lazy 180-degree turn before heading back north again, through hardwoods and the newer homes and neighborhoods that now completely enclose the golf course and the lake. Cul-de-sacs and circles sprout from it along its course. The acreage of the area around River Road is only slightly less than that of the grid that is Cottondale, but with only about one-fourth as many people.

"Well," Mattie said two years ago when Walker told her that, "I guess they don't have golf courses and lakes and all eating into their land down there. Plus mowing the yard must be a breeze."

A way of establishing your place in the pecking order of St. Andrews is to let it be known that you live east of Sycamore, by the river, it being understood that those west of the town's only country club, while not cursed enough to live in the bottoms of Cottondale or the newer, treeless tracts north of Route 30 or out by the mall, are the *arrivistes*, the new money.

It's 4.6 miles from Big Walker and Dottie's to the paper

going this way, but it's a beautiful drive. It always pains Walker to pass out of this canopied womb and into the world of commerce. The back entrance to the *Standard* offices is only a hundred yards beyond the gate that marks the west entrance to what is loosely called Old St. Andrews. The *Standard* is at the intersection of Route 30 and River Road West. From the parking lot, Walker can see through the early-September haze the unbroken white monolith where most of St. Andrews, old and new, does its shopping now: Rich Valley Mall.

Seeing the mall makes Walker think of Harold Neely, which in turn makes him wonder if he was wrong about the day's low point.

Walker takes the backstairs up to his second-floor office, right next to Big Walker's. He sees that, even though he left home first, his father has beaten him to work, will no doubt want to know where he's been.

The red light on his phone is blinking, as it is every morning. Walker has a secretary, but Big Walker insists that they both have their office numbers listed on Page 2 of the *Standard* and that they, not the secretaries, deal with what Big Walker always calls "the public," as if, Walker thinks, it's more than a few dozen of the same damn people calling to complain about dropping *Mary Worth* from the comics or using too-small type for the weather ear on Page 1.

This morning, the neutral, grating recording tells him he has "seven new messages." Three of them had hung up without leaving their names or numbers, one is a supporter of stock-car racing who's dropping his subscription because the *Standard* had Dale Earnhardt driving a Ford instead of a Chevy in the agate this morning, two are people whose papers didn't get delivered on time. Walker transfers these three to the sports and circulation departments.

The seventh call is his secretary, telling him what he has already remembered: he has a ten-o'clock meeting with the rest of the board of directors.

The board of directors of *The St. Andrews Standard* consists of Walker, Big Walker, Grant Adkins from Garnet Bank, David Melvin, senior partner in Melvin, Melvin, and Bates, and Harold Neely.

Harold Neely's family founded the mill that kept Cottondale alive after the Civil War, at the same time that the Fanns were starting the town's newspaper. Walker guesses that there have been Fanns and Neelys sitting on each other's boards of something or other for more than a century.

Harold is ten years older than Walker. The two have never gotten along; Neely is more inclined than his father, who was ten years older than Big Walker, to wield his family's advertising impact like a cudgel.

Harold Neely is at least passably deferential to Big Walker, calling him "Mr. Fann" even when he is insisting on having his way. With Walker, he's no more than civil, often less.

Today's meeting was called by Neely. Big Walker told his son the reason for it the day before. One of the new reporters, a bright young woman just one year out of the University of North Carolina journalism school, did a story, a rather good one, Walker thought, about the slave museum. It ran in Thursday's paper.

The trouble is, there weren't supposed to be any stories about the slave museum, just Ry Tucker's sarcastic editorials about troublemakers who won't let the past die. Walker curses to himself. Ry Tucker, telling the *Standard*'s readers not to look back, sometimes leaves early on Friday for Civil War reenactments up in Virginia.

With the museum referendum just four days away, the

article is bound to have caused Harold Neely some distress, and Walker is sure this meeting is to spread that distress around.

Big Walker had told his son to instruct Ed McLaurin, the managing editor, that there would be no more stories on Rasheed Aziz or anyone else involved in the movement to get the Old Market turned into a museum on slavery.

"Hell," he'd said, "if we don't nip this stuff in the bud right now, they'll be wanting reparations and all."

But Walker had taken halfway measures, told his managing editor to "go easy" on the issue, and that had been a month earlier. And McLaurin is gone this week, probably didn't even tell the assistant M.E. what Walker had said.

The meeting starts ten minutes late, because of Harold Neely. Neely is always the last person to arrive for whatever meeting he's attending, has been known to leave the room and come back if anyone else is later than he is.

They make small talk about advertising linage and the upcoming rise in newsprint prices, then Neely clears his throat and the others turn his way. It makes Walker crazy to see how he dominates the room. He isn't a big man, maybe five-ten, 160 pounds, with a pockmarked face and perpetual dyspeptic frown. Walker likes to believe that all Harold Neely's clout comes from his money, that he commands no more respect than his pocketbook can pay for. But he isn't sure.

"What I came here for," he says, looking at Walker rather than his father, "is to find out what the hell we're doing running that liberal piece of tripe about that damn tomb of the unknown nigger?"

There is some nervous laughter from Adkins and Melvin, even a chuckle from Big Walker. A small part of the plans for the slavery museum is a monument to the victims of the 1919 race riot, a plaque or something, Walker recalls. But

Neely has picked up on this and uses it for laughs at the club and elsewhere.

"Now, Harold," Big Walker says, putting one of his big paws on Neely's arm, "she didn't know any better. It won't happen again. I've told Walker to make sure it doesn't."

"I thought he made sure last time," Neely says.

Walker feels his face flush. "The managing editor was gone this week."

"It wasn't the managing editor's responsibility."

What infuriates Walker is that Neely is right. He knows he should have either stood his ground with Big Walker or with Ed McLaurin.

There is an uneasy silence.

"Harold," Big Walker says, "it won't happen again. I promise."

The Fanns have argued this issue to dust more than once. Walker used to be caught in the middle, between Mattie and Big Walker, when the issue was first taking hold in the mostly black Cottondale bottom. He wishes that Mattie were here now. Walker has never been quick with words; Mattie and Big Walker could both outargue him.

Walker sits through the rest of the meeting without saying a word. When it concludes, the other three men leave, and the Fanns are alone. Big Walker walks over and shuts the door, then turns back to his son.

"I thought this was settled," he says. "I thought we had an understanding."

Walker doesn't speak for several seconds.

"We have an understanding," he says finally. "Do you think I didn't tell Ed to go easy on the slave museum?"

"Nah, I don't think that. I just think you have an awful hard time dropping the hammer. I think you feel like you ought to apologize for being a Fann, for owning this damn place."

"Well, sometimes I do. It's not like I built it myself."

"Hell, son, I didn't build it myself either, but I've kept it going. And here's the thing. You can think what you want to about what happened before your granddaddy was even born, when your great-granddaddy was in knee britches, but it don't have a goddamn thing to do with what's happening now, or it shouldn't. What matters now is St. Andrews and this newspaper. And if we wind up as some kind of damn symbol of all the terrible things that've been done to all those poor, humble, hard-working African-Americans, it'll hurt every business in town. And God help us if Harold Neely thinks we cost him that Sudduth's store."

The year before, the Rich Valley Mall had lost one of its three anchors. A large department-store chain that had been in Cottondale and then St. Andrews for more than sixty years decided that, as its spokeswoman said, "the demographics dictate that we should close our unit here." Feldman-Gray and Sears remained, but the two-story hull on the mall's north side was an open wound to St. Andrews in general and Harold Neely in particular.

Then, in April, Neely seemed to have solved his problem. Sudduth's, a major chain out of Birmingham, was ready to fill the void, he told the *Standard* and the local TV reporter. He appeared to be almost happy. Sudduth's was not a great store, not the kind of store that would preclude trips to Raleigh for Christmas shopping. For St. Andrews, though, it would do. Tax incentives were promised by Neely, on behalf of the city council. A small celebration was planned.

The day before the papers were to be signed, however, Neely called a frantic meeting with the Fanns. The deal was in limbo, he told them, banging his fist on the conference-room table. Henry Sudduth had found out about the slave museum movement.

The information didn't come from Sudduth himself, of course. An anonymous caller told Neely how things stood, why Sudduth had not flown in earlier that day as planned. The man himself never said a word about it.

Sudduth still controlled just about everything involving his chain of stores. He had been a big supporter of George Wallace in the sixties and was appalled when Wallace reversed himself in his old age on the issue of his earlier racism. According to the anonymous friend, when Henry Sudduth found out that his newest store might be in the same town with a museum built to broadcast the horrors of slavery, his new love affair with St. Andrews chilled. The caller told Harold Neely that he couldn't speak for Henry Sudduth, but that he'd bet that the deal was off until Mr. Sudduth found out which way things were going to fall.

Big Walker made a call to Sudduth and assured him that the *Standard* would guarantee that the museum didn't materialize, as Walker sat silent, teeth clenched, two chairs away. Sudduth said nothing, never conceding that this might be a factor in his thinking, claimed that some last-minute information on the town's "economic viability" had made him have second thoughts. Mostly, he just listened. At the end, he said, "Well, let's wait and see what happens."

The slow dance had gone on through spring and summer. Twice, it appeared that Sudduth's was coming, but Henry Sudduth never committed. Finally, it became clear to Harold Neely if no one else that only the defeat of the slavery museum referendum would produce a tenant to make his mall whole again.

Even Big Walker was cool toward Sudduth's after he heard from a publishing friend at a convention in June that Sudduth had once pulled all his advertising from the Birmingham paper for three months because his daughter's wedding picture had appeared next to that of a black woman, only relenting when the offending editor was fired. St. Andrews, he told Walker, ought to be able to do better than that.

"But if Harold Neely thinks we cost him that store," he told Walker, "he'll call in every chip he's got to run us out of business."

Walker wishes sometimes that he'd done the thing Mattie wanted him to do—the thing he wanted to do—when he graduated from Duke.

He'd done summer internships at the Raleigh and Baltimore papers when he was in college, because Big Walker wanted him to have some experience at larger places. He'd shown promise. It especially pleased him that he was so appreciated at *The Baltimore Sun*, in a city that was far outside the sphere of any of Big Walker's friends (Big Walker had wanted him to intern at Charlotte that summer), in a place where he was Walker Fann instead of "Walker Fann's boy."

He'd done so well, in fact, that the managing editor at the *Sun* had used him as a stringer his senior year at Duke. Walker had done outstanding work covering a famous on-campus murder for the *Sun* that winter. When he'd call Big Walker and tell him of writing some news story for the *Sun* or the other two papers who occasionally used his services, though, or show him bylines from the *Sun*, his father seemed somewhat reserved in his praise.

In the spring of 1974, the *Sun*'s managing editor called Walker—who'd sent him a résumé in December without Big Walker's knowledge—and offered him a job. It was the classic entry-level newspaper position, covering cops and crime, working the graveyard shift, looking at burned and drowned and bullet-abused bodies, interviewing the next of kin. But Walker knew what a break it was. Nobody he knew was going to a paper that large right out of college, not even the journalism majors over in Chapel Hill.

Walker called Mattie that night at her dorm at Millen and told her the news, asked her if she'd like to live in Baltimore. She said she'd love to live in Baltimore. He told her to mention it to no one, that he still had to tell Big Walker about it. Then he called the managing editor and accepted the job. Come May 29, he'd go to work full time for *The Baltimore Sun*. Walker had never felt so worthy.

He realized later that he hadn't really thought it through.

When he called Big Walker and Dottie, he was prepared for some resistance. He was prepared to tell Big Walker that he would probably eventually come back to the *Standard*, but that he couldn't turn down an opportunity like this.

He was not prepared, though, for utter, immutable rejection.

If you go to Baltimore, Big Walker told him not two minutes into the conversation, *The St. Andrews Standard* will not be here for you when you decide to come back.

"I don't have time for any prodigal sons," he told Walker before he hung up.

Walker, the only child, had never imagined the possibility of utter darkness, the possibility of being shut off from his family. He spent the next month in a daze, missing half his classes and drinking heavily. He and Mattie, who were planning to marry in August, debated and sometimes argued.

Dottie came up in early May, a week before exams were to begin.

Walker had never known his mother to drive this far by herself, but there she was, standing at the door of the apartment he and a fraternity brother were renting. It was 11 A.M., but Walker knew he looked like someone who'd been sound asleep two minutes earlier.

Dottie came inside. She was still an attractive woman, with blond hair turning to gray, but with her features turning soft with age and weight. She looked as if she'd been crying on the way up.

"Honey," she said, "this is killing your daddy. If you go to Baltimore, you might just as well shoot him right now."

Walker knew he was doomed. He could possibly, with Mattie's support, survive his father's spiritual disinheritance. But Dottie, the soft one, was the one who always got her way. She didn't ask for much, because she didn't have to ask for much. It was part of the Fanns' unspoken creed that when Dottie cried, people around her did whatever they could do to make her stop crying.

Walker asked her, without much hope, if she couldn't intercede with Big Walker, explain that it wouldn't be forever, that someday he'd come back to run things.

"But he thinks it will be forever," Dottie said, sniffling. "He's sure that he'll be the last Fann to run the *Standard*, that you won't ever come back. He just sits and stares at that television."

Dottie moved a little closer on the couch, conspiratorially, and even before she spoke again, Walker was thinking, "Don't . . . don't."

"You mustn't ever tell him I told you this," she said, lowering her voice as if the empty apartment walls were listening, "but I'm worried about your daddy. He has these pains in his arms and his chest, and he won't go see the doctor, says there isn't any use in it."

It's easy now, twenty years later, to look back on all this and see the transparent play on his emotions. It wasn't so easy then, even with Mattie's help.

He went back to St. Andrews, of course, and *The*

Baltimore Sun hired another May graduate. Walker saw, eight years later, that his replacement had won a Pulitzer Prize for one of the New York papers.

Walker, upon returning, insisted that his father go to a doctor immediately. The doctor apparently found nothing wrong with Big Walker that diet and exercise wouldn't cure. After worrying about his father's health for the five years following his graduation from Duke, Walker came to understand that there was nothing, short of his son's leaving for Baltimore, that might bring on a major heart attack and shorten Big Walker's life.

The real key, though, was Mattie. If she had stood her ground, the way she did at the start, and flatly refused to marry Walker if he moved back to St. Andrews, he would have had to choose between the only sources of love he knew at that time.

But Mattie weakened, too. She didn't want the burden of Big Walker's and Dottie's broken hearts on her shoulders, either, and she didn't want to lose Walker Fann, whom she had come to truly love and knew she would continue to love. She feared that she would be blamed for Walker's exile, by both sides. In the end, the gamble was too much, and she told Walker she would love him and marry him no matter where they lived.

Over the years since then, Big Walker has been very generous to Walker and Mattie, as were the Grays. Mattie was their only child to stay in St. Andrews. At times, Walker almost admired his father's determination to keep the paper within the family, no matter what, and he saw the event that not so much directed as cemented his future twenty years ago as evidence of the tough cord of endurance that ran through Big Walker.

Other times, though, he couldn't help but wonder if some of it wasn't pure selfishness.

*   *   *

Big Walker reaches for the doorknob.

"Want to get something to eat?" he asks. Walker shakes his head and doesn't move.

Big Walker shrugs and frowns. He starts out the door, then stops.

"By the way, how come you took so long to get in this morning? Car trouble?"

Walker doesn't answer.

5

WALKER PASSES THROUGH THE NEWSROOM LONG ENOUGH TO TELL THE ASSISTANT MANAGING EDITOR, A RATHER HUMORLESS woman in her late twenties, that any future stories about the slavery museum must be approved by him. He can see the censure in her eyes that she dares not put into words. He leaves an electronic message in Ed McLaurin's computer to the same effect, then leaves.

It's a beautiful day, better than early September has any right to be this far south, Walker thinks, breathing in deeply. A cool front has cleared out the humidity, and the noon sky is robin's-egg blue. It is almost enough, Walker thinks, as he walks down the front steps and heads around the building to his car. Almost enough.

He doesn't remember any conscious decision to turn east on Route 30, toward Cottondale.

As he nears the bridge, he passes the faded wood storefronts that used to house a variety of businesses on both sides of the river but are now abandoned behind sidewalks half conquered by weeds.

The river, neutralized by a dam farther up, is a muddy brown, still flushing out the week's rains.

The original town of Cottondale was built here because

the first barrier to ships was the falls, a mile north of the bridge, but now there is no reason to continue dredging the river; trucks and trains can do anything the ships once did, cheaper and quicker.

The only clue that the Rich River once was Cottondale's main link to the outside world is the deteriorating cargo ship that was left docked within sight of the bridge in 1968, impounded because the captain was hauling several tons of marijuana.

Someone set fire to the ship before anyone could figure what to do with it, and it sank as far as it could. A sweet burning smell lingered over the town for several days afterward. But part of the deck still is above water, even when the river is running high. To Walker, it looks as if it has sunk a little deeper in the mud since the last time he noticed it.

Past the bridge is the swampy area where a second, smaller bridge spans Cotton Creek. To the right is Neely Industries' mill buildings, sitting on a peninsula between the creek and the river. The main structure is three blocks long and sixty feet high, built on concrete pilings one story high to keep floodwater out. Near it, next to the highway, are more abandoned buildings, mostly restaurants, snack shops, bars, and loan companies, whose business dwindled and died as the mill laid off more and more people.

The road, now Main Street, rises an almost-imperceptible fifteen feet as Walker enters the old downtown, Cottondale itself.

The Old Market comes into view, three blocks away, as Walker nears the top of the small rise that used to separate what was under water from what wasn't when the Rich River would flood.

The building sits in the middle of a traffic circle where Main and Third streets intersect. The shopping district gets only slightly better as Walker nears what was until the past twenty years the center of town. A few small clothing stores and restaurants, a thrift shop, a furniture company, a hardware store—most bordered by one or more deserted buildings—keep up appearances. They seem to be holding the fort, waiting for the reinforcements that will once again make Cottondale's downtown a factor in what the *Standard* calls "the tri-county area."

On the other side of the Old Market, a new courthouse brings a couple of hundred white workers downtown five days a week, giving the area at least a part-time integration. After five o'clock, though, the area along Main Street east of the river is all black; the only signs of life are neon ones hanging outside bars and pool halls. Cottondale is eight blocks wide, twenty blocks deep, laid out on a grid that was expanded when Alexander Neely built his cotton mill in 1883 and started bringing in hungry, cheap help, first white, later some black workers as well. Main Street is only five blocks from the north end of the grid because the cotton mill, and the millhands, stretched the original town ten blocks to the south.

Walker notices that there are graffiti painted on the bricks of the Old Market's first floor. The one he can read, in bright blue letters, says, BURN IT DOWN. Aimless-looking black children hang around the cool area underneath the enclosed second floor, outside boarded-up windows.

The Old Market was built in 1820, and there is no doubt that African slaves were sold there, that those already in America were commodities here on market days, like cotton or tobacco. Even Big Walker will concede that; even Harold Neely couldn't deny it. But Big Walker used to argue with not so much his son as his daughter-in-law, What can you do about that? Send 'em back to Africa? Hell, he'd tell his son and daughter-in-law, I'd pay higher taxes to do that.

When the museum movement started, first directed hopelessly by a few old black preachers, white people up on the hill laughed at them. Then Rasheed Aziz, not long back from the University of Maryland law school, took it over, and it became more than a joke.

As his car turns right down Third Street, he feels he is under the influence of some unseen ouija board, moving without any discernible effort or will on his part. Skirting the Old Market on its southwest side, Walker wishes the whole issue could somehow disappear. He can't foresee a conclusion on Tuesday that will make anything better for black or white St. Andrews.

Walker knows where he's going now, guesses he knew all along.

The east-west streets south of Main were named long ago for Cottondale's mayors, starting with Malcolm McRae in 1806. Philly Justus's house, Walker has little trouble remembering, is at 804 South Second Street, between Simmons and Wade. Walker figures that, if he is going to make any kind of peace with R.J., he has to find him first. And he can only think of one place to start: R.J.'s mother.

In the brief time, his senior year in high school, when Walker and Raymond Justus were actually friends, at least in Walker's mind, he spent so much time at the old house he now beholds from his idling car that Big Walker forbade him to go there. Walker would just park his '67 Mustang a block away, down toward the river.

Philadelphia Justus was raising five children, mostly by herself, but Walker never felt that he was intruding, never felt that his coming by for dinner or to visit was an imposition. R.J. was her second-oldest.

Sometimes, Glen Murphy or Kenny Graham would come over with him. Sometimes, some of the black kids on the football team would come over, too. It was almost the only place the black and white members of St. Andrews's state football championship team of 1969 ever met away from school.

Now, looking at the rambling, weathered house, Walker is amazed at the flood of memories it brings. Philly's pork chops and fried chicken, the way she'd shake the boards of the old house with her laughter. How she'd always refer to the little bit of spending money she kept from the nearby store she and her children ran as "chump change," how her house was the only place Walker ever ate where the blessing was asked before every meal.

It ended with little fanfare when they all went off to college or the war. Walker only spent one summer back home during college, and he seldom ran into R.J. then. When their paths did cross, the old frequency had been lost. Conversation was affected and difficult.

Walker sees that the house next to Philly's, at 802, is halfway through a paint job. The structure, which was probably worse off than Philly's, also has a new tin roof now. Both houses have screened front porches, and Walker sees a boy get up and go inside 802.

He becomes aware that he's the object of stares from passers-by, and he figures the best thing to do, other than leave, is get out of the car and go up to Philly Justus's front door.

He knocks on the screen-porch post several times before an enormous woman, wearing sandals, a smock, and an incongruous black beret, comes waddling to the door.

"Just a minute," she mutters, then looks out at him through Coke-bottle glasses.

"Missus Justus," Walker says hesitantly from the other side of the screen as Philly reaches for the hook-and-eye latch, "it's Walker Fann. You might not remember me, but I used to be friends with Raymond. . . ."

"I remember you, all right," the black woman says,

putting her right hand on her hip. "Carneal remembered you for me this morning, when he told me you had him put in jail last night."

"That's what I came over here about . . ." Walker starts, already regretting the attempt to patch things up.

Philly Justus, Walker sees, is that rare thing from his past that hasn't shrunk with age. If anything, Philly is larger than ever. She was always a big woman, but she must be well over three hundred pounds now, and she obviously has no desire to hear anything Walker has to say.

Philly turns her head to the side and calls, "Cracker!" Almost instantly, a dingy-looking but very inspired mongrel, mostly chow, comes out from under the house. Walker is amazed that he didn't charge him before. He wonders if the South is the only place where racism extends even to pets: it's understood around St. Andrews that any white person's dog will chase blacks, and vice versa.

Walker is trapped on the top step leading to the screen porch, the chow's teeth a foot away. He leaps off the step and into the front yard, hoping to make a run for the car, but the dog herds him away from the street.

In the side yard, next to the renovated structure next door, Walker sees a pump house, perhaps thirty inches high. He runs toward and leaps on it. Standing in the middle, he can barely evade the chow's lunges.

It is in this perilous state that Walker Fann meets Raymond Justus for the second time in a day.

"Cracker! You get away from there!"

The dog has to be ordered three times before he will back off. Finally, he leaves slowly, giving one last growl, to reclaim his spot underneath the house. Walker turns and faces his savior.

"You can get down now," R.J. says, then turns to go back toward his house.

"You should of let him eat him!" Philly yells from the porch next door.

Walker goes toward her son.

"R.J., wait. Isn't there anything I can do to make it right?"

Walker follows Raymond Justus almost to his front door before the black man turns and acknowledges his presence.

"It don't matter," he says. "Don't think nothin' about it. The boy shouldn't of stole your glove."

Walker sees a face quickly move from one of the house's front windows. He's sure it's the boy he had arrested the night before.

"I just wasn't thinking," Walker says. Then thrashing about for something, anything to excuse himself: "It's been a bad year."

"Yeah," R.J. says. "I heard. I'm sorry."

There is a pause, then he adds, "Well, you're here. Why don't you come on up?"

Walker follows his former teammate inside.

"Carneal! Come here!"

The same boy finally comes slinking out of one of the side rooms.

"Now," R.J. says, "I want you to tell this man you're sorry you stole his glove. That might get you at least one step on the right track with me."

The boy mumbles an apology, and Walker tells him it's O.K.

"No," R.J. corrects, "it's not O.K. And he's goin' to be at your front door tomorrow morning, just like I said. He's going to work it off."

Carneal's lower lip seems to poke out a bit farther at this news, but he is silent as his father glares at him.

R.J. turns to Walker. "Beer?"

Walker gratefully accepts, and they go back out to the front porch, where they attempt to catch up, as much as possible, on their lives since they made St. Andrews High briefly famous.

Raymond Justus and Walker Fann first met in August of 1966. They were both freshmen at St. Andrews High. It was the first year of school integration, and R.J. was one of twenty students who came over from Carver. He was one of two blacks trying out for the junior varsity football team. R.J. had been the quarterback for all his teams since fifth grade, and Dexter Cates was his best friend, a ferocious boy, who would lead the St. Andrews defense that gave up thirty points their entire senior season.

Coach Kell, the varsity coach, had made sure that R.J. and Dexter came over. He'd scouted the black junior high games as soon as he realized that integration was inevitable, and he knew these two could get him the state championship he'd always coveted. He didn't tell them how hard their lot would be, though.

The junior varsity coach was a short man with a crew-cut who always seemed irritated. Ricky Johnson was a twenty-four-year-old phys ed teacher who had grown up in St. Andrews, and no one beyond tenth grade ever called him "Coach" except under extreme duress. He had power over the freshmen, though—until he was fired two years later for having an affair with a tenth-grade girl—and he used it with great relish.

He made life especially hard for the two black players, and most of their white teammates were glad for the distraction. If Dexter Cates missed a tackle, they could revel in somebody else's mistake. If Raymond Justus overthrew a receiver, it was his ass and not theirs that was being chewed.

From the beginning, Walker and Raymond had been the obvious competitors for quarterback, and from the beginning, it was obvious that Walker would probably win. It was one thing, the coaches knew, to integrate. It was quite another to have a black boy telling the white boys what to do, even if the plays did come in from the bench. Besides, Coach Kell believed that Raymond Justus would be all-state no matter what position he played.

It was Coach Kell, not Ricky Johnson, who called R.J. into his office and told him he was going to be an end.

R.J. shook his head.

"Coach," he said. "I'm a quarterback."

"You're whatever I say you are," the varsity coach told him, poking his finger into his chest.

R.J. backed off slightly, then said, "Just give me a chance, coach."

Coach Kell was impressed that any ninth-grader, especially a black one, would dispute his word. He'd once made a sophomore tackle wet his pants just by yelling at him.

In the end, he promised R.J., who he knew could throw farther and more accurately and run faster than Walker Fann, that he would get a fair chance at quarterback next year on the varsity if he'd just play end right now. R.J. reluctantly went along. There was really no other choice—Philly was determined that her son would remain at the St. Andrews High, where everything from teachers to school lunches was far superior to the black high school.

His speed and large, supple hands made Walker Fann a star.

Coach Kell knew that he would never start R.J. at quarterback. The toughest man in St. Andrews knew he wasn't tough enough to pull that off. But nobody told R.J., at least until it was unavoidable.

Raymond Justus and Walker Fann both were listed as backup quarterbacks on the varsity their sophomore year, but while Walker rode the bench and took more snaps in practice, R.J. was already starting at wide receiver. He was better than any upperclassman on the team, catching six touchdown passes and making a mediocre senior quarterback look good. Walker Fann was still waiting to grow into his body.

The summer before their junior year, Coach Kell could stall no longer. R.J. and Walker had been sharing time at quarterback in the August practice sessions.

The day Walker was announced as the starting quarterback, the eight black players who now graced the St. Andrews varsity boycotted practice. Walker went to Coach Kell's office and offered to let R.J. have the starting job, which he didn't feel he deserved, no matter how many times Big Walker told him he did.

Coach Kell told Walker to grow up, to stop giving things away. He made sure, though, that his teammates knew what Walker had done, and it gave the player the blacks had scornfully called "Rich Boy" a finger hold on credibility. Walker's natural likability and R.J.'s unwillingness to put himself ahead of "the team" did the rest. Dexter Cates wanted to organize a season-long boycott, but R.J. wouldn't let him.

Walker and R.J. only talked about it once.

In the fall of 1969, halfway through their senior season, Walker had given R.J. and Dexter Cates a ride home from practice. He'd done this several times before; many of the black players didn't have cars.

This time, R.J. invited him inside, and Walker accepted. He met Philly; she was cooking, an activity that seemed to consume most of her hours away from the store, but she took time to make him feel welcome. She was able and willing, unlike the maids and gardeners with whom Walker had tried to be pleasant, to look him in the eye and talk as one person to another. Perhaps, Walker thought, it was because she was on home territory. But it was hard to imagine Philly Justus out of her element anywhere. She would use a wooden soupspoon, a butcher knife, or whatever other cooking implement she had in her hand to emphasize her point. She loved to laugh, and she always had a houseful of children, some hers, some others'.

Walker was drawn to her as much as to R.J. and his raucous siblings. He continued to come over once or twice a week, sometimes bringing a couple of his white friends with him. Philly's store was half a block away, and sometimes they'd play tag football, right there in Second Street, with Philly's property line as one goal and the back of the store as the other, little children and old men watching from the sidewalks.

One day, they were competing to determine who could kick and throw the farthest. Walker, who had to depend on accuracy more than strength, heaved the ball a good fifty yards; it landed near the rear of an unfortunately parked Lincoln Continental. No one else had thrown the ball farther.

"R.J. can do that left-handed," Dexter Cates had said, turning away. R.J., Walker noticed, didn't say anything, didn't even seem interested in joining the contest. Then Glen Murphy goaded him, foolishly bet him $5 that he couldn't top that. Walker wanted to stop him, knew it was a sucker bet.

R.J. was not about to turn down $5. He reached down, gathering some dust to rub on his hands. He took the ball, stepped back three steps, did a quarter turn, and sprang forward. Walker could hear a little snap as he released the ball. It landed a full ten feet in front of the Lincoln, a good ten yards beyond Walker's throw.

Later that day, when Philly asked R.J. to go get his older brother at the store, Walker went with him.

"Look," Walker said, when they were out of earshot, "you know and I know that you ought to have been the quarterback. I'm sorry it worked out like it did."

R.J. shrugged, then stopped. Walker stopped.

"You know," R.J. said, "I've been waiting for over a year now to hear somebody white say that. You know what, though? It don't make me feel a damn bit better."

They walked on to the store. On the way back, R.J. spoke again.

"Don't feel bad about it, Walker. It isn't your fault. If it was going to be anybody, I'd just as soon it was you."

There was nothing else to say.

They had both prospered, in their own fashion. Walker was a meticulous, moderately athletic type who could get people to do what he wanted without even having to ask. Raymond Justus was, simply, the best athlete in the tri-county area.

That senior season, St. Andrews did what it had never done before and hasn't done since. The Saints won the state championship in football, beating the largest school in Winston-Salem 27–14 in their fourteenth and last game of a perfect season.

Walker was all-conference at quarterback. Raymond Justus was all-world at wide receiver. When Walker went to Duke and left football behind, R.J. signed with Southeastern University. He was one of Southeastern's first black recruits, and Walker had heard, in bits and pieces, the story of his unraveling career there. Today, he was hearing it all in one piece for the first time. Later, he would reflect that he had never heard Raymond Justus talk so much at one time.

First, they moved him to defensive back, a position he'd never played.

"We ain't quite ready for a nigger to score a touchdown,"

a big freckle-faced offensive lineman had told him the day they changed his position.

Later, he injured his knee. He was made to feel that he had to play hurt, and he injured himself worse.

He had been an average high school student. At Southeastern, he slid by, taking all the courses prescribed by his academic advisor, a man who would later be fired, reluctantly, when it was revealed that he had tried to bribe a geology professor into changing a player's grade. He didn't realize how pitifully little actual college credit he had until the end of the fall semester in 1973. He had another year of football eligibility because he'd been redshirted his freshman season, but the coaches at Southeastern decided that he was never going to get any better, on what had become two bad knees.

It was up to the academic advisor to sit Raymond Justus down and explain to him that he was still a freshman academically, that he was never going to graduate, that he was never going to be able to take another crip course, that he might as well clear out right then.

It was one of the great regrets of R.J.'s life that he didn't slap the little man, that he didn't sue the school or go to *Sports Illustrated* or something. But he didn't. His pride wounded, he headed back to St. Andrews with twenty-four hours of college credit. He had started two games in three seasons.

Walker has a theory about old jocks. They always embellish their careers. If he ran into a guy playing golf who said he was all-Southeastern Conference at Auburn, chances were he'd been a scrub. If he just said he was on the team, it meant he'd never played past high school. Walker doesn't even believe it's intentional. He thinks that men deceive even themselves over the years. Maybe it comes from watching too much sports on TV. He and

Mattie used to talk about it; she swore that women never did that, that it was purely a male failing. Walker never admitted it, but he was fairly sure she was right.

There'd always been something about R.J., though. Even as a kid, he had a quietness about him that was not the intimidation of being in a tiny, unwanted minority. You always had the feeling that there was nothing R.J. feared. Even Dexter Cates, who outweighed him by fifty pounds and could bench-press twice his weight, would be quiet when R.J. told him to shut up. And nobody ever doubted anything Raymond Justus said.

If R.J. says, in so many words, that he was screwed by Southeastern University, Walker is pretty sure that was the case.

They don't broach the subject of the slavery museum until after three o'clock, when Walker realizes he should either call someone or go back to the paper.

He's looking for an excuse to leave when he sees Philly come waddling across the yard.

She doesn't say anything to Walker at first, claims she's just bringing R.J. his supper, some sort of gumbo in a battered pot. She takes it inside, then comes back and takes a seat on the porch. Finally, she does acknowledge her son's visitor.

"I don't reckon I should of sicced Cracker on you," she mumbles, "although I wanted to do worse when I heard about Carneal."

Walker apologizes again, and she seems to accept it.

The boy himself, who left the house as soon as his father would let him, comes back from up the street, drawn by the smell of his grandmother's cooking, Walker figures. He sits, cautiously, on the edge of a wrought-iron rocking chair.

They make small talk for a few minutes. Then, when Walker is ready again to leave, Philly says, apropos of nothing, "Well, I reckon your newspaper is going to whip that slave museum right into the ground."

Walker sits back in his chair.

"Momma," R.J. says, "I want you to mind your manners. This man is our guest."

"I know he's your guest," Philly says. "He's eat at my house a few times, too. But I know what's right, too."

Walker starts to speak, but R.J. cuts him off.

"He's got his job, and we got ours," he tells his mother. "There isn't anybody gets to get up every day and just make it up the way they want it."

Amen to that, Walker is thinking.

"Tell me about the slave museum," he says. "Mind you, it isn't going to do any good. I don't think I could change things even if I wanted to. They'd shut us down if we backed something like that."

Walker isn't sure he's telling the truth, isn't sure he and his father aren't just too greedy or too scared to find out.

"Who's your great-granddaddy?" Philly asks Walker, turning to him suddenly, fixing him with a laser stare from behind her thick glasses. He's taken aback for a moment, then tells her Hector McNeill Fann. He can also name the other three.

"How 'bout your great-great granddaddy?"

Walker still isn't sure where this is leading. He can name two, though.

"And where did you all come from?"

Walker guesses she means what country, and he says England by way of Ireland by way of Pennsylvania.

Philly sits back and crosses her arms.

"Well," she says, "I know as much about my folks as anybody in Cottondale. You know how many of my great-grandparents I know the names of?"

She holds her index finger and thumb in a circle.

"None. Zero. I never even known who my daddy was, and the only name I got for my momma's folks is what they told me, because none of 'em could write.

"We ain't got any Jamestown or Plymouth Rock, or one of them fancy family trees that goes back to Jesus. All we got is old dim, distant Africa, that nobody remembers nothing about."

Philly leans closer and lowers her voice. Walker sees that the boy, Carneal, is listening intently. R.J. is looking away, embarrassed.

"What we want is some history," she says, almost whispering, but all her three-hundred-plus pounds bearing down on the words. "It might not be pretty history, but it's ours. What else we got?"

R.J. stirs. "Come on, Momma," he says, helping her up. "You've given Walker enough hell for one day."

"There's plenty more where that came from," she says, and suddenly, for the first time in more than twenty years, Walker hears that laugh, the laugh that seemingly could drown out all the pain in the world, the laugh that conjures up smells of collard greens and hot ironing boards.

When Philly has gotten back across the yard to her own porch, R.J. says to Walker, both of them standing now, "I'm sorry about that. Momma gets fired up about the slave museum."

He hesitates for a couple of seconds, then adds, "Well, hell. You might as well know. I'm pretty fired up about it, too. Fired up as I get about anything."

It turns out that R.J. has been helping the former Dexter Cates, the current Rasheed Aziz, organize people in Cottondale, getting names on petitions, calling and visiting to make people aware of the vote coming up on Tuesday.

There is an awkwardness when they part that is different from the one of a few hours earlier. Then Walker felt that he just needed to make himself understood, to explain how he wasn't quite the white devil Raymond Justus and his family thought he'd turned out to be.

Now, though, Walker knows there is something between him and his old teammate that words won't fix.

He's halfway to his car when R.J. calls after him, "Carneal will be there in the morning, nine o'clock. You get your money's worth out of him, hear?"

Walker waves, the parting words like an extended hand, buoying him.

6

BY THE TIME WALKER LEAVES, IT'S AFTER FOUR. HE CALLS BECKY WHICKER, HIS SECRETARY, BEFORE HE LEAVES AND TELLS HER HE won't be at the four-thirty meeting, where editors try to put the most positive spin on their departments' offerings for the next day's paper. He could have gotten there just in time, but he knows that the assistant managing editor probably welcomes the opportunity to assert some authority, and he doesn't feel he can give his full attention to *The St. Andrews Standard* just now, can't ask the right questions to let the editors know he's not just a rich man's son playing newspaper publisher.

Walker is sure Becky will tell his father that he called. Big Walker is not accustomed to his son's taking the afternoon off without a word.

Walker drives past Philly's store on the way home. A half-dozen young black kids are outside as he drives past, trying to stare him down. He wonders if even Raymond Justus can make Carneal show up at his house to work the next morning. The store looks a little dilapidated, and Walker doubts that it is large enough to be an actual, full-service grocery store. But Philly has had gas pumps put in at some point, and there are four cars parked outside. The name has changed, too: it used to be PHILLY'S CASH 'N' CARY. Now it's JUSTUS'S CASH 'N' CARRY. Someone, he guesses R.J., has corrected the spelling, and he supposes that the change from "Philly" to "Justus" reflects R.J.'s role in helping run the store now.

He hopes Philly is turning the reins over to R.J. more easily than Big Walker is turning them over to him.

When Walker bent to his father's will and came home with his English degree from Duke, Big Walker had everything planned. It was the first time Walker was made aware of his father's plan.

Walker would work in advertising for a year, circulation for a year, then serve as a reporter for two years—which turned out to be probably his happiest years at the *Standard*. The day after Walker had won two state newspaper-association writing awards, Big Walker moved him to assistant city editor, a job that required him to work until midnight five nights a week.

Well into his twenties, he was "Little Walker" to many of the older—and some of the younger—*Standard* employees, as well as much of the population of Sycamore Country Club. Walker liked to think that his good work as a reporter and then as a subeditor helped to eventually train everyone in town except his father's oldest cronies to call him Walker. By then, though, his father had been promoted to "Big Walker." Some, like Ry Tucker, still used "Little Walker" in front of others, but it was generally out of fashion to do this by the time Walker, at twenty-eight, became the managing editor.

Walker likes to think he is molding a better *Standard* than the one with which he started. The paper has two more black reporters than it did when he came back after college—for a total of two. Walker would like to have more black employees, but every time he recruits a good one, he or she seems to be gone nine months later to a larger paper or a friendlier town. He wonders if his editors are recruiting hard enough. There are many women on the staff, including the assistant managing editor and a department editor, but he knows that the real power at the *Standard*, as in St. Andrews, is white and male, and he can't see how it's going to be different any time soon.

When Big Walker made his son the publisher at thirty-five, seven years ago, Walker and Mattie flew to New York for a long weekend. Walker would have preferred a trip to Myrtle Beach or Hilton Head, if anywhere at all, but this time Mattie insisted.

In an expensive restaurant on Park Avenue, they had a bottle of champagne with their appetizer and first course before switching to a good Bordeaux. Made expansive by the alcohol, Walker told the waiter they were celebrating. The waiter, a young man who looked and acted as if he were between auditions, asked him what they were celebrating, and Walker told him he'd just been made publisher of the newspaper for which he worked.

"Publisher," the waiter said, nodding. "Publisher of a newspaper. Congratulations. How do you go about being a newspaper publisher?"

Mattie, made silly by all the champagne and wine, spoke without thinking. "It helps if your daddy was the publisher before you," she said, giggling, then immediately knew she'd ruined the weekend.

The waiter laughed politely and slipped away. Walker, knowing how right she was, blamed her no matter how much she apologized. What hurt him was that, if Mattie, his soulmate and love, could say something like that, even after sharing a bottle of champagne and a bottle of wine, then everyone in St. Andrews must take it for pure fact. Walker knew right then, sitting at a table in a Manhattan restaurant, that he was always going to be, no matter what people back home said to his face, Little Walker. If he succeeded, he was just building on what Big Walker and his father and grandfather before him had started and nurtured. If he failed, he was a double failure, someone who not only didn't build on what he was given but pissed away what he started with.

He thought of Jesus' parable of the talents, of the poor soul who not only failed to profit but lost even what was given to him.

Walker retraces his route back to the Old Market and then west. With the afternoon sun beating down, bringing some heat to the waning day, he still tastes the first beer he's had in a year, a vow broken without even thinking. What the hell, he thinks as he draws near Charley's, a low white cinderblock building just across Route 30 from River Road. He puts on his right-turn signal and rolls into the dirt parking lot.

Charley's is where many River Road executives go for a quick drink after work. They feel in touch with the common man here, as they wouldn't at the club. The common man is often sitting in the next booth or on the next stool, just off his shift at the mill or killing time at the end of some dead-end day on a mindless job. Walker can't help but think that the common man is working his butt off so he can get into Walker's club.

Walker has on short sleeves, and the cool darkness chills his sweaty arms. He gives a general nod to the ten or so people inside, none of whom he knows, although he's sure some of them know him. "Life During Wartime" is playing on the jukebox. The jukebox at Charley's is schizophrenic, half the time replaying the rock 'n' roll past of guys in golf shirts, the other half twanging out country ballads for men whose names are cursive-scripted on their work shirts.

Walker goes to the end of the bar, sits down, and orders a long-neck Miller. Charley's is the only place in town he can get them, and Charley Lampros keeps them about one degree above freezing.

Walker kills the first tall bottle in two swallows and is halfway through the next when the black man comes in.

He doesn't look like a worker, more like somebody on his way to the beach. He's wearing casual clothes, as if he'd just finished playing golf, although Walker is pretty sure not at Sycamore, which has no black members and damn few black guests, just the occasional token assistant manager at the mill being treated by his boss.

The man is a silhouette against the outer brightness, and Walker doesn't even know how he knew he was black. Maybe the hesitancy at the door, the bushy hair in outline, maybe the way he walks.

Walker can't remember ever seeing an African-American in Charley's before. It's odd that he hasn't, because the bar is right on a national highway, albeit an underused one, in a thirty-five-mile-per-hour zone where you see it in plenty of time to stop. Is there a secret mark on the door, like the blood of the lamb, he wonders, warning black people to pass Charley's by? And if so, why didn't this guy see it? The bars in town are pretty much segregated by custom, but outsiders do go through St. Andrews occasionally.

The man sits down three stools from Walker and two from a dusty-looking laborer, who turns and stares, not acknowledging the new arrival's nod. In the back, by the mirror behind the bar, Walker can see three men, barely old enough to drink, it appears. They have been playing a pinball machine, but now the machine goes quiet, and in the long seconds between songs there is a dead silence, so loud Walker can hear the scrape of an ashtray farther down the bar.

Finally, a George Strait song comes on, as Charley brings the black man his Budweiser, taking the money right then rather than starting a tab. The song hasn't been on more than ten seconds when somebody by the pinball machines says something indecipherable, and three voices join in raucous laughter.

Walker finishes his second beer and glances into the mirror at the black man. The man is large, probably the largest person in the room, and Walker can see what looks like a college ring on his left hand, an expensive-looking watch on his right arm. The man is staring straight at his bottle, drinking it in quick, determined gulps. Walker wants to speak to him but doesn't know what to say. Before he can think of anything, the man has finished his beer and, with exaggerated calm, has gotten off his stool and walked, as if on eggshells, toward the door.

Five minutes after he came in, he's gone. Walker can see a late-model Honda go past in the dirt and hear a brief squeal of tires as it hits the blacktop.

Charley Lampros and he make eye contact briefly in the mirror. Charley raises his eyebrows, and Walker sees the edge of a smirk on his mouth.

Nobody at the bar says anything. Behind him, Walker hears one of the young men say, "And stay out," and they all break up in laughter again.

It's another beer and five-thirty when Walker pulls into Big Walker and Dottie's driveway. Big Walker pulls up right behind him, straight home from the office. Walker would have preferred to have a few minutes to himself before his father's arrival, but he knows he has only himself and that third Miller to blame.

Big Walker crawls out of the big Cadillac, shuts the door, and locks up. He walks slowly toward Walker, who is waiting for him.

"Where did you get to?" he asks his son. "I thought you had some work to do this afternoon."

Big Walker moves closer and sniffs. "I reckon you were doing some community-service work down at Charley's," he says. It is not a rebuke. Big Walker believes in an honest day's work, even from his son, but he sees a three-beer break at Charley's as a return to better times.

"Went by to see Raymond Justus," he says, turning to walk inside.

"Raymond . . . That, that sassy so-and-so that I almost had to arrest this morning? Raymond Justus?"

"I put his son in jail, Big Man."

"I don't care. I'd of put him in jail myself. Good godalmighty. The boy stole your glove, same glove you've had since you were Mac's age. I don't blame you a bit."

Walker stops just short of the front door. "I know," he says. "I blame myself, though."

"You always did," Big Walker says, following and shaking his head.

Walker changes into jeans and a polo shirt. Dottie won't have dinner ready for another forty-five minutes, so he goes out in the backyard, where he hears young voices.

The yard slopes down to the river. Walker can just glimpse it through the sycamores. Walker's house had a flatter backyard, level enough for Mac to have a basketball court. Walker wonders if his son ever goes over to their old house, just to shoot hoops. He misses doing that with his son; misses that among many things.

Walker recognizes his son's voice somewhere down there. He's too close to turn back when he realizes his son is with a girl, Mary Ann or Mary Ellen, whatever, Gillman from the cul-de-sac across the street.

Walker stops, stunned by the sight of Mac and the girl on an old Army blanket they got from somewhere. She sees him before Mac does and pulls down her dress as Mac looks back. Walker turns quickly and retreats up the hill, feeling his own innocence strangely violated. He hadn't even been aware that Mac was noticing girls, and he curses his self-absorption, wonders what little Ginger is up to that he doesn't know about, either.

He vows to be better, to stop wallowing in his own loss. He tells himself that Mac and Ginger are at difficult ages, that even with Mattie it would be hard. He knows they need hugs and he knows they would push him away right now if he tried something so uncool.

Mattie, dammit, he's thinking, you took us from two parents to zero.

At dinner, Dottie and Big Walker keep trying to rise above the awkward silence, but Mac is either embarrassed or sulking, and Walker is preoccupied. Ginger seems oblivious to it all, quietly chewing away. Walker has to fight the urge to tell her to eat more slowly, or less.

Afterward, Big Walker invites his son to come sit on the back porch with him. He pours himself a cognac, offers one to Walker for the first time in many months, but his son refuses.

"Guess you don't want to break all the rules in one day," he says with a chuckle, then sees that Walker sees nothing funny in it at all.

Big Walker sets his glass down.

"Hell, son," he says, putting his hand on Walker's knee, "it's good that you're starting to do some of the old things. It was a good life. It can be a good life again."

But Walker just stares across the darkness above the river. Finally, he says, "R.J. was talking about the museum."

He can hear his father sigh.

"You know he's in league with that damn Rasheed Aziz, don't you? Every time somebody's paper lands on the roof, he's got 'em suing us. He wants to put us out of business."

Walker nods. "Yeah, I know about Dexter Cates. I know about R.J., too. I know R.J. isn't anybody's fool. If Raymond Justus is for something, it probably isn't all bad."

"Damn, damn, damn," his father says softly. "Raymond Justus might of been a good boy at one time, but Grant Adkins could tell you some stories that'd make you think otherwise."

Walker looks over.

"What the hell does Grant Adkins know about R.J.?"

"I mentioned it today, that stuff this morning at the house. He says he's been on drugs, his wife's left him, now he's spending time with that damn Black Muslim."

Walker has heard the stories, third-hand, about how R.J. didn't turn out well after he came home from Southeastern, and he would give them more weight, probably, if he hadn't spent several hours with R.J. that afternoon, if it hadn't seemed for all the world like the old R.J., just a little more tired.

Walker realizes that he hasn't had a serious argument with his father in the past year. He thinks it might be time to go back to one more old habit, too, except this time he's alone.

"Big Man," he says, "I wonder what would happen if they did get the slave museum. Would it be the end of the world? R.J.'s mother . . . "

"No, son," Big Walker says, leaning forward in his chair. "It wouldn't be the end of the world. It would be just one little domino falling and hitting one other little domino.

"But as soon as those dominoes start falling, there's no reversing, no turning back. And at the end of all the dominoes that have got to fall because that first one did, there's one with 'End of the World' written all over it. Might not even happen while you're working. Might fall on Mac's watch instead.

"Besides," Big Walker adds, "even if it was the best thing in the world, how are you going to sell that to Harold Neely? And do you think Henry Sudduth's going to think a slavery museum is such a hot idea?"

Big Walker has always assumed that Mac will take over the paper someday, and Walker doesn't know who he aggravates more by saying it, Mac or Ginger. It used to drive Mattie crazy.

"Well, I don't think it'll be the end of anything," Walker says, wishing for that cognac now, missing the weight of the balloon glass in his hand that was always part of these arguments. "I think it would be a gesture, a symbolic gesture . . ."

"I think it would be a symbolic gesture that the Fanns had gone soft," Big Walker cuts in. "I think it would be a symbolic gesture to all the businessmen, to Harold Neely and everybody else, that the paper wasn't there for them anymore. And then maybe they wouldn't be here for us. I know sure as hell Neely wouldn't be."

Walker has never been easy with the paper's stance on the slavery museum, but like so many things, it has slipped past him in the last year, when the battle really heated up, when the bumper stickers started appearing, along with the spray-painted water towers and billboards. He knows his father is right about Neely and Henry Sudduth, but he can't let it go.

"Big Man," he asks, "do you think the *Standard* has the same obligation to every reader, no matter how rich or poor he is? Isn't that what the motto says: 'Every man's voice'? Is that just a joke?"

Big Walker sets his drink down.

"Naw, son," he says, "that isn't a joke. It wasn't a joke when my granddaddy got beat up for opposing the union. We supported them that wanted to make up their own mind. It wasn't a joke when we had to get the National Guard in here during the King riots to keep 'em from burning the building down because we were defending men's rights to have a business and not worry about some criminal animal breaking in and stealing everything they have.

"It ain't no joke, son, and you'd better not think it is. We are serious as a heart attack, I mean to tell you."

Sometimes, Big Walker uses "we" in a way that chills his son, because the "we" is some group that doesn't include Walker, a "we" that Walker isn't sure he'll ever be a part of, that he's afraid he someday will be a part of.

They are quiet for half an hour or more, then Walker goes inside, politely turning down his father's entreaty to watch a John Wayne movie with him. The baseball strike has greatly diminished Big Walker's enjoyment of television and taken away a major vehicle for getting father and son in the same room in a social setting.

Despite putting in almost no time at his job this day, Walker is tired. It's not much past ten o'clock, but he says goodnight to Dottie, half-asleep on the Eames chair she appropriates when Big Walker is elsewhere, a P. D. James novel in her lap.

"So early on a Friday night?" she says, frowning. "You ought to get out more, honey. You're a young man."

"I wish I was as young as you think I am," Walker says, kissing her cheek.

His children have their own rooms and their own TVs, just like in the old place. He stops at Ginger's door long enough to hear some mindless sitcom as background to a phone conversation. Ginger's phone calls can stretch for an hour or more, which is why she and her brother also have their own lines. Otherwise, no one would ever be able to reach the adult Fanns after school hours. It's something Walker would never have allowed a year earlier. He can hear the crinkle of a plastic bag, the crunch of junk food.

Mac's door is also closed. There is music, although Walker has no idea who his son is listening to. Angry music.

Another line that's been cut. The only time he can talk with Mac about music is when his son gets plugged into the Rolling Stones or some other remnant of Walker's youth. Lately, though, he finds that his reminiscences of long-ago rock concerts are met with rolled eyes or, at best, tolerance. Someone, a mother he met at a PTA meeting last spring, told him junior high was the worst, that kids today mature so fast that they outgrow jerkiness by the time they enter high school. Walker hopes she's right. Mac has just started the ninth grade.

Walker hesitates at the door. He never knows anymore which Mac he might interrupt. He wonders if his son jerks off much, fears he'll catch him in some shameful act that will make the two of them even more distant. This afternoon, stumbling on his son with a girl, was painful to Walker. He has never had "that little talk," as Dottie diplomatically put it once, has just assumed that, in 1994 America, there isn't much he can tell Mac that he hasn't already picked up from television, movies, school, or the information highway.

Walker almost passes by. He's tired, just wants this day over. But what kind of message does he send if he just pretends he never saw anything? He'd like more than anything for his world to spin in an orderly, uninterrupted orbit, free of trouble for just a little while longer, but he's passed by doors too many times lately. He knocks.

There is no sound for a few seconds. Just as Walker starts to knock again, more forcefully, he hears the bed springs creak, then loud, somewhat clumsy, heavy-footed steps.

The door opens a foot or so.

"Yeah?"

"Can we talk?" Walker says it like Joan Rivers used to, "tawk" instead of "talk," hoping to get at least a smile.

Mac shrugs, and Walker comes inside the door that seems to give way grudgingly.

Mac returns and collapses on the bed. Walker sits backward in the chair next to his son's desk.

"I didn't mean to walk up on you this afternoon," he says.

"Dad . . ." Mac's face reddens. "It was nothing, O.K.? We don't have to talk or anything. We were just, you know, messing around."

Walker is pretty sure that his son meant to say "screwing around" but caught himself.

"Mac," he says, "it's O.K. Just be careful. O.K.?"

Mac nods his head, relieved that this will soon be over.

"And please," Walker says, rising to leave, "don't let Big Walker or Dottie stumble over you. We don't want to give 'em a heart attack."

The idea of his grandparents finding him with a girl makes the boy smile and stifle a laugh. Walker realizes it's the closest he's seen his son come to laughter in some time.

"Is everything else all right?" he asks, made sad by the memory of a Mac who once smiled most of the time.

"Yeah." Mac shrugs, looking away.

"How about Ginger? She just seems like she's disappearing from me."

"She's a pain in the butt," Mac says. "I'm glad I'm in high school so I don't have to see her anymore."

Walker has been aware that his children don't always play well together, although they did when they were younger. Mac's vehemence surprises him, though.

"Well, you know, she's been through it all, too."

"But can't you do something about her eating all the time?" Mac says, rolling over on the double bed. "I mean, she's fat, Dad."

"She'll grow out of it," Walker says and hopes he's right. As hard as it is to talk with Mac these days, the idea of broaching the subject of his twelve-year-old's eating habits fills him with even more dread. Maybe Dottie can do it.

"I just want us to be happy," Walker says.

"I know," Mac says. Walker can hear his voice catch. He moves toward the boy, but Mac waves him away.

"I'm O.K. Just, you know, don't worry. I'll be careful, Dad. Don't worry."

Walker wants to comfort his son, wants him to cry in his arms the way he did the time the puppy got run over, but neither one of them can manage that right now. Walker leaves.

Safe in his own room, Walker throws his clothes across a chair, too tired even to hang them up. He gets into the queen-sized bed and turns on the TV with the remote control. The local news is just starting, and the main item is the Museum of Slavery. There is a sound bite with Rasheed Aziz urging everyone to vote on Tuesday, to approve the referendum. Walker thinks he can see R.J. in the background, but before he's sure, the cameras have gone on to Dick West, one of the city councilmen opposing the museum. West, who owns a chain of convenience stores, says he's against spending tax dollars to dig up a past best left buried.

Walker stays awake through the news, weather, and sports, then catches Leno's monologue before switching the set off.

In a year, he's never learned to sleep by himself. Sometimes, he'll wake up and find that he's done a ninety-degree turn, thrashing out wildly into space as he tries to locate a ringing alarm clock somewhere to his right or left. Dog-tired, he knows he'd better read for a while or face an endless hour of tossing and turning in the dark.

He reads twenty pages of a biography of Stonewall Jackson, giving up finally when he realizes he's read the same paragraph three times.

Before Walker Fann falls asleep, his brain dredges up one Raymond Justus story he hasn't thought of in years, one that only he or R.J. could tell.

Raymond Justus's freshman year at St. Andrews High was even more miserable in the classroom than on the athletic fields, where at least he could excel.

He was an average student, but because he was black, every mistake, every mispronounced word or math error, was magnified. In classes where R.J. was the only African-American, he sat alone. It got better as more black students transferred or were bused in, and most of the whites got used to it, but ninth grade was hell.

Shop was the worst of all.

Almost all the ninth-grade boys had to take either agriculture or shop. The St. Andrews principal, then in his early seventies and in his twenty-fourth year at the school, felt that boys should get their hands dirty.

It was an inconvenience to Walker and other college-bound boys, but Big Walker and the paper backed the policy. Just as he felt his son should go to public school, he also believed he should mingle with the future millworkers and carpenters, at least this once.

To Raymond Justus and the other black freshmen, though, it was more than aggravation; it was pure agony.

Purvis Freeman had been teaching shop almost as long as the principal had been at St. Andrews. He was a rough, weather-beaten man with few academic credentials. His students spent much of their time building things for Freeman or one of his friends.

Nobody at St. Andrews High, though, really understood, before integration, just how much Purvis Freeman hated black people.

R.J. and Walker were in the same shop class, second period. The first day, Freeman started in on R.J. right away.

They were in the classroom, in the same small, two-room building as the shop itself.

"Mr. Justus, come up here," he said not two minutes after the bell rang.

R.J. came hesitantly to the front of the room.

"Mr. Justus," he said, his drawl even more pronounced than usual, playing to the crowd, "what is this?" And he reached into his pocket, pulling out a Brazil nut.

No one in white St. Andrews, to Walker's knowledge, ever referred to the dark brown crescents as "Brazil nuts," though. To the Fanns and every other white family, they were "nigger toes."

"I don't know," R.J. said quietly as the rest of the class, all white, caught on and began laughing.

"What? Speak up, Mr. Justus. I cain't hear you."

"I don't know."

"You don't know? Well, you ought to, boy. Class, can you all tell Mr. Justus here what this is?"

Twenty-five voices, including Walker's, sang out, "Nigger toe!"

Raymond Justus just stood there, not frowning, not smiling, until he was told to return to his seat.

"I tell you what," the teacher said. "I'm gonna leave this,

uh, Brazil nut, up here on my desk so you won't forget what it is, Mr. Justus."

And it never seemed to let up. Anything R.J. did was carefully scrutinized for mistakes by Freeman. And when a mistake was made, he would stop everyone in the middle of their shoeboxes and planters and other projects to hold R.J. up as an example of what not to do.

Walker was amazed, thinking back on it later, that R.J. didn't complain to someone. He just seemed to take it. Things were bad in general for the black students at St. Andrews High, but the shop was a world to itself. Purvis Freeman had a full-size Confederate flag hanging over the entrance to the shop, and no one ever thought about taking it down until Raymond Justus and Dexter Cates made it a moot point.

Cates was in a later class, and he no doubt caught more grief than even Raymond, because he did not have his friend's coolness under fire.

Walker figures, even twenty-eight years later, that he is the only white person who knows what happened to Purvis Freeman's little kingdom.

It was late November, and several of the freshman basketball players had been scrimmaging in the gym. They'd all played football and were trying to break in a new set of muscles, with the junior varsity season only a week off, and Glen Murphy had been able to talk the janitor into letting them stay and lock up.

They didn't stop until after ten o'clock. Afterward, Walker told Glen he'd get Big Walker to come get them— Glen lived just a few houses down. So Glen stayed at the front of the gym while Walker cut through the alley between the gym and the shop, headed for the phone booth at the edge of the school parking lot.

It was a moonless night, and the area between the two

buildings was darker than black. Walker heard a door close in front of him, at the back of the shop. Then, in the glow of the parking-lot lights, he saw Dexter Cates and Raymond Justus. Dexter didn't look back, might not have even heard the footsteps coming toward them, but R.J. did. He jumped, only a twitch really, when he saw Walker, and then he was under control again.

It was the first time Walker had ever seen his black teammate show any real emotion. Then Raymond Justus did something that froze Walker where he stood. He held his index finger to his lips, as if he didn't want his friend to know they'd been seen. Walker stopped, dead silent, long enough for them to slip into the darkness down toward the river. Then he walked on, toward the phone booth, wondering what he had just seen.

He was halfway across the parking lot when he smelled smoke, and he could see the red reflecting off one of the shop's back windows.

He used the telephone to call the fire department, but by the time the engines got there, the little building was beyond saving.

It was obviously arson, and the police questioned Walker at length. Surely he must have seen someone leaving the building. This wasn't a prank that got out of hand, was it? Could it have been one of those colored boys?

Walker told them nothing. He wasn't sure why he kept silent. Maybe it was because he didn't like Purvis Freeman much better than R.J. did; as a well-cared-for River Road boy, he took plenty of abuse, too. Maybe it just seemed good to know something everyone else didn't.

As it turned out, it was the end of shop as a required course. The classroom took until the next school year to rebuild, and by then what had been seen as a necessary evil was rebelled against. A couple of parents filed suit to keep their sons from having to waste valuable time making book-cases, and the principal gave in. Given the choice, almost no one opted to take ninth-grade shop, and by Walker's senior year it was no longer part of the curriculum.

Purvis Freeman was almost certain he knew who burned down his shop and eventually brought an end to his useful-ness, but six other boys in Cottondale said they'd been hanging out with Raymond Justus and Dexter Cates at ten o'clock that night, two miles away. And no eyewitness came forth.

It was a strange conspiracy. Walker didn't know if R.J. had even told Dexter Cates of the white boy who saw their getaway, and neither of the two would-be quarterbacks ever talked about it, not even when Walker started spend-ing time at Philly's and they talked about other things almost as important. They'd nod in the hallway at school, usually speak, and that was about it.

The only time R.J. ever hinted at their shared secret was the day the Saints won the state football championship.

It had been the kind of day most people don't get even once in a lifetime. Even now, Walker and Glen Murphy or Rudy Blake or one of their other teammates will agree, after a couple of drinks, that their lives probably reached apogee that day.

St. Andrews beat the school from Winston-Salem on a cold, windy December afternoon. Walker threw two touchdown passes to Raymond Justus and sneaked for another one.

The game had been played in Winston-Salem, and St. Andrews was a huge underdog. By the time the boys had dressed and the bus had returned them to St. Andrews, it was after nine o'clock on a Saturday night.

They first noticed the crowd as they neared the school. They heard horns blowing and, looking back, saw a string of cars that had waited at the city limits to escort them.

They kept going, past the school. There were people two deep on the River Bridge, three deep on Main Street itself.

The bus stopped at the Old Market, and the boys were given a dozen ovations by a crowd that the *Standard* later estimated at three thousand. Glen Murphy was the first to jump on the hood of the bus, then climb on the roof, and soon the whole team was up there. Dexter Cates and Tom Maddry, another lineman, waved the trophy, but the biggest cheers were for Walker and R.J.

Someone had rigged up a microphone down below, and Coach Kell took it.

"You won't need to turn those jerseys in, men," he said. "You keep those jerseys, and tell your children and your grandchildren what you achieved. Tell them you were the best St. Andrews ever had."

It was the only time anyone had ever seen the toughest man in St. Andrews choke up.

Walker was sitting yoga-style on top of the bus. As he glanced over to his left, he saw R.J. standing quietly amid all the tumult. For a brief second, they made eye contact.

Raymond Justus held up his index finger to his lips, Walker did the same, and that was that.

Now, drifting into sleep, Walker wonders why he would remember such a thing now, and how he had ever forgotten it.

7

WALKER AND I THOUGHT OUR LUCK WOULD HOLD FOREVER.
OUR LIFE TOGETHER WASN'T COMPLETELY SEAMLESS. WE DID break up once, for three days.

It was our freshman year in college. He was at Duke and I was at Millen, feeling a little intimidated by all those New York and California girls that Walker suddenly had as "pals." And then he'd get jealous if I even mentioned some boy from State or Carolina who happened to buy me a beer.

We had a big argument over the phone because he told me he had to study all weekend and couldn't take me to the Duke-Carolina football game. I told him I guessed I'd have to find another date then, not even believing I was saying it.

It was quiet for so long I thought we'd been disconnected.

Finally, he said, "Well, I guess that's that."

"That's what?" I asked him.

More silence.

"Do you want your ring back?" I asked him, not believing he'd say yes.

"I guess so."

I waited another few seconds, then hung up.

I cried all night, then started again in the morning when I mailed that big fat St. Andrews High School ring back to him. I threw it into a manilla envelope and, when it hit the bottom of the mail box outside our dorm with a thud, it sounded like my life ending.

Who knows what would have happened if I had used sufficient postage?

The thing came back two days later. Sandy Kyle, my roommate, said it was a Freudian slip, putting just a fifteen-cent stamp on that clod-knocker of a ring, and that I didn't really want to break up with Walker. She was probably right.

Walker called me that night. He told me he'd waited three days to get that ring, and when he didn't, he'd figured that maybe I wasn't completely fed up with him.

It was years before I told him about the insufficient postage. We probably would have made up anyhow, eventually, but the idea that we might have split up for good over something that stupid could bring tears to my eyes twenty years later.

I'd see college friends break up over this and that all the time, just like our married friends were all the time getting divorced later on. Sometimes you had the feeling that they were better off apart, after all the misery they'd put each other through.

People thought Walker and Mattie Fann were the luckiest souls in the world, to have found that one perfect partner right from the start. We thought our luck would never change. But it wasn't like we had mental telepathy or something. It wasn't as if one of us would get an itch and the other would start scratching. We had our own identities—at least, I think we did—and we each had our own what our friends were forever calling "space." Walker could spend the afternoon playing golf or I could go down to Charleston with the girls for the weekend without either of us going into a coma.

But I can honestly say that probably very few people achieved the contentment and happiness I had just drifting off to sleep every night with Walker curled like a spoon around my back. I doubt that many people enjoyed evenings at Sardi's any better than I enjoyed stretching out on the couch in our den with Walker leaning back against me. I could measure his aging by how much the bald spot on the top of his head was growing, the one he didn't know was there until he saw a picture of himself from behind one day. He was horrified, but I didn't care. It suited me fine to grow quietly old with Walker Fann.

Anyway, when he called me, Walker apologized and told me he'd stay up all night if he had to, but that he intended to take me to the Duke-Carolina game, that he hadn't known how much it meant to me. I told him, I don't even like football; I just want to be with you. And, I was thinking, to be sure you're not with one of those Yankee floozie "pals" of yours, studying anatomy. I was a little bit insecure back then, a little too afraid of losing a good thing. I like to think Walker was, too.

The thing is, Walker was so serious about his studies. He wasn't a natural genius or anything; he just got ahead in school by outworking people. That, more than money, was his real inheritance from his daddy. People always had this image of Walker Fann as some kind of dandy, a rich man's son who probably slid through with gentlemanly Cs. Hell, Walker graduated with a 3.5 from Duke. Walker was smart, is smart. Sometimes, many times, I'd wish he'd been some poor boy who had to get it all on his own. Then he'd have felt more like he earned it.

It would have made a lot of other things more simple, too. Like race.

Walker was what you would call a liberal when we graduated, and he might have stayed one if we'd gone on to Baltimore, said to heck with family and obligations, delved into the big old world instead of just St. Andrews. I guess it was easier to be a liberal then, with the oppressed damn happy to get any kind of break they could, after all they'd been through, especially black people.

It was easier for me. Momma and Daddy were more understanding than most around here, and after Walker and I got married, it was expected that I would be involved in good deeds of various kinds. But around River Road, being a liberal is viewed as a sign of weakness, and men are definitely not supposed to be weak. Never mind that it would have taken a lot more real strength to just tell Big Walker to take *The St. Andrews Standard* and shove it.

What few arguments Walker and I had, a goodly percentage started over something or other on the *Standard*'s editorial pages. That awful Ry Tucker or one of his toadies would write something against aid for dependent children, or something implying that poor people deserved to be that way, and I'd be waiting when Walker got home. We'd talk about it, him conceding that Ry Tucker was wrong but that Big Walker insisted that it run. I'd stay after it like a fox terrier, not letting go until Walker started taking it personal. He'd say something like, "Well, why don't we leave St. Andrews, then? Hell, I don't need all this crap," and I didn't know whether he meant the crap I was giving him or our material possessions.

But when push came to shove, neither one of us had guts enough to leave, after a while. First, it would break our parents' hearts. Then, we had the kids to think about. Finally, we'd just agree with each other that we were too damn old to start over somewhere else, that we could do more good trying to make things better in St. Andrews. The paper was getting better, slowly but surely; my charity work surely must be making life down in Cottondale a little better.

Truth is, though, we didn't do half enough.

Walker was caught in the middle, no doubt about that. The way we were raised, you don't just quit having parents because you don't agree with their politics, and Big Walker . . . well, he was, is, the kind of man that would pay his gardener's hospital bills anonymously, then approve an editorial that denounced national health care as Communism, pure and simple.

Big Walker wanted to give; he is not an ungenerous man. He refused to be taken from, though. Trouble was, he didn't always give enough, or encourage his cronies to give enough, quickly enough. Change came hard to Big Walker and the rest on River Road, partly because they had it so good any change to their self-contained world almost had to be for the worse. And then when the federal government would try to make them change, they'd fight it like it was Gettysburg all over again.

The worst was the slavery museum.

The first time I heard of it, back when Rasheed Aziz and some of the black ministers were just getting the idea off the ground, I saw it as something that St. Andrews could be proud of, a bridge. It sounded good to Walker at first, too, but soon his interest seemed to be slipping. He and Big Walker had arguments over it; Big Walker and I had arguments over it. Funny thing about Walker's daddy: he always treated me like the daughter he never had, and he'd let me get away with saying just outrageously rude things. Looking back, part of it was that Big Walker didn't take me seriously enough. He was humoring me.

The women's club backed off from supporting it after a while. The official line was that it would hurt racial harmony, which I told Peggy Sellers meant "happy niggers," which caused us not to speak to each other for a few months.

I did door-to-door campaigning to get up a petition forcing a referendum, and I wish I could have been there to see it happen. It hurt me that Walker wouldn't help much at all, and it hurt him, I'm sure, that I'd embarrass him by going up to strangers and asking them to support something the *Standard* was diametrically against. But he knew, and I knew that he knew, that this was right. If all this business with Harold Neely and the anchor store at his damn mall hadn't come up, and if I had been there to fight, to prod Walker and Big Walker both, it might have turned out differently.

If I could have changed the love of my life in any one way, I'd have made him care less about what other people thought. Looking back, I might have made myself care a little less, too.

Runner-up in the If-I-Could-Have-Changed-Walker contest: I would have made him a little more adventuresome. It would be me, all through our college years, who would have to coerce Walker into having fun. Once you got him to the dance, or the beach, or the ballgame, he was fine. But he needed a push.

We got married in August of 1974, two months after graduation. We'd already been sleeping together for four years, since the summer after we finished high school, and it is a tribute to Walker's carefulness that we didn't "have to" get married. But the thrill of living together was something else.

We rented an apartment in Country Club Gardens, right next to the golf course. It was a place where the newly-divorced and newlywed lived side by side. It was two stories, two bedrooms, and two baths. Sometimes, friends of Walker's would stop by for a beer in the middle of a round; golf balls used to bounce off the side of the apartment building and wake us up.

It didn't exactly suit either one of us to be back in St. Andrews, but we surely did have a good time with each other. Walker would write me poetry. He'd remember not only our anniversary but also the day we started going steady. He told me he loved me about five times a day, and I told him about ten. I'd get the blues sometimes just thinking about what would have happened if we'd broken up.

I worked for five years as a teacher. By then, Big Walker was paying Walker enough for us to move onto River Road,

just down from him and Dottie. I quit when I got pregnant with Mac and never went back. Did some charity
work and raised a family.

The children were a joy, for the most part, but the lack
of challenge, the blandness of life at home with two
young ones, made me want to get out and explore more
than Walker did.

He always said he didn't want to go anywhere that he
couldn't eat barbecue and work on his tan. I did get him
to Bermuda once, and in our mid-thirties we started going
to the Bahamas every winter for a week.

But I'd always dreamed of going to Italy, ever since I
was a little girl. Walker put me off for nineteen years, and
if it had been up to him, we never would have gone.
Walker Fann just flatly did not like to travel. He got more
like that every year, it seemed to me. I wonder sometimes
what would have happened if Big Walker hadn't forced
him to come home after graduation instead of taking that
job in Baltimore. It was almost like Walker said to himself,
Well, if they won't let me go where I want to go, I just
won't go anywhere at all.

Big Walker, he loved to travel. They'd go to England or
France, take a cruise to Scandinavia or Greece, but Walker
was happiest, I believe, when he was either sitting around
the house with me and the children or over at the club,
playing golf or poker or shooting the breeze with the
same boys he'd known all his life.

It was up to me to get him out of that, to not let him
sink into the kind of rut our friends seemed stuck in. Well,
I got him to Italy, all right.

*   *   *

How did I do it? Simple. I went down to the travel agency, the one that booked our trip to the islands every winter, and bought us two tickets to Rome. I'd already checked with Big Walker and Dottie about keeping the kids.

Walker couldn't believe it.

"I can't just take off," he said, when I told him. "I'm the publisher of a newspaper."

"Well, I just checked with the chairman of the board, and he said it was O.K. with him."

Walker just shook his head.

"I can't speak Italian. I can't stand to sit that long in an airplane. What if we crash? Who's going to take care of the kids?"

I told him Big Walker and Dottie would until they could find an orphanage for them.

Walker just shook his head, but he knew he was trapped.

He actually worked up some enthusiasm, once he accepted his fate. I bought the tickets in April, and we went in August, as sort of an anniversary present to each other. It was the first time we'd gone more than two days without taking the kids; they'd always been with us when we went to the islands. But this time I wanted to be alone with my husband.

Walker started listening to language tapes in the car, would proudly show me how well he could count in Italian, would tell me an easy way to convert lire into dollars in your head. There were times when I wanted to tell him, when he was planning our itinerary down to the minute, to slow down, take it easy, let it happen.

The thing about Walker was—is, I guess—that he

wants to be in control. He can't stand to not know what's around the corner. He was always after me for buying something that we could easily afford, telling me how much that $300 I'd spent for a chair would be worth if he left it in a money market for forty years. Like Big Walker wasn't going to leave him more money than the two of us, and our children, could ever spend. But it wasn't that Walker was a skinflint. He didn't mind spending great sums of money, mostly on what I wanted, because his tastes were as simple as you could find on River Road. But he wanted it all planned. It was the unscheduled purchase, the uncharted trip, that made him crazy.

Me, I was the wild child, Ms. Midlife Crisis of 1994. My role, as I saw it, was to push Walker Fann, a sweet, generous man, who pleased all my senses except the one of adventure, to new frontiers.

We left on August 19, our anniversary. It wasn't supposed to be a long trip. We'd return on the 29th, in time to get the kids back in school.

Nothing seemed to go right, at the start. It rained all morning, and Walker got soaked. All the luggage wouldn't fit in the trunk, so he put it onto the rack up top, then covered it with a tarp and tied it down.

We weren't two miles from the house, heading for the Raleigh-Durham airport, when a man in a dilapidated station wagon did a U-turn and pulled right in front of the tractor-trailer beside us. The truck drifted all the way into our lane, and we went bumping along on the edge of the pavement with rain coming down so hard we could barely see.

We came to a stop on the shoulder, traffic whipping past us, throwing water on us so hard it made a whumping sound as it hit the side of the car.

At the airport, we had to go to an auxiliary lot, and we both got soaked this time. By the time we reached the terminal, we looked like a couple of drowned rats.

We got in the world's longest check-in line, behind some kind of Indian youth group that seemed to have neither tickets nor destination, from the amount of time it took to sort things out.

Finally, we got checked in and reached our gate, stopping for a couple of stiff bourbon-and-waters on the way.

The flight would go first to London, then to Rome. Miraculously, it was more or less on time. As they called our row and we stood up, clutching our carry-on bags, Walker looked at me, dog-tired from defying death on the highway and fighting the monsoon.

"Last chance to back out," I told him, reaching up to smooth out his hair.

"Forget it," he said. "They've already got our luggage. If my underwear's going to be in Rome, that's where I want to be, too."

8

W ALKER HAS ALREADY BEEN UP THREE HOURS WHEN THE DOOR-
BELL RINGS.

He rises at six on Tuesdays, Thursdays, and Saturdays to run the 3-mile loop around the golf course and country club. He has it all figured out: 9 miles times 52 weeks, at 30 miles per pound, equals 15 or 16 pounds a year. If he's training for the 10K in October, he'll step it up to 4, 5, and 6 miles at a time, but usually he clocks a steady 25-minute 3-mile run 3 times a week, no matter the weather. In the winter, he runs on the street because it's lighted. In the spring, summer, and fall, it's the golf course.

When he doesn't run, he feels guilty. Even after Italy, he missed exactly two weeks.

This morning, though, something happened that he hadn't experienced in a long time.

Usually, he'll hit a stretch, even in the 3-mile course, where he really wants to quit, where there is something pessimistic, almost like panic, within his body telling him he's not getting enough air, his legs are too heavy, he'll never make it. He used to even have dreams about it, before more monstrous visitations preempted them.

But it's always a small victory for him that he overcomes that moment, which usually comes on a long, tedious hill almost a mile from the finish.

This morning, he quit. He can't explain exactly why he yielded to the siren song this time, why he didn't run through the pain. He took a last few stumbling steps and then just walked the rest of the way to the clubhouse, a couple of fellow joggers slipping past him on the way. He has told himself all year that he won't give in to it, and now he feels that he has. The small defeat will nag him the rest of what started out to be the kind of cool, dry Saturday he waits for all summer.

He remembers Big Walker admonishing him once for stopping just a few yards short of the finish line in a swim meet, when he was no more than nine years old.

"Son," Big Walker had told him when they got back to the car to go home, "don't you ever quit on me again. You can not start, although I'd rather you always tried, but once you do start, you keep going. You hear me?" His fingers dug into Walker's shoulders. They never talked about it again.

Now Walker has showered and dressed, opting not to shave, a luxury he seldom gives himself, even on Saturdays, despite his light beard. He's had breakfast with Dottie and Big Walker, who had just returned from the health club. Big Walker used to jog with his son, until his knees gave out. These days, he tries in vain to get Walker to swim laps with him.

Another great day is predicted by the weatherman— bright blue skies, highs in the upper sixties.

As Walker sits in the den, reading the *Standard* and the *News & Observer* from Raleigh, still hounded by that last mile he didn't run, he feels a touch of the old excitement he used to get when the weather would take that first turn from the humidity of Southern summer.

"Don't forget," Big Walker tells him, walking past at a brisk clip in search of yard work. "We've got a two-o'clock tee time."

Walker plays golf most Saturdays with either his friends, his father's, or both. It works best when they have one of each. Big Walker and Glen Murphy or one of Walker's other friends are usually a good match for Walker and one of his father's business buddies. Today, it's Walker and Billy Holland against Big Walker and Glen.

"Two o'clock," he repeats to his father's rapidly retreating footsteps.

He's been there for some time, reading and then just staring out into the space across and above the river, when the bell rings.

Dottie has gone out to visit her sister at the retirement home, and the kids are upstairs; Walker can hear both Ginger's television and Mac's CD player. Big Walker, whose hearing seems to be slipping, is in the backyard. Walker sighs, gets up out of the Eames chair and goes to answer the door.

Opening it, he wonders if he has slipped into a real-life version of a horrible movie he rented recently, in which the main actor was doomed to live the same day over and over until he got it right.

"R.J.," he says, somehow not surprised.

Raymond nods his head. He's dressed in work clothes.

"You seen Carneal?"

It's the first time Walker has thought of the boy this morning. He should have known that Raymond Justus would be as good as his word, that he would send his son over here to do yard work if he'd said he would.

"Ah, no, R.J. He hasn't been here. What time did you send him over?"

"Eight o'clock. And I didn't send him over. I dropped him off two doors down and told him to walk his nasty self up here and ring that doorbell like a man."

Walker can see that R.J. is disappointed but not totally surprised. For a split second, he sees a "kids-what-can-you-do?" look, like the fraternity of parents' secret handshake, pass across his old classmate's face, then the scowl returns.

"Well," R.J. says, "I reckon that means I got some tracking to do."

He starts to turn, but Walker grabs his arm.

"R.J., can I come with you?" He realizes it sounds like a plea, and that it is one. "I mean, I don't feel so good about this. I shouldn't have had him thrown in jail."

The black man stares, then something behind Walker catches his attention. Walker turns and sees Mac, still somewhat sleepy-faced, staring at them from the bottom of the stairs.

R.J. turns back to Walker.

"You want to come on a wild-goose chase? I thought you'd have better things to do on a Saturday morning."

Walker turns to go and get his wallet off the table in the den.

"Dad," Mac says to him, exasperated, "you're supposed to take me to the Y at nine-thirty. Remember?"

Walker tells Raymond Justus to just leave his car out front, that he'll drive them in their search for Carneal. That way, he can drop Mac off at the YMCA too.

"Nah," R.J. says. "Better let me drive. I'll drop the boy off. I'm afraid to leave my car in a neighborhood like this." He winks at Mac, to whom he has not been formally introduced, and motions for father and son to follow him.

Mac crawls into the backseat of the two-door Buick. Walker prays that he won't complain about being seen in such a boat; you could probably knock someone down ten feet away just by opening the door. It's the kind of car Walker and his children joke about when they see one near them in a parking lot. There are, Walker notes thankfully, no dice or other artifacts hanging from the rearview mirror.

"Where're you all going?" Mac asks from the cavernous backseat.

"We're looking for somebody," R.J. says. The car starts on the second try.

"Can I come?"

Walker turns to look at his son. It's been a long time since the boy asked to go anywhere with him, and he wishes he had chosen a more pleasant and predictable trip. He has no idea where Raymond Justus's red Buick might take them.

"I thought you were going to the Y. Aren't you meeting somebody there?"

Mac shrugs his shoulders. "Nah. They can get along without me for one day, I think."

R.J. looks over at Walker, who says, "It's O.K. with me if it's O.K. with you."

"All right, then," he says, wheeling out into River Road, "let's go on a scavenger hunt. See if we can find us a Carneal."

"Is Carneal your son?" Mac asks.

"Yeah. You know him?"

"I know of him. He's a great running back."

"When I get through with him, he might have to go on injured reserve."

It's obvious to Walker that this isn't the first time Raymond Justus has gone out in search of his son. He makes a swing through the mall first, stopping once to call a boy about Carneal's age over to the car and question him. They stop so R.J. can use the pay phone next to Charley's. While they're alone in the car, Mac says, "Dad, I know that kid. Carneal Justus, right?"

"Right."

"He's the one you had thrown in jail?"

"Right."

"Man." Walker can't tell whether his son is expressing disgust or surprise.

"He's really some kind of football player."

"Well, his father wasn't bad, either."

"They threw him out of junior high for a week last year. For fighting or something."

Walker turns around to look at his son. Mac stares back at him.

"But you still shouldn't have had him thrown in jail."

R.J. comes back to the car and the conversation ceases.

"Miss Willie McDuffie says he called her boy and asked him to come get him at the mall. He must of run all the way back down River Road."

"So you know where he is?" Walker asks him.

"Well, Miss Willie's boy didn't come back, so they might be anywhere from here to Raleigh. But I got a few ideas."

They cross the bridge and cruise past the abandoned storefronts. R.J. turns left a block from the Old Market and drives three blocks away, to where the pavement turns to dirt. He goes another block, then turns left again.

Where this dirt street, which doesn't even have a name, stops, there is an old house that would appear abandoned except for the three late-model cars outside.

R.J. gets out and motions for Walker and Mac to stay.

"Some bad niggers hang out here sometimes," he says. Walker is relieved that he isn't expected to follow but asks R.J. if he's sure. Walker is fairly certain that this is the street where the out-of-town man in a Jeep Cherokee turned up dead the week before, shot through the head, in what his police reporter referred to as a DDGB: Drug Deal Gone Bad.

R.J. is met by another black man, pencil-thin, wearing dreadlocks, at the front door. Walker can tell, just by the deference R.J. shows him, that he is armed. They talk for a few moments, then R.J. comes back to the car, puts it in reverse, and backs out to the nearest north-south street.

Walker wants to sound interested but not nosy. He is saddened to think of the young-old boy he met two nights before in such a place. "Does he go there?"

R.J. gives him a tired, pained look.

"No, but it don't take but one time."

They try another house, almost as menacing as the first.

"Well," R.J. says as he gets in the car again, "I reckon we might as well try the Old Market."

The Old Market has become a meeting spot for teenagers, mostly black, mostly from the Cottondale bottoms. While Rasheed Aziz and his group are trying to get the building turned into a museum, Ry Tucker has been writing editorials in favor of demolishing the structure entirely, claiming that it is "an eyesore, a hazard to navigation, and a magnet for undesirable elements."

It certainly has been a hazard to navigation, Walker concedes. Rarely does a month go by that someone doesn't run into the circular brick wall that encloses it. One night last spring, a truck driver from Sanford was killed when he hit it head on, going forty miles an hour. His rig destroyed much of the brick barrier on the west side, coming to rest against the building itself, which was afterward equipped with a flashing red light. The light, strung across a second-floor window, gives Walker the eerie feeling, every time he sees it after dark, that the place is on fire.

And it would be hard to argue, this morning, that the Old Market doesn't draw its share of what the *Standard*'s editorial writers would call undesirable elements. There are about a dozen black kids, the youngest appearing to be no more than twelve, the oldest well past sixteen, leaning against the pillars that hold the building up, talking loudly, scowling with practiced perfection. The foot traffic that still frequents the few surviving shops around the square seems to be giving the market a wide berth.

But Walker would argue that the Old Market is no eyesore, even after decades of neglect.

The copper roof has been green for as long as anyone can remember, the city fights a losing war against graffiti, and the inside, consisting of one room at the middle of the ground-floor open area and a four-room second story, hasn't been used since the chamber of commerce moved out to a new building near the mall in 1977. The old clock on top hasn't worked for almost that long. The rooms are pretty much trashed from occasional, mindless vandalism.

Still, Walker appreciates the building, its Palladian arches, eight to a side, its four-square, solid, old-brick Colonial architecture. He even likes the weather vane on top, just about the only thing about the old building that seems to still work. Today, it twirls smartly in the brisk breeze. He likes what he thinks it gives St. Andrews, a town that didn't even have its present name until after World War II: individuality. He would like, from an aesthetic standpoint, to see the old downtown bustling again, as it was when he was a child, but he keeps such thoughts secret from Harold Neely and the other shapers of St. Andrews's future.

The only time he ever broached the subject at a board meeting, advocating that the paper support the town's attempts to get state and federal funding for a downtown renovation project, Neely left the room without a word. Walker had been naive then, in his late twenties and relatively new to what his father called the management end of things.

Big Walker asked him to stay afterward.

"Son," he said, staring at him solemnly across the big meeting table, talking slowly as if to a small child, "if these folks wanted to bring back downtown, do you reckon they'd be putting their life savings into building malls and housing developments and such out on 30 West? Do you want to put the paper's future in the hands of a bunch of black would-be entrepreneurs that wouldn't piss on us to put it out if we were on fire? Do you want to lose every advertiser we've got that pays their bills on time?"

Walker said he thought there was room for St. Andrews to have a shopping mall and a downtown too.

Big Walker just shook his head.

"Where do you think we live, son? Charleston? Savannah? San Francisco? Look around you. What if they bring a Belk's back to downtown? What if they open a theater or two? Ain't anybody going to be flocking to see quaint old St. Andrews.

"I love this place, son." Here, Big Walker lowered his voice as if the room might be bugged. "But I love it like you love your old maiden aunt, warts and peculiar ways and all."

Big Walker then went off on one of his favorite theories: how Southern towns and cities spread out from their centers, leaving the old downtowns to rot away, because of the white Southerner's natural desire to have some space around him, push out to new frontiers. It had nothing to do with not being able or willing to mix with blacks.

Walker would often argue this point with his father, to no avail, and he seldom went to the enclosed, Muzak-filled Rich Valley Mall, where the temperature was always the same, where old people did their morning walks without their feet ever touching the earth, that he didn't think of Big Walker's theory on Southern frontierism.

Mattie was fond of walking inside the mall doors, into the indiscriminate roar of the place, holding out her hands and turning her head upward, and exclaiming, "No claustrophobic downtown streets for me. Give me the wide-open spaces. Don't fence me in!"

Raymond Justus parks the car on the southwest corner of the traffic circle surrounding the market, and the three of them get out.

R.J. comes around to the passenger side, where Walker and Mac are standing.

"You all might want to wait here," he says. "I won't be long."

"Come on," Walker tells his son. "I think there's a shop up the street that sells baseball cards."

He knows his son has almost surely reached the age where such a hobby is a source of embarrassment, where Walker will have to store the complete sets Mac used to collect until he passes into adulthood and remembers to miss them someday. But he wants an excuse to do something other than stand on the Main Street sidewalk with his hands in his pockets. And he doesn't want to be there when R.J. confronts his own son, who is probably among the crowd holding the Old Market's pillars up.

Mac goes with him. Sure enough, there is a sports collectibles shop, spelled "collectables," near the end of the block, but there is little there to interest either father or son. Inexplicably, the shop, in a nearly all-black shopping district, seems to mostly concentrate on stock-car racing memorabilia.

They come out five minutes after they entered. They see Raymond Justus and his smaller, younger likeness waiting, leaning against the side of the car. The father seems to be doing all the talking; the son, next to him, is motionless, except for his head, which jerks up every few seconds as a "Look at me!" cuts through the noontime air, then sinks slowly downward again.

"Come on," Walker says. "Let's give them a couple more minutes."

He and Mac walk around the block, passing three dozen buildings, of which only eight or nine are open. McRae, the street parallel to Main, has been dubbed "Antique Row," but it's really a sad collection of secondhand stores, most with "On Consignment" placards in the windows. Any true antique in the area would never find its way down here, Walker surmises, and if it did, it would be bought cheap by a more savvy dealer from one of the places out on Route 48 that cater to the only people in town who can afford the real things.

Mac stops suddenly in front of one building that looks vaguely familiar to Walker, too.

"This is the store!" Mac says excitedly. "This is the one where Mom bought me the train that time. . . ."

Walker remembers. It wasn't even Mac's birthday. But she and Mac, who was probably only seven then, had been downtown at the dentist's. Mac had broken a tooth off in a fight at school, and it had to be ground down and capped. Mattie had promised the boy, who was terrified of doctors of all kinds, that he could choose any toy he wanted for enduring his hour in Dr. Forrest's chair. Dr. Forrest was the only white dentist still within a block of the Old Market, even then.

Afterward, they walked back to the car, a block away, headed for the mall and Mac's reward. But Mattie had parked right in front of Taylor's Hobby Shoppe, and before she could get Mac inside the car, he'd seen the train set.

Mac had never expressed any interest in electric trains,

and it somehow never occurred to Walker to buy him one. He'd never had one himself. But Mac fell immediately in love with the Lionel set in the window. Mattie said to Walker later, when she told him how much it cost, that Mac had gotten so excited that he bit his numbed jaw hard enough to draw blood. The sight of her son doubled over in pain, trying manfully not to cry out, was too much. So she bought him a gift about twenty times more expensive than she had planned, then had to buy Ginger a dollhouse to even things up.

Walker helped Mac set the train up, the two of them discovering it together, Big Walker even putting in his two cents' worth, but the boy seemed to enjoy assembling the track and trestles in interesting and convoluted ways more than he actually liked to watch the train run. For a few months, though, it had been Mac's most cherished possession. Walker wonders where it is now.

Father and son look at the window, which still has TAYLOR'S HOBBY SHOPPE painted on it with FOR CHILDREN OF ALL AGE'S underneath, but the shop has, like many of its former neighbors, fled to the mall. A nearly empty bottle of Thunderbird wine lies next to the door, and the entrance-way is littered with tiny shards of green and white glass.

Walker would give anything right now if he could close his eyes, open them, and see McRae Street—and this little store in particular—alive and well.

"Come on," he says, finally, and Mac follows him down the street, around the corner, and back to where the Justuses are sitting in the car, waiting for them.

R.J. tells his son to get in the backseat. Mac gets in the back, too, nodding at Carneal, who is looking out the window. Walker slides into the front passenger's seat.

"Sorry," he says to R.J. "We were taking a nostalgia trip."

Raymond Justus looks at him impassively.

"You nostalgic for this?" he says, waving his left arm out the window to encompass the Old Market and what surrounds it.

"Like it was," Walker says. "I used to just about live down here on Saturdays. We'd go to the Colony for a movie, or over to the library or to Neely Park to play ball."

"All the king's horses and all the king's men . . ." R.J. says, and starts the car.

"Do you think the museum would help?" Walker asks him.

R.J. stares at him as if he's just asked whether fire burns.

"What do you think?" he says after a long silence.

It hadn't occurred to Walker that Raymond might still be set on making his son work off the ancient glove he stole, until they head west, toward the bridge and River Road.

"R.J.," he says, quietly, "he doesn't have to do anything. This has gone far enough, don't you think?"

R.J. has his jaw clenched, eyes straight ahead.

"No," he says, finally, "it hasn't."

Nobody says anything else until the red Buick coasts to a stop beside Big Walker and Dottie's house. It's nearly one o'clock, and Walker realizes that he is hungry.

R.J. gets out and motions for Carneal to do the same.

"You work him," R.J. says to Walker. "I'll be back here at six, and we'll see what he's done."

"R.J. . . ." Walker begins, but his old teammate shushes him.

"Work him," he repeats, quietly.

And then he drives off, before Walker can even offer him lunch.

Carneal is standing in the street, his arms folded, the same stoic, faraway expression on his face that he'd had when the policeman was questioning him two nights earlier.

Walker and Mac look at each other.

"Come on," Walker says after half a minute. "Let's get you some lunch and then put you to work." He tries to make it sound light, but Walker has never been good at ordering others to work, has never had Big Walker's assumption that "some were made to do things for others."

He turns to go inside, followed by Mac and, finally, by Carneal.

Big Walker is in the kitchen, looking out the window. He's been watching them.

"What you doing back here again, boy?" he asks when they come inside.

Carneal says nothing, although he visible stiffens at "boy."

A light bulb comes on in Walker's head.

"Again?" he says to his father. "Did this . . . did Carneal come around here this morning?"

"He come around here when you were upstairs takin' your shower," Big Walker says. "Trying to sell something, no doubt."

"And you ran him off."

"Damn right. Told him we don't allow soliciting in this neighborhood."

"Do you remember," Walker asks, "when Raymond Justus said yesterday that he'd send his son over to work off that glove?"

Big Walker looks dumbstruck.

"You mean this here is Raymond Justus's son?"

Walker nods his head. He can hardly blame his father, since he himself forgot the promise until R.J. showed up.

He turns to Carneal.

"Did you tell your father that?" he asks. Carneal nods his head.

"He didn't believe you?"

Carneal says nothing, just looks straight ahead.

Big Walker walks off, mumbling to himself. He stops and turns.

"Be ready to go in thirty minutes," he tells his son, who has forgotten about golf.

Walker turns to Carneal, who is standing beside Mac next to the kitchen table.

"Look," he says, "I'm sorry. I'll tell your father it was all a mistake. He'll believe me. Meanwhile, we'll get you something to eat, and then Mac can show you what needs doing."

Mac gives his father a quizzical look.

Walker improvises.

"We need the yard mowed around our old house," he says, "and maybe you could clip the hedges? That ought to be enough to pay for a raggedy-ass old glove."

Carneal almost smiles.

"Carneal," Walker says, and the boy looks up at him.

"I'm sorry. You're catching more grief than you ought to over that glove."

"S'all right," Carneal shrugs. "I shouldn't of took it anyways."

Walker leaves Mac, who glares at him for putting him in charge of a boy almost as old as him, to make them some sandwiches, then he gratefully flees to dress for golf.

As he and Big Walker leave, golf bags slung over their shoulders, they see that Mac and Carneal are in the garage, gathering up a lawn mower and some hedge clippers. They are talking, but they grow quiet when the two adults come near. Amazingly, Ginger is with them, sipping on a soft drink, about as animated as he ever sees her anymore.

Big Walker harrumphs as they put their bags in the car, just out of earshot. "I just hope the little so-and-so doesn't steal the TV or my car while we're gone."

Walker almost tells his father to go violate himself, and Big Walker can see that he's out of bounds.

"O.K., O.K.," he says, holding his arms up. "Forget it. Forget I said anything."

At the club, Walker calls and tells Raymond Justus about the misunderstanding. As a gesture of mollification, he tells R.J. that he'll drive Carneal home "since you're probably out of gas after this morning anyhow."

R.J. grunts but doesn't object.

Please, Walker prays as he heads for the putting green, please let that boy do something before we come back, so Raymond Justus will call this debt paid.

9

T HE ROUND OF GOLF GOES SLOWLY, WITH HALF OF RIVER ROAD TAKING ADVANTAGE OF THE BLUE, BEAUTIFUL DAY. IT'S SIX-FIFTEEN before Walker returns. He's left Big Walker back at the club to be driven home by Billy Holland after his usual two bourbon-and-waters.

In the lengthening shadows, Walker sees that his entry into the garage is blocked by his children and Carneal Justus, sitting there in lawn chairs, looking like three little adults.

He also sees, for a second, how soon they will be gone and how much he will miss them.

"So," he says, energized by the sight of his two children actually interacting with each other instead of disappearing into their rooms the way they usually do these days, "did you all get the old home place looking like the Taj Mahal?"

"Go take a look," Mac says. Carneal doesn't say anything, but he looks pleased with himself.

"Daddy," Ginger says, "did you know Carneal can dunk a basketball?"

Walker looks skeptical.

Both boys speak at once, saying the exact thing a half-beat apart: "It's just a nine-foot goal!"

They look at each other and both laugh.

"Better than I could do," Walker shrugs. "Come on."

The four of them take the short walk up River Road to the old house. The yard and the shrubbery look the best they've looked all summer. The dead branches that fell during the July and August thunderstorms have been hauled somewhere.

"Good work," Walker says. "That ought to satisfy your daddy, Carneal."

"I sure hope so," the boy mutters.

"Well, I guess we'd better get you home."

Both his children ask if they can come, too. Walker allows it, making them first let Dottie know where they're going.

He wants to ask his children if they don't have anything better to do on a Saturday night, but he knows it would just start an argument. Besides, he thinks it might not be the worst thing in the world for them to see somebody else's neighborhood.

Raymond Justus is sitting on his front porch when they get there, acting as if he hasn't been waiting for them.

Walker gets out of the car, and R.J. comes out to meet them. Mac and Ginger follow Carneal, standing uncertainly on the edge of the front yard.

"Where you-all been?" R.J. asks, his hands in his pockets.

"My fault," Walker says. "I didn't get back until fifteen minutes ago. He did a fine job, R.J. We're even." He hopes his old teammate won't debate that.

"I understand you and old Mr. Fann had a little misunderstanding," R.J. says to his son.

"That's what I TOLD you," Carneal says.

"I know that's what you TOLD me," his father replies, "but you've done told me so much bullshit that I don't believe half of it anymore."

Carneal says nothing, just turns and walks toward the house.

R.J. follows him with his eyes and shakes his head.

"Why don't you all go on inside?" he says to Walker's children. "You can watch TV or something."

"Oh, we can't stay," Walker says.

"Come on, Dad," Ginger says. "Just for a few minutes? Please?"

R.J. looks amused.

"Looks like you're outnumbered. Come on. I'll fix you all something to drink."

The Fann children go inside. R.J. follows them in, then comes back to join Walker on the porch, where it's almost too cool for sitting. He has a couple of beers with him.

They've been there no more than five minutes when they hear heavy footsteps coming up the walk. It's Philly, bearing a plate covered with tinfoil.

"Evening, Momma," R.J. says. "You comin' over to spy?"

Philly fixes her son with her most evil eye, nods neutrally at Walker.

"Miz Justus," Walker says, standing slightly.

"You all stay where you are," she says. "I just wanted to bring some spareribs over. Made more than we needed."

Walker isn't sure who exactly is living at Philly's. He has seen people of both sexes and all ages coming and going, some of them helping run the store, some young enough to be Philly's grandchildren or even great-grandchildren. The house next to R.J.'s seems as pungently alive and vital as it did when he was a teenager. Everywhere Walker goes these days, he sees diminishment. Large, rollicking families are shrunk to a few older left-behinds. Mattie's mother lives alone in the huge house that once was filled with five Grays and assorted friends. Towns like St. Andrews tread water, neither gaining nor losing much population from one census to the next. But they look so much smaller to Walker because it's all out there on the fringes—malls and subdivisions. Even city hall is now out near the *Standard* building; downtown Cottondale after dark makes many whites uneasy. It pleases Walker to see Philly Justus, and Philly's brood, bigger and more alive than ever.

Walker sees that it isn't just his imagination—the house really is bigger than it used to be. He remarks on this to the matriarch herself, who is also having a beer that she commanded R.J. to fetch for her.

"Yes," she says, frowning in recollection. "I suppose we added a bedroom and bathroom since then, when R.J. and that woman came back down here from New York."

"Momma, she has a name. Janette."

"She HAD a name."

R.J. and his mother lapse into silence.

They get the conversation back on track, steering it toward safer subjects like Philly's store (supporting its third and fourth generations now) and, when Walker spies the large grill made from an old barrel in her backyard, barbecuing.

"Son," she says to Walker, "when you got as many eating at your house as I have, you better be able to cook big slabs of meat in a hurry."

She leaves in half an hour, after Walker and R.J. have had another beer each.

"Got to go back and make some more phone calls," she says, on the way out. "Referendum's Tuesday, and we don't want to let that museum die on the vine, do we?"

Walker feels himself flush in the oncoming darkness.

"Momma," R.J. says, but she waves away his remonstration and waddles back home.

"She's something," Walker says, shaking his head.

"How old you think she is?" R.J. asks him.

Walker says he guesses about sixty-seven, sixty-eight. He's thinking early seventies at least but wants to be polite.

"Fifty-nine," R.J. says.

Walker does some quick math. R.J.'s older brother, Matthias, the one who was killed in Vietnam when they were still in high school, was a year or two older. He figures Philly must have had her first child at fifteen.

"She's a tough old gal," R.J. says, shaking his head. Behind them, they can hear their children's voices occasionally interrupting the TV's drone. A couple of Carneal's cousins from next door have wandered over.

R.J. gives Walker a rundown on what's happened to his three younger siblings. One sister and her husband are living at Philly's with their three children and helping run the store. One of their children, a girl of eighteen, has a baby of her own now, Philly's first great-grandchild. Another sister took her degree from East Carolina to Chicago with her. A younger brother, whom Walker remembers following R.J. and Matthias everywhere, is working for what's left of the mill, living part of the time at Philly's with his girlfriend and their two children.

In a lull, Walker asks R.J. about Janette.

"We'd better save that one till after supper," R.J. says. "It's a long, sad story."

Walker says they can't impose on them for supper, and he's sure there aren't enough ribs for five people, especially when two of them eat like his kids do.

"Carneal," R.J. calls out, and his son comes to the door, followed by Walker's children, "how about running down to the store and getting one of those fifteen-piece buckets. Get some slaw and rolls, too." He hands the boy a twenty-dollar bill. Walker tries to get him to take a ten from him, but he refuses. Philly's three grandchildren, Mac, and Ginger head down the street to the store.

They clean out most of the chicken and ribs, sitting at the big table in R.J.'s dining room.

Afterward, as Walker is again getting ready to leave, R.J. goes to the refrigerator, comes back with two more beers, and says, "Come on. Let's take a walk." Walker follows him outside.

They walk up toward the middle of town, passing other men, mostly in groups, all black except Walker, all polite to R.J.'s friend.

"You asked me about Janette," R.J. says.

There wasn't much to do, he tells Walker, after he found out his academic career at Southeastern was made of smoke. Not much to do except come home and work for Neely Mills.

He fell in with other young black men who didn't seem to have a way out, and they passed the time with fortified wine and dope. R.J. sold an ounce to an undercover agent, who offered to let him off with probation if he'd finger the man he got it from, which R.J., afraid of going to jail, did.

"It was the most dishonorable thing I ever did in my life, up to then," he tells Walker and shakes his head.

Raymond Justus, the hope and pride of Cottondale, his old state championship jersey enclosed in a glass frame at Philly's, was reduced to just another character who would name names.

The brother of the man R.J. gave up to stay out of jail tried to kill him one night.

"It was before all these Uzis and all," R.J. says, kicking a small stone into the gutter. "Back then, you had to get up close and personal, with a switchblade or something. It took guts and time. Otherwise, I'd probably be dead."

The man pulled a knife on R.J. as he walked out of a neighborhood bar at Third and Knowles ("Right over there," he says, pointing to a now-deserted building less than a block away). R.J. was saved because a neighborhood boy was walking by with a baseball bat in his hand. R.J. grabbed the bat and, in the ensuing fight, escaped with superficial wounds. He beat the brother of the man he sent to jail so badly that the man never regained consciousness.

"They probably wouldn't have done anything with me," R.J. says, "but I already had the one thing on my record."

So they gave him six months in a work camp. He was out in three, but he felt he had run out of any luck he might have once had in Cottondale. Besides, he was ashamed. The day after Raymond Justus was released from the work camp, he left for Newport News, Virginia, where one of Philly's brothers worked for the shipyards.

He spent three years in Virginia, finally losing his high-paying job at the shipyard when it started interfering with his partying.

"By then," R.J. says, "we were living in DST—Dope Standard Time. We would go to work stoned on dope, just got so that stoned was the normal way to live. Get up, get breakfast, get stoned, stay stoned.

"And then we got introduced to cocaine. It wasn't any crack or nothing back then, just snort it off the mirror like the rich folks did. Couldn't afford much of it; couldn't afford to snort it off no hundred-dollar bills. And, my God, it was sooo good. If I ever get some incurable illness, I hope I've got enough money to go out on cocaine."

A friend had a friend in New York, and that's where Raymond Justus moved in 1977, after he was fired at the shipyard. He got a job driving a taxi ("got robbed at gunpoint six times in two years") and then was hired by Tyron Key, who was in the home-renovation business, something R.J. had learned something about from working with another uncle when he was in high school. His new boss had a daughter named Janette.

Tyron Key had migrated up from North Carolina in the sixties, and he felt a kinship with Raymond Justus. Like Raymond, he had been a high school football star. Back then, he told R.J., you didn't even think about any Southeastern University, just hauled your butt up North as soon as you got out of high school.

Janette was just seventeen when Raymond met her in 1980.

"She was the prettiest thing I had ever seen," R.J. says. "Beautiful skin, eyes that just shone all the time, great sense of humor, body that wouldn't quit. I was in LOVE."

They were married six months later, with Tyron's blessing ("He thought he'd found him someone to take over the business from him") and with Janette already two months pregnant.

"Lord have mercy, I loved that girl," R.J. says, bending down to pick up the parts of a broken bottle and deposit them in the trash can at the corner. "I would have done just about anything to be with her."

Carneal was born in 1981. They had a girl, Sonya, two years later.

"We thought we had it made," R.J. says. "Good job. Living in a not-bad neighborhood over in Brooklyn. But even then we were headin' down that slippery slope."

They did cocaine a couple of times a week, as did most of their friends.

"It was like you knew everything, like you had all the answers, like everybody was your friend. And the sex! Great god almighty!" He shakes his head.

From that, it was a straight line, R.J. explains, to the brave new world of crack.

At first, crack seemed like the answer to the only problem they thought they had with cocaine: how to afford it.

"Hell, little children, kids younger than Carneal, could afford it."

But before long, the friends, the sex, and everything else got to be second-best to the rush itself, and the rush was over almost before it began, followed by ever-deepening lows.

"We woke up one day," R.J. says, looking straight at Walker through his no-nonsense glasses, "and we were addicts.

"What was it like? What it was like was Atlantic City. You know, you can go to the slot machines and you say, well, I'll just spend this much, and then, if I don't hit, I'm gone.

"And then you wake up and you've done lost two thousand dollars that you don't even remember. And all you want to do is play some more."

By the time they left New York, on a Greyhound bus in the spring of 1986, they had stolen enough from Tyron Key to drive the business he'd worked twenty years to build up into bankruptcy, had more or less abandoned their own children, had been in and out of rehabilitation programs three times, and had pretty much worn out their welcome in New York City.

The last night they spent in Brooklyn, Tyron Key, who had just discovered what happened to the '82 Volvo he'd thought was stolen, called R.J. aside. R.J. and Janette and the children were now living with Tyron and Sandra.

He put $200 in R.J.'s hands.

"You got family down in North Carolina," he said. "Take my daughter and my grandchildren and go on back down there. You're not going to get straightened out up here. You might not get straightened out down there, either, but you've got nothing to lose. You can't stay here anymore."

Tyron had chosen a weekend when his wife was visiting

family in New Jersey. He told R.J. he'd deal with Sandra.

"You know something?" he told his son-in-law. "I don't have any idea whether you all will make it or not. That's a terrible thing to say, that you're sending your daughter out to fend for herself. But we're tired. You all have just about ruined us. And we don't have time to raise no grandchildren."

R.J. says he wondered if Philly would even let them move back. He'd been too embarrassed to stay in touch since he left for Virginia, only calling on Christmas, visiting seldom, sending large, generous gifts sporadically.

Janette didn't want to go, said she'd take the children and live somewhere, somehow. She wasn't going to the place from which her husband and father had fled. But R.J. knew Janette had the itch even worse than he did, would do even worse without him than with him. And then there were the children. He stayed up all night convincing her. They left in the morning without saying goodbye to Tyron.

They showed up on Philly's doorstep on a raw April evening. They'd managed to score in the D.C. bus station, right before R.J. called to tell his mother they were coming, but their nerves had been shot since about Richmond. R.J. was surprised to look around, when they got up to get off the bus, and see his children standing patiently behind them, waiting to get off, too. Neither he nor Janette had really been aware of their existence for some miles.

Philly had only seen her daughter-in-law once, at the wedding. The only trip R.J. had made back to North Carolina since then he had made alone. She had never seen Carneal and Sonya, who were five and three then.

"I told her, 'Momma, we need help. We need help bad.'"

Philly Justus had seen the ravages of crack even in Cottondale, seen neighborhood children turn into addicts and thieves.

Philly made up a bed for her son and his wife, put

Carneal and Sonya up on a foldout couch, and sat up most of the night praying.

The next morning, bleary-eyed, she called Ramona Hairfield, who ran the city's drug-prevention program.

"Ramona," she said, "I want you to help me save my family."

There were five times as many addicts, even in St. Andrews, as the clinic could possibly help. But Ramona Hairfield was Philly's niece; she and her mother had lived with Philly in the big house on Second Street for a couple of years when Philly's sister had nowhere else to go.

"Aunt Philly," her niece said, "I'm here."

They got Raymond and Janette Justus into the drug rehabilitation program at Rich Valley Hospital. The odds were heavily against them, but they also had Philly, who took in the grandchildren she'd never met and raised them like her own, who never censured her son and daughter-in-law, because Ramona told her that wouldn't do anything except hurt, who saw to it that they both stayed busy, working at the store and, in R.J.'s case, helping another distant relative in his cabinet shop.

"It worked, somehow," R.J. says now. "For a long time, I thought it would keep on working."

The beginning of the end was when Janette, who was still, despite the private war she'd been fighting, an attractive woman, got a job in sales, something with which she'd had experience in New York.

Even around St. Andrews, there was enough of a burgeoning black middle class so that Randle Realtors figured it could do worse than to hire a bright young African-American woman. Janette, on a tip from a friend of Philly's, took some courses and got her real-estate license, and there was a job waiting for her.

R.J. says, walking slower now as if to make his story and

their walk end at the same time, that he guesses it was the need to be bright and alive and funny that made Janette fall back. Even he never knew all of it.

For a time, Janette was the star of the company, selling twice as many houses as the average realtor. The first warning sign for R.J. was the gap between what Janette said she was earning and what was actually showing up in their bank account. He wrote it off for months, figuring that if Janette was making that much money, she was entitled to spend some of it on clothes and such, even though her clothes didn't look all that new to him. He was helping run the store and picking up pretty good money working nights and weekends as a cabinetmaker, but Janette was the one pulling in the real money—at least on paper.

By Christmas of 1990, he couldn't ignore it anymore. She hardly seemed to notice Carneal and Sonya, and R.J. had stopped working so many nights and weekends so one of them could spend some time with their children. She would come home sometimes after 2 A.M., claiming that she'd been with clients or at seminars, finally not explaining at all.

Two days before Christmas, when she came in after one in the morning, her husband was waiting for her. She was wild, her hair and clothes rumpled. When he accused her of running around on him, she just laughed. He slapped her, and she tripped and fell into Philly's Christmas tree, smashing a couple of the gifts that were piled around it. R.J. looked up and saw Philly standing at the entrance to the living room, their two children peeking around her broad frame at the mess that was their parents.

Philly and R.J. put her into a rehab center against her will, but she was out again almost immediately. They tried three times.

In April, R.J. got a call at the store, where he was doing inventory.

"Daddy," Carneal said, "Momma and Sonya are gone."

He asked him, "Gone where?" and Carneal didn't say anything.

The boy was sitting on the steps of Philly's house when he got there; they were just finishing the renovations R.J. had started on the house next door, where R.J. and Carneal live now.

It was the last time Raymond Justus would see his son cry.

He called Tyron Key, finally reaching him a week later. Janette's father was under the impression that R.J. had gotten them back on crack, and he told his son-in-law that he would shoot him if he ever saw his sorry ass again, that he would never, ever see Sonya again, and that it would be his goal in life to get custody of Carneal, too.

So far, the long and aging arm of Tyron Key hasn't threatened R.J.'s custody of his son, but he has not spoken with either his wife or his daughter since that April day three and a half years ago.

"I try to remember," R.J. says. "I try to remember the last time I saw Sonya, and for the life of me I can't. She was probably sitting there in the kitchen eating her breakfast. She was almost eight then. I was probably too busy, half asleep, not even thinking I might never see her again."

Half a block from their starting point, he says he doesn't know which was worse: that Janette would take their daughter back to New York with her, or that she would leave their son.

"Hell, who am I kidding?" he says as they stop in the street. "I'm most hurt that she left me, that she couldn't beat it. Hell, I beat it, and I ain't Superman. Why couldn't she do it?" He looks away, down the street.

*   *   *

It's after eleven when Walker, Mac, and Ginger go home. He looks in the backseat, where Ginger sits alone, and sees that she is dozing, the way a younger child would, her rosebud lips slightly open, the cynicism and stealth of the last year wiped away. He wonders where that year went, and how he can keep the next one from going the same way.

10

ROME DID NOT DISAPPOINT.

WE WERE THERE FOR FIVE DAYS, FAR TOO LITTLE. I COULD HAVE spent my whole life just wandering through the ruins around the Colosseum with a guidebook in my hand, imagining what it was like two thousand years ago. The best thing we did was hire a driver. He was expensive, but a friend of ours at the club had used this same man, barely more than a boy really, and Walker was sure he would be worth it.

His name was Giancarlo, and he spoke English better than he understood, something we came to understand by trial and error, but he showed us Rome in one ten-hour day. The Vatican, the Colosseum, the Piazza Navona, the Pantheon, the Catacombs, the Appian Way. All the high spots.

Walker probably enjoyed the whole experience less than I did. He didn't like it that the hotel, which had promised air conditioning, had only these dinky little portable units—Walker called them space coolers—that you had to get up and empty the water out of every four hours or so.

He was a little disappointed that the Italian pasta wasn't as rich as that cheesy stuff you get in the States. He said he was going to have Pasta Meatballs back in St. Andrews send them a pizza so they would know what one tasted like. I told him I didn't think the Pasta Meatballs delivered that far.

Mainly, it took him the whole time we were in Rome to get used to the fact that, no matter how well he planned things, nothing ever came off the way he expected. It wasn't that we didn't do everything we really wanted to do; it was just that the Italians have their own pace and didn't change it just for Walker and Mattie Fann of St. Andrews, North Carolina, U.S.A.

The driver was to pick us up at 9 A.M.; he arrived at 9:45, with Walker standing outside the little hotel near the Spanish Steps, muttering about people who don't keep their word. But Giancarlo only charged us for the time we were in his car.

The road to the Pope's summer palace was blocked by strikers, but they soon tired of the heat and left.

The shop just up the street with the wonderful gifts in the window never seemed to be open, but on our last day there, it was.

An excellent restaurant off the Via Sistina lost our reservations, but the maître d', or whatever they call them in Italy, shrugged, smiled, and said "No problem," and it wasn't.

"No problem" seems to be the national creed of Italy.

All in all, things were going well. We came, we saw, we shopped. All of Walker's hard work, learning an amazing amount of Italian in a few weeks, was pretty much for naught, because everyone spoke English better than we spoke Italian. The low point of Walker's efforts to speak Italian was when he asked for *otto francobolli*, eight stamps, and the lady gave him three—*trey*. He pretty much gave up on language control after that.

We did have some of the best sex we'd had in some time, though. Getting away from family for a while—although we did call home every other night—was a release, and Walker always seems to get a little turned on by hotel rooms, like we're doing something a little naughty instead of the same old twice-a-week routine.

High point of my trip?

We'd seen all these Italian kids sitting on walls, her straddling him, the two of them locked together at the groins and the lips, swaying to some interior rhythm.

Well, the last night we were in Rome before we headed for Sorrento, I told Walker I wanted to go for a walk along the Tiber. The little restaurant we were going to was near the Vatican, barely a mile from our hotel, so it wasn't much out of the way.

I'm pretty straitlaced back home, but this was Rome, and it seemed like we should do at least one outrageous thing. We walked a block along the river, and then I figured this was as good a place as any.

I had Walker sit on one of those stone walls. When he was situated, I straddled him just like I'd seen those teenagers do. He didn't realize that I wasn't wearing any panties until then.

It was twilight. There weren't that many people walking by, although there were plenty of cars along the street. I unzipped his pants and hopped right on. I have to tell you, it was the hottest we'd been in a long time, made all the better by the tension of trying not to look like we were doing what we were doing. To tell you the truth, the occasional leer from a passing Italian man, or the driver who blew his horn and yelled something in Italian I couldn't understand, didn't hurt, either.

Walker came twice, never withdrawing, just getting large again inside me on that stone wall in a city half a world away. I came twice, too. We almost knocked each other out banging heads.

We barely had enough energy to walk to the restaurant. We arrived, famished, thirty minutes late. It was, of course, "no problem."

I always tried, in large and small ways, to make Walker loosen up. Sometimes, I see the same little boy who threw up the first time we met, back in second grade. He's wound very tight.

The first two years we were married, we would occasionally smoke a joint. It was almost expected among the people we partied with, young adults who were in college in the late sixties and early seventies. Walker didn't want to at first, but he finally gave in to peer pressure.

Walker would never bring it home, though, even before I became pregnant with Mac. I wouldn't have minded having an ounce around the bedroom myself, for special occasions, but Walker said it just made him "stupid," which meant out of control.

A lot of it was learned behavior, of course. The funny thing is, I've heard that Big Walker was a hellion in his younger days, but he rode Walker hard, even after he was grown. He was always going on, after he'd had a couple of drinks and was out of control himself, about the "obligations of privilege." Sometimes I'd be there when he'd start in, and sometimes we'd argue. I'd tell Big Walker that if he really felt some kind of obligation, he ought to get after the city to do something about the schools in Cottondale, or the streets down there. Hell, half of the ones on the south end, down where everything dead-ends at the edge of town, still aren't paved.

And Big Walker would rant and rave about how people in the River Road district paid five times as much city and county taxes as the residents of Cottondale, and weren't they entitled to better service?

So what is it you feel obligated to do? I'd ask him.

"My obligation," he said more than once, with minor variations, "is to see that everybody gets a chance to be somebody. What they do with it depends on them."

And I think he really believed it. He never went down there and saw how some of the people lived. He never did volunteer work at Harbor House and saw the mothers who wanted to work but couldn't get their kids into a day-care program that wasn't one-third big enough for all the women it was supposed to help. He never saw the people I saw when I worked with the AIDS ministry, a lot of them dying in pain and shame because of nature or bad luck.

I'm not sure Walker really saw it, either, although I tried to show him. I sensed, a little better than he did, how much of life is the luck of the draw, how just because your luck has been good doesn't mean it always will be, how all the planning in the world can't save you sometimes.

"Look at Flip Sandlin," Walker would say to me when I indicated that I thought we'd been dealt a pretty good hand ourselves. "I could've turned out like Flip Sandlin. I didn't have to work hard."

George Mathers Sandlin IV. We went to elementary and high school with him. He fried his brains on acid at UNC, and his father, who owns three car dealerships, disowned him. He died of exposure in Seattle, Washington.

No, I'd tell him, you could have turned out worse. Do you get a medal for that?

Thing is, though, I wasn't really ready to walk the walk, either. I'd do volunteer work for a while, then get "burned out," like it was harder on me to have to tell those young black women no than it was for them to hear it. Mostly, I'd talk about it at cocktail parties, where my diatribes sometimes made Walker uneasy.

Last year, though, I was forty-one years old, and I wasn't studying the poor and oppressed back home. I was reaching the point where you just want to save what's inside your own happy home. I wanted to be good to Walker, my children, and the rest of the world, with the first two tied for first and the other a distant third.

Going out of Rome, on our sixth day in Italy, we were both as relaxed as a couple of small-town Southerners can be their first time in a place where you can't get hush puppies or iced tea with sugar.

We'd hired Giancarlo to drive us down the coast. The original plan was to take the train to Naples, then another train to Sorrento. But it seemed complicated. The two trains didn't run on the same line, and the idea of hauling all that luggage through the Naples train station and trying to find the Circumvesuviano line seemed daunting.

"What the hell," I told Walker. "Let's spend a little money. Let Giancarlo do it."

So we paid him to drive us to Sorrento, then pick us up five days later in Positano, on the opposite side of the peninsula.

It seemed the ultimate in luxury and decadence that morning to get into the Mercedes and ride south.

It took us three hours to get to Sorrento, with Giancarlo going 160 kilometers an hour on the expressway and getting lost trying to find the main road along the coast, then getting lost again in Sorrento before we finally, magically, rolled up to our hotel.

We were sucking on those liter water bottles like babies all the way down, and it was summer-hot when we got out. But then we were escorted to our room, and we forgot any inconvenience we'd experienced. All we could see, through the billowing white curtains, was the Bay of Naples, with Vesuvius, which we'd passed at a hundred miles an hour, a darker blue outline in the distance.

We luxuriated there for two days, taking a day trip back to Pompeii, but mainly alternating between the beach below, the pool on the other side, the best shopping town I'd ever seen, and our room.

We spent another day on Capri, where it was more of the same, deeper and deeper into the heart of paradise.

We thought it couldn't get any better. When we had another Italian Maalox moment the next morning leaving Capri, involving luggage that was supposed to be delivered to the dock but wasn't, we felt that the best was behind us.

"No problem," the overweight functionary on the dock told us, strolling casually as he ushered us toward the hovercraft and assuring us that our luggage would follow "very soon, very soon." But watching Capri recede, with our clothes and airline tickets at the mercy of Italian efficiency, we doubted that even the gospel of No Problem could save the bacon this time. Walker said the Italians reminded him of a basketball team that was always falling behind early and having to pull the game out with a miracle shot at the buzzer.

"The Italians," he said, "are always playing catch-up."

We forgot the luggage, though, when the hovercraft rounded the last jut along the Amalfi coast and we saw the harbor at Positano, our destination. We'd seen pictures, of course, but they didn't do it justice. The place looked like a wedding cake, pastel buildings starting at the inky blue water and rising to a point somewhere just short of heaven. Maybe the stress of not knowing where our luggage was, of almost missing the hovercraft, somehow made the vision of Positano all the more welcome.

"My God," Walker muttered. "This is the most beautiful place I've ever seen in my life."

The look he had was the exact one Mac had the time Walker got them both tickets to a Redskins-Cowboys game in Washington. It was the look of an eight-year-old who is genuinely, unexpectedly delighted.

11

SYCAMORE BAPTIST CHURCH IS AT THE BOTTOM OF THE LARGE U THAT IS RIVER ROAD. THE LOCATION WAS MEANT TO SYMBOLIZE its distance from the marketplace that starts where the points of the U attach to U.S. 30.

Actually, however, much of affluent St. Andrews's real business is conducted in the churchyard after Sunday services.

Some of the city's "movers and shakers" worship elsewhere, of course. There is a fine Presbyterian church (although a little too modernistic and liberal for Big Walker's liking) on the west side of the loop. There is a good Methodist sanctuary, although frequented mostly by those who live in the suburbs north of the mall. There are plenty of Protestant churches of all denominations down in Cottondale and in the surrounding county. There is a Catholic church, St. Anne's. There's even a synagogue. The Sycamore Country Club has two Jewish members and three Catholics, Big Walker is proud to point out.

"But, son," he told Walker once when his son protested the club's blackballing of Murray Fesperman, a well-heeled merchant with uncomfortably leftist views (by St. Andrews standards), "this is a Christian town, a Protestant town—

hell, a Baptist town. It's all right to have a little spice, but there ain't nothing wrong with a good piece of tenderloin as is. And that's St. Andrews. Nothing fancy, just good, plain, quality people who want a decent town."

This Sunday is no different from most. When services let out, the families slowly leave the imposing brick building, saved from plainness by the best stained-glass windows the congregation could buy. They shake hands with the Reverend Graham and shield their eyes from the sun. Some wander off to talk about the sick and shut-in, about the latest divorce or sexual-orientation scandal. Some talk business.

Walker rides to church with his father and Dottie. He still makes the children come with them, although he wonders how much longer he can face them down every Sunday morning.

Today, he and Big Walker gravitate toward several men in loose groups alongside the windows on the sanctuary's west side, where the sun hasn't stolen all the shade yet. They've been doing this, Walker realizes, since he came home from college in 1974. He used to only occasionally join his father in these after-church rituals, but now it's expected. He and Mattie seemed to know from the start that, once they were grown and out of college, he'd drift toward the businessmen and she'd wander over toward the women, often the wives of Walker's and Big Walker's companions.

Today, Walker sees Bert Evans in a too-intense conversation with Grant Adkins from the bank, and he knows, just from the downward angle of Bert's head and the way he nods occasionally in quick little spasms, that the man is overextended, that he's going to have to declare bankruptcy again.

Over next to the building are three deacons, one talking and the other two leaning against the bricks and nodding somberly. The one talking, Johnny Cowles, is a trouble-maker, a preacher's worst nightmare, and Walker knows that Reverend Graham had better watch his back.

He feels a light, almost delicate touch on his arm as his father guides him toward their destination today: Harold Neely and Buck Sandlin.

Between the stores at the mall and Sandlin's car dealer-ships, the two account for much of the *Standard*'s advertis-ing revenue.

Walker's favorite thing about his brief exposure to the world of big-city journalism was the power. The paper in Baltimore had been large enough to do what it felt was right, no matter if it was unpopular with the kind of peo-ple who would pull hundreds of thousands of advertising dollars because they didn't like the drift of a certain edito-rial.

One day, he witnessed an argument between his city edi-tor and the owner of a fairly large grocery-store chain. The owner wasn't happy at all over a story the paper had just run about tainted meat in his stores, and he'd come all the way to the newsroom to tell someone about it.

Walker's desk in Baltimore was right next to the city edi-tor's office, and he could hear politeness fail and turn into a full-blown argument, the kind that Walker would always associate with the Northeast—loud, angry, always just short of a full-blown fistfight, it seemed. In St. Andrews, such talk could get you shot.

Finally, the city editor, a man with steel-gray hair plas-tered back on his skull, who always wore short-sleeved white shirts with prodigious sweat stains, banged his coffee cup on his desk.

"Now you listen to me," he told the man—by this time,

half the newsroom had turned to watch with no pretense of doing anything else. "If you continue to harass and threaten me, I will have no choice but to instruct the advertising department to refuse to accept any more of your ads.

"Furthermore, I will tell the circulation department that we can no longer take your subscription money."

The grocery-chain owner's mouth dropped slightly, and he was actually speechless for a few seconds. He'd just been threatening to drop his advertising, but nobody, by God, could tell him that his money was no good.

"You'll be hearing from my lawyer," he yelled as he stormed toward the elevator. "You can't tell me where I can and can't advertise. This is America, goddammit!"

The minute the doors had closed on the man, still yelling and using his cigar as an exclamation point, the reporters and subeditors burst into such cheering that Walker felt certain no adult human beings had as much fun as newspaper people.

The city editor had no power or desire to do what he threatened, of course, and he did get a mild reproach from the managing editor, but the man never dropped his advertising, and the paper certainly didn't refuse his money.

"He needs us," the city editor told a group of reporters at the crab house they sometimes frequented after work, "more than we need him."

Walker wished then, and wishes perhaps even more now, that little papers like *The St. Andrews Standard* had that kind of power. Perhaps then he could do what he had always wanted to do: tell Harold Neely and his friends where to stick their money.

"Harold. Buck," Big Walker nods pleasantly to the two men, who nod back, hands in pockets. "What you reckon Johnny Cowles is cooking up over there?"

"Looks like the preacher better gird his loins," Buck

Sandlin says, shaking his head. "Lord, I wish we could find one that could keep everybody happy."

"I don't know if Jesus could do that," Walker says. The other three men just shake their heads.

They exchange small talk for a couple of minutes, then it grows quiet.

Buck breaks the silence.

"Ah, Big Walker—and you too, Walker—what we need to know is, What are you all going to say about that slave museum mess? In the paper, I mean."

"We're a little worried," Harold Neely cuts in. He turns to face Walker straight on. "You've been spending a lot of time with your old classmate lately. . . ."

"Raymond Justus. What about it?" Walker is amazed at how little gets past Neely, who must have his mean little eyes trained on every neighborhood, black and white, in St. Andrews.

Neely looks down and clears his throat.

"What about it is this: We do not—repeat, do not—want that referendum to pass. We know that you all can keep it from passing. We've gone over and over this, and I'm still not easy about whose side you're on. We know for a fact that Justus and his momma are involved with Rasheed Asshole and all that nigger-loving crap they're trying to drum up."

"But, Harold," Walker says, shaking his head, "they are niggers. Aren't they allowed to love themselves?"

"Yeah," Neely says, "but you don't have to go laying a big old wet one on them yourself. Look, I don't care how you spend your time. It ain't my business. But this close to that referendum, what's it look like? We don't want to become the goddamn—'scuse me—nigger-history capital of the United States. Hell, I know for a fact that at least a dozen people on River Road will have For Sale signs up within a week if that thing passes. We'll be mecca for every nappy-headed malcontent on the East Coast. 'Come on down to St. Andrews; they love us down there.'"

Walker doubts that turning the Old Market into a slavery museum will have much impact one way or the other on the future of St. Andrews. If anything, he feels that it might actually be a breath of fresh air for a town whose racial legacy is gamy at best. He wonders, too, if St. Andrews can bend far enough backward to entice Henry Sudduth and his department store to Rich Valley Mall.

Walker thinks, not for the first time, that so much of what Harold Neely, Buck Sandlin, and their friends care about is power. He's almost sure that, if you gave Neely truth serum, he'd confess that what he really wants is to know that his power is considerable, at least in the small world where he lives.

"Now hold on, Harold," Big Walker says, putting a hand on the man's shoulder, "we've already told you what we're going to do. I know Walker's already made sure ol' Ry Tucker will blast this mess out of the water Monday *and* Tuesday morning."

"I don't have any worries about you, Big Man," Neely says, and Sandlin nods in agreement. "What I worry about is him," and he jerks his head toward Walker.

"We'll print what we think is right," Walker says, his jaw clenched tight. Very few things make him lose control, but Harold Neely comes closer than most. "I'm not sure just yet what that will be, but I'm sure you can read it in tomorrow's *Standard*."

Walker knows his father well enough to doubt that anything could make Big Walker let him endorse the slave museum, but he wants to leave some doubt in the other men's minds, just for spite.

Neely, squinting as the sun breaks over the top of the

church roof, puts his hands back in his pockets and shakes his head as if amazed at the stubbornness of a child who refuses to accept the immutable wisdom of his logic and must be subjected to less pleasant methods.

"You don't understand," he says to Walker, "without us, there won't be any *Standard*. We've been carrying your sorry ass for years."

"Carryin' us! Now you hold on, Harold Neely . . ." Big Walker sputters.

"Easy. Easy," Sandlin steps between the two men.

"You know me," the older man says. "You know what I will and won't do. Then you come out here and insult me." Other men are stealing glances toward the four.

"I know you, Big Walker," Neely says. "And I didn't mean to hurt your feelings. What I don't know"—and he turns toward Walker again—"is him."

"Harold," Walker says quietly, then finally utters the words he's wanted to say for twenty years, "you need us more than we need you."

Neely's eyes widen, and Walker wonders if he'll actually have to fight the man he's disliked for so much of his life. Then Neely catches himself and even manages a lifeless smile.

"Bullshit," he says, then turns and walks off, Buck Sandlin following him.

Walker and his father don't speak all the way home. They barely acknowledge each other during Dottie's Sunday dinner.

Afterward, the two men go outside on the porch. Big Walker sits on the chaise longue, using the remote control to turn on the TV. It's the second weekend of the pro football season. One of the constants in Walker's life, even in the past miserable year, has been this Sunday-afternoon ritual. Sometimes Mac joins them, but today he and two friends got a ride to the mall cinemas. Walker and Big Walker are "football nuts," as Dottie describes them. From now until the chill of late October drives them inside, they'll spend their Sundays this way. Walker never feels closer to his father than when they're cheering for the Washington Redskins and against the Dallas Cowboys. Even the editorial Walker ran two years ago without Big Walker's permission or knowledge, advocating a less offensive name for their favorite team, hadn't ruined this ritual.

Today, though, they say nothing until the first rash of commercials.

"Son," Big Walker says, setting his cigar down, "I'm not keeping this paper going for me. It's for you, and for Mac, and for his children. . . ."

Walker's heard this before. Big Walker's Sometimes We Can't Do What We Want to Do speech. He has to admit that it has more urgency now than at many times in the past. Newsprint prices are expected to rise more than forty percent in the new year, and it will hurt small independents like the *Standard* worse than the large papers and chains. Market penetration is shrinking. Sometimes, when Walker sees all the ways his children have to entertain themselves, he wonders if all the conciliation, all the adjustments in the world can save the *Standard.*

Just last month, the Creed chain, a group with no local ties, so ultra-conservative that even Harold Neely might be appeased, approached Big Walker for a second time. They already own several papers in the region, mostly in towns like St. Andrews. Their routine is to cut the newsroom staff as much as possible and depend on wire-service stories and freelance writers.

But Big Walker, to his credit, swears he won't ever sell the *Standard.* Unfortunately, in Walker's opinion, his father also won't look into the things that the *Standard* needs to survive long enough for Mac or Ginger to run it. The *Standard* was the last paper in the state to run television grids; Big Walker felt he would be helping the competition. He doesn't seem to grasp the whole concept of going on line; he's constantly resisted even a phone system that would allow readers to get useful information from the paper on everything from school lunches to the stock market.

"Why the hell should we give information away?" he said the last time he was approached.

"We're just teasing them," Walker told him. "They'll want to read the paper more than ever, to get the rest of the story."

"We'll tease ourselves right out of business" was Big Walker's last response.

But Walker lets his father go through what they both know, and it always comes back to the same thing: Despite what Walker said, they do need their advertisers more than the advertisers need them.

"I'm tired, son," Big Walker says. "I'm not going to fight you on much from here on out. I don't mean to be hanging over your shoulder for much longer. But we have to do this. We just flat have to do it."

Walker is quiet for several minutes, until Washington gives up a touchdown and there's another round of commercials.

"Big Man," he says then, "I just don't know." He's thinking about Philly and R.J. and Carneal. None of them has really leaned on Walker at all, but he realizes that he's been touched by some unspoken eloquence in their lives. And he's more clearly aware than he's ever been that it would be wonderful, just once, if white St. Andrews would do something voluntarily to make life better across the river.

He tries to put this in words for his father—how the establishment and the paper had opposed integration, the abolishment of the poll tax, the removal of the Confederate flag from the courthouse, and what Ry Tucker called, in 1966, "the unwarranted persecution of a group of white citizens who merely want to aid their local officials in repelling an invasion by the federal government." This last pronouncement came a week before a black teenager was shot and killed by white men in sheets as he walked down the Wigginton Road, an act for which no one was ever convicted.

Going through the microfiche in the paper's library, Walker had learned long ago that the *Standard* even tried to defend the white race riots of 1919.

"What a wonderful thing," he says, looking out across the river as the Redskins' quarterback throws his second interception, "if we could do one kind, decent thing, without anybody having to beat us over the head first."

"Beat us over the head?" Big Walker sits up in the chaise longue. "Hell, son. We've done good things. Look at the Christmas charity drive. A lot of those little buggers wouldn't even have any presents if it weren't for that. And the Shriners' hospital. Who built that? White folks, that's who. And what about when that boy got burned at the mill last year? Who raised most of the money to send him to Duke to get treated?

"You want to go back to 1861 or 1919 or 1965 and hold everybody up to the standards of right now, today. Well, it can't be done. It doesn't work that way. You do what you can at the time, and you don't go back later whining and begging for forgiveness."

No, Walker thinks to himself. No. All I want is for us to do something, once, that we can look back on fifty years from now and not be ashamed.

But he holds his tongue.

Near the end of the third quarter, with the Redskins hopelessly behind, Big Walker surprises him by turning off the TV.

"I'll tell you what I'm going to do," he says to his son. "I'm going to put the ball right directly in your court."

"Meaning what?"

"It's your decision. I've been hearing you talk about this for so long, I'm tired of it. Do like the man in the commercial says: You make the call. Whatever we run editorially about this slave museum mess on Tuesday, it'll be your doing."

Big Walker gets up to go inside, but he stops at the sliding glass doors and looks back.

"If you want to be the one that puts us on our backs, so Creed can buy us cheap, then go ahead. There'll still be enough money for me and Dottie to retire on comfortably. And then you can explain to your children and their children what happened to that newspaper your family once owned."

Walker can see that his father's eyes are moist as he goes inside. He knows he probably should go after him, but he doesn't, hoping instead that Big Walker will come back outside. Fifteen minutes later, he hears the door slide open, but when he looks up, it's his daughter.

"Dad," she says, "it's Carneal's father. He wants to talk to you."

Walker picks up the cellular phone.

"Hello?"

"Yeah. Walker? This is R.J. Ah, look, I'm sorry to be doin' this, but there's some people over here that want to meet you."

Walker is reminded of the feckless would-be friends he and Mattie once had, who tried to get them to an Amway meeting with that same come-on.

"You're not trying to sell me anything, are you, R.J.?"

"Not exactly. Man, I hate this. But it's ... well, it's Rasheed. He just wanted to talk with you. And Momma thought I might could get you over here."

Shit, Walker thinks to himself. Shit. Hell. Goddamn. The last thing in the world he wants to do is be harangued, as he's sure he will be, by the most truculent black man in Cottondale. But he hears himself lecturing his father not an hour before on race relations, and he wonders if this isn't God saying, Put up or shut up.

"Sure," he tells Raymond Justus at last, with a sigh. "Why not?"

12

RASHEED AZIZ HAS SHRUNK.

WALKER HAS SEEN HIM ON THE STREET, NOW AND THEN, FOR years. He was at the town meeting two years earlier, which Aziz turned into a personal attack on the *Standard*.

But now, dressed in Levi's and a knit shirt instead of a suit or a dashiki, he looks as if he can't weigh more than 140 pounds. When he was a two-way all-conference tackle in high school, he was almost a hundred pounds heavier. He appears to be lost inside his clothes. His glasses, even his ears, seem made for a larger man. Word has it he eats no meat and drinks no alcohol. He has been a Muslim since law school, and Walker wonders if his religion proscribes smiling as well.

Walker arrives at Raymond Justus's house shortly after seven-thirty, because that's when R.J. has told him evening services at Beulah Baptist Church, two blocks away, will be over.

As he gets out of his car, he sees a crowd coming up Second Street from the direction of the church. Before it reaches R.J.'s house, three small groups peel off, and then, when they get to Philly's, the matriarch herself, R.J., his sister, her husband, and several children leave the quickly thinning congregation to the sound of various goodbyes and blessings. They steal glances at Walker as if they've just been talking about him for the last hour.

Walker sees Carneal continue down the street with two friends, seemingly trying to escape his father's notice, but the boy does nod and ask Walker where Mac and Ginger are. Walker didn't tell his children he was coming, even though he passed Mac coming in on his way out, because he figured they'd gladly forgo their homework to accompany him. Now he wishes he'd brought them. For some reason, they seem to take to this boy who has nothing in common with them except a zip code.

Walker hears a car door slam behind him, turns and sees Rasheed Aziz, who must have been sitting there since before Walker arrived. Just watching, damn him, Walker thinks.

The two men nod neutrally. Even in high school, even when he was coming over to Philly's on a regular basis and hanging out with a crowd that usually included Dexter Cates, Walker always felt uneasy, always felt he was being sized up every time he talked or moved.

Raymond Justus always had a calm dignity about him that seemed to allow for differences and past and present offenses. Dexter Cates just seemed pissed off, always one word away from a confrontation. Walker remembers one incident their senior season. He had never had a strong arm, and one day in practice he threw a pass to R.J. that was too soft and too high. R.J. caught it, as he'd caught many mediocre passes before, but he had to jump and stretch for it. As he wrapped his fingers around the ball, a linebacker hit him low, flipping him. R.J. landed hard and lay on the field for a few seconds, then started to get up on his own, shaking the cobwebs out of his head.

Dexter Cates went to see if his friend was all right, then turned to Walker, who had also gone to check on his favorite receiver.

"Man," he said, "why the fuck don't you throw something besides medicine balls?"

Walker didn't say anything. It was Glen Murphy who asked what a medicine ball was.

"He throws 'em," Cates said, jerking his thumb backward in Walker's direction, "and R.J. has to go get him some medicine."

Even Coach Kell broke up, but Dexter Cates never cracked a smile.

Now, as the shrunken Rasheed Aziz, he seems to have boiled all that anger into a black essence, the bile more potent, as the bite of a small rattlesnake is said to be more venomous than that of a larger one.

Philly, on her front steps, hollers to the two men, and to R.J., who is walking toward them.

"You all come on over here and get something to eat. We got aplenty."

The three men join the other family members and two other men whom Walker didn't see walking up from the alleyway across the street.

"R.J.," Walker says quietly, moving up to fall in step with him as they head toward Philly's, "are you ambushing me?"

"No, man, I ain't ambushin' nobody. Look, Rasheed asked me could you come listen. That's all."

Rasheed Aziz moves up even with them.

"That's right," he says. "It won't hurt you to listen to a few of your subscribers, will it, Mr. Fann, suh?"

Walker starts to turn around right there at Philly's front gate and go home. To hell with them.

"Shut up, Rasheed," R.J. says to his friend, who falls

silent and, at R.J.'s command, goes inside. Despite the fact that Raymond Justus is a part-time cabinetmaker helping his mother run a convenience store and Rasheed Aziz is a lawyer, it is obvious to Walker that the pecking order of their youth has not changed, a phenomenon he has observed more than once among St. Andrews natives. The final word, then and now, belongs to R.J.

"Look," he says to Walker when he's led him out into the street, "this isn't going to take long. They just want to tell you—just you, not some citizens' panel or the chamber of commerce or nothin' like that—how they feel. This is important to them, Walker."

"And how about you, R.J.? Is it important to you?"

R.J. looks up—the two men have been talking into the ground.

"Hell, yes, it's important to me. This is my town, too. I want to feel like part of it belongs to me."

Walker is surprised at the unaccustomed heat in his old teammate's words.

"Let's go in," R.J. says after a few seconds' silence. "They'll be waiting for us."

Inside, various meats, vegetables, and desserts are laid out on a twelve-foot oak table that dominates the living-dining room. People are helping themselves, but they make sure Walker gets a plate right away, and they usher him into the line.

An older man, the Reverend Tabor, who is Beulah's minister, introduces himself, as does Jackson Mims, who owns the largest black insurance company in St. Andrews.

The adults sit in various chairs and on a large couch. The Reverend Mims says a long blessing before they begin eating, something Walker hasn't experienced in so long that he almost takes his first bite before R.J. catches his eye and saves him.

The children's table is in the kitchen. The adults make small talk, which Walker feels is strained because of his presence. Some of the men go back for seconds, and everyone has dessert, complimenting Philly and her daughter on the food.

Rasheed Aziz sits quietly in the corner, eating corn and field peas with cornbread, passing on dessert.

Finally, Philly stands up. All talk quickly ceases.

"I suppose you all know why we're here," she says. "I want to thank Mr. Fann for coming tonight. We always appreciate it when folks are willing to listen."

She sits down, and Aziz stands, as if they'd rehearsed.

He wipes his mouth deliberately with a paper napkin, doesn't say a word for several seconds. Walker has the feeling that he's using some of his courtroom tactics.

"What we're here for," he says when he finally speaks, "is justice. What we want from you is to help us get it.

"Why would you want to help black folks in Cottondale get their due? Well, you might do it because you wanted to do something right, something that sends a message that St. Andrews isn't two different places, tugging at each other."

Rasheed Aziz pauses, then starts in again.

"Failing that, you might want to help because we all have to live together. You might do it because people up on River Road might sleep a little easier, might not have to spend all their money on burglar alarms and rottweilers, worrying about another damn race riot."

He takes off his glasses and wipes them slowly, carefully with a clean white handkerchief.

"You know," he says, "my great-uncle Conway Cates was one of the ones they threw off that bridge. Landed on a sandbar and broke his goddamn neck—excuse me, Miss Philly. My momma used to tell me about white folks coming through our neighborhood afterward at night, yelling about 'Anybody want to go bridge diving tonight? Got any niggers wants to do some bridge diving?'"

The riots are an indelible part of the town's history. Walker remembers the last one. The days after Martin Luther King's assassination were filled with smoke and sirens. Most of the damage was in the Cottondale bottoms. Even Philly's store was looted. But enough white businesses near the Old Market were damaged so that it made Harold Neely's idea for a big mall on the west side of the river a very palatable one.

The one before that, the one Walker's grandfather used to tell him about, happened in 1919. The Cottondale Massacre. Walker can still remember the way the old man's eyes shone when he'd get into the heat of the story.

The mill drew farmers' sons and daughters for miles around, and it was just about the only thing in a four-county area that wasn't segregated. Blacks and whites worked together; there was hardly time to look up and see who was next to you anyhow. There were separate bathrooms and water fountains, and the cafeteria was whites-only. Black workers had to bring their lunches and eat where they could find a place to sit. Mostly, though, the Neely Mill was a peaceful place to work.

World War I changed that. When the white soldiers came back from Europe, they wanted jobs, and it didn't sit well with them that black men were drawing salaries while they waited for openings. Harold Neely's grandfather had been considered progressive, and he wouldn't fire black workers for no reason.

One warm spring day, a black man, Maximus Widney, was walking home after the seven-to-three shift. Several unemployed white men, who had been hanging around the outside of the plant, followed him for two blocks, then attacked him, beating and kicking him so brutally that he was never able to work at the mill again.

The next day, a white man who was alleged to have been one of the attackers, Sandy McKeithan, was pulled into an alley and beaten senseless. There were no witnesses, but it was assumed that the culprits were black. Cottondale's blacks were considered to be "uppity" by area standards, "jumped up" by the wages they were getting at the mill, but this, it was decided, was too much.

Things were calm for four days, and Walker's grandfather said anyone in town could have told you what was coming.

"It's like that sticky, humid feeling you get before a hurricane" is how he explained it.

It happened on a Sunday afternoon. There was a fine mist falling as the congregation of the Jordan Baptist Church left the sanctuary. The church was one of the few things that black Cottondale ventured west of the river for, and then for only a few hundred feet.

The church was on the west bank of the river, at a spot that made baptisms easy to perform. That afternoon just before one, the *Standard* reported later that several dozen men, women, and children left the church after services, most of them headed east, back across the bridge.

When they reached the highest part of the bridge, they saw the white mob, their faces covered with masks and sheets, coming toward them from the east. Looking back for sanctuary, the black churchgoers saw another group of masked men closing on them from that direction. They had waited down the highway a safe distance, in cars and trucks, then moved in when their prey started for home.

The whole incident lasted no more than ten minutes. None of the black people were armed; several of the whites were. There was more beating than shooting, but there was enough beating to go around.

It wasn't the beating, though, that would stand out in people's minds and give the Cottondale Massacre an identity beyond the usual Klan brutality, leading, many would say, to the white leaders' changing the town's name to St. Andrews thirty years later.

The men in the congregation tried to fight back, and then word spread from somewhere that a white man had been thrown from the bridge. The River Bridge, now long since replaced, was a good sixty feet above the river, and there were rocks and sandbars all through the water. A person being thrown from the bridge would almost certainly either die or be horribly crippled.

The first black man to be hurled screaming from the bridge was Bristol Philyaw, a deacon and father of three. He landed on a rock that would be stained with his blood until the next rise of the river. Before the killing stopped, ten black men and a black woman, trying to save her husband, were thrown off the bridge. One had his hands tied behind his back. Six died and two were crippled.

Every white person growing up in St. Andrews had heard the story. Along River Road, no one's father or grandfather had actually been there, but everyone seemed to know the story by heart, how the white crowd was gone as soon as it came, leaving a wailing black mass in the middle of the bridge.

Two men were actually convicted of assault, and one of them, a man whose mask had come completely off and who was observed by several witnesses to help throw a black man off the bridge, served one year in Central Prison.

The main effect of the massacre, though, was to scare Harold Neely's grandfather into hiring white veterans immediately. He didn't have to actually lay off very many black workers, since many of them were either dead, injured, or scared out of town. Over the years, more black workers were hired at the mill, but there was a feeling in Cottondale that no black person got a job there for the next forty years unless no qualified white person could be found in a thirty-mile radius. It took another world war to get black people back in the Neely Mill again in sizable numbers.

"What if the referendum passes?" Walker asks the black lawyer. "Won't that just stir things up more, just dig up hard feelings?"

Rasheed Aziz and a couple of the men laugh, short and unpleasant. Rasheed speaks, soft and slow. Even the children in the next room grow quiet.

"It ain't likely that voting money for the St. Andrews Museum of Slavery will do much for 'feelings' one way or the other," he says, "except to maybe make black folks think somebody on your side of the bridge wants to apologize. People on my side ain't ever forgot a damn thing."

"It'll help that you're calling it St. Andrews instead of Cottondale," Walker offers, although he knows most of his neighbors wouldn't vote in favor of the museum if it had Jesus' name tied to it.

"Well, we don't care much about that," Rasheed Aziz says. "Although the whole place ought to be Cottondale, but that's another story, and I don't want to get sidetracked."

Cottondale, more or less owned by Neely Mills, had actually been run by Neely-picked town councilmen. At the time it lost its name, the town, by then sixty percent black, was run by one black and four white councilmen, all answerable to the Neelys.

After World War II, more and more whites moved to the bluffs west of the Rich River, an area that had incorporated as St. Andrews in the thirties as a bow to its Scottish heritage. The River Road leaders and the people who ran Cottondale for the Neelys got together and managed to absorb the much older Cottondale bottoms into St.

Andrews. Cottondale disappeared from the map. Efforts in recent years to split the two were resisted by black and white leaders. The African-American community could see what a blow such a move would be to a dwindling tax base; the whites resisted because the small tax break they would get would be offset by the loss of status, political clout, and image inherent in halving their town's population.

And so, in the mid-1990s, white St. Andrews and the former Cottondale limped along like feuding Siamese twins.

R.J. leans forward, puts his big hands together and clears his throat.

"Walker," he says, "the people down here don't want a whole lot. What they're talking about is a few thousand dollars, matched by federal money, matched by a few business people we've already got signed on. I know you don't think like Harold Neely and them, but it won't matter much, if this thing doesn't pass.

"And it isn't like these folks'll get insulted and move off somewhere else if they don't get their slave museum. Hell, where they gonna go to? They'll just be here, for somebody to deal with."

"What about the Cottondale Massacre monument?"

"You mean the Tomb of the Unknown Nigger?" Rasheed Aziz says, smirking at Walker's discomfort. "It ain't anything but a historical marker. They have one telling you where Sherman went through. They got one where some raggedy-ass house used to sit on the river, where your ancestors used to own mine. My God, they got one by the mill to tell people it's a historical mill."

Walker is silent. He has lived his entire life in St. Andrews, and he's known for his adult life that most of what these people are telling him is dead true. But he has never been hit between the eyes with it before.

"Mr. Fann," the Reverend Tabor says, "we understand your position. We just asked you here tonight to understand ours. We know you might not support us, but we wish you would."

"Amen," Philly and several others say in unison.

Rasheed Aziz snorts and turns angrily away.

Walker decides to plunge in deeper.

"Do you know what most of my neighbors up there think?" he asks. "Do you all know what all the white people who buy advertising think is going to happen if that referendum passes?"

"No," Rasheed says quietly, suddenly sounding tired. "I wish you would tell us."

"They think," Walker says, swallowing hard, "they think that the town will be some kind of a symbol of evil, like Dachau or something, that it will be a rallying point for black people all over, that it will dig everything up again that they want buried. That they and everything they've made will be diminished."

"What!?" Aziz's head pops back up. "First of all, what in the world would there be in St. Andrews or Cottondale to bring black people running here? All it might do is bring some good people back that gave up and moved away. We might get more people like Raymond Justus to come home.

"Second, I don't know how much you study demographics, Walker"—Walker takes it as a good sign that the man has actually used his first name finally—"but if you look at the trends, you have got to know that nobody in this country, black, white, yellow, or paisley, is going to get along for much longer if he can't deal with different kinds of people. You tell that damn Harold Neely and all the rest of them that they better start exploring interplanetary travel if they want to go somewhere where they don't have to deal with folks that ain't white. Hell, even South Africa won't work for them anymore."

Several people chuckle appreciatively.

Walker tells them, too, about Harold Neely and the department store that Neely believes hangs on the referendum's outcome, but no black person, he is aware, cares whether Rich Valley Mall burns to the ground or not.

After that, there isn't much left to say. They talk for a few more minutes. Walker finds the give-and-take to be more bearable than he'd thought, but he knows, too, what he's up against on the hill. Not for the first time in his life, he wishes he had no agenda, no side to defend. Not for the first time, he realizes that he isn't eager to make the sacrifices needed to gain that kind of freedom.

"I'll do what I can," he says as he leaves. Only R.J. gets up to walk him to his car.

"I know you'll do your best" is all his old teammate says as they shake hands.

Heading back north toward the bridge, Walker can see, across the river, the lights off River Road. He asks himself if he has ever really given anything his best.

Lately, he's been having this dream: Mattie is still with him. They're playing in the sea off Positano, just bobbing along like two corks in the briny water. There was a boat, but it's somehow disappeared, and he realizes they're slowly sinking. He grabs Mattie's hands, because she's going down faster than he is.

"Let me go," she says. "Let me go." He does, and suddenly she's gone. He goes down, down, down after her, but he can't stay under the water. It isn't his lungs; he's too buoyant, popping up again and again.

He's always shouting the same words when he wakes up.

"Take me with you! Don't leave me."

And he always wonders what he could have done better.

13

THE LI GALLI WERE WHERE THE SIRENS SANG, LURING SAILORS TO THEIR DOOM.

You could see them from our balcony at Le Sirenuse, little bumps way out in the Gulf of Salerno, above and just to one side of the duomo down below us. When Walker found out that we could take a tour to the Li Galli, he immediately wanted to go. You always worry about a trip on which you've more or less kidnapped someone else, so it was pleasing to see Walker take the initiative. If he wanted to see the Li Galli up close and personal, fine by me.

"Could we be any farther from St. Andrews?" he asked me as we were luxuriating on the oversized mattresses on the poolside chaise longues, the breeze tickling our feet, those same islands out there between the faultless sky and the ink-blue water. He said it as if this were a positive. I envisioned other trips. France. The Greek isles. China.

We took the tour our second day there. The night before, we had one of the best meals either of us had ever eaten, fresh fish and pasta, good cheap Italian wine, without the sulfites that always gave me a headache back home. Afterward, Walker made love to me with admirable passion, back in our room with the breeze from the sea ruffling the curtains, the sound of an occasional fishing boat in the distance only adding to the feeling of, for once in our lives, no strings, no obligations, no cares.

Oh, I know it sounds ridiculous to talk about poor, poor, pitiful us, forced to live a life of wealth and privilege in a small Southern town. It sounds ridiculous to me, hearing myself say it. Still, though, it did feel like escape, like Positano was a magic castle where we could just be Walker and Mattie, where we could play. You could look out the window at night and the whole town was there, rising in lighted layers. It was a town where you could wander for half an hour along vine-covered walkways, past little shops selling *limoncello* and music boxes, suddenly emerging onto the beach, where you could have a glass of wine and watch the world go by.

The day we went to the Li Galli, we had lunch at Chez Black, real Italian pizza. We had a bottle of white wine and were feeling a little goofy by the time the little launch showed up that would take us on our trip.

I was a little leery of this excursion, because it was so cheap. My daddy had taught me that you get nothing for nothing.

This time, though, Daddy seemed to have missed the boat, so to speak. We rode out with two other American couples. It took us almost an hour to get there. One of the other couples had brought two more bottles of wine with them and shared it with us. We sat back on soft cushions and watched Positano recede. There was a light breeze; the other two couples and the two Italians manning the boat were charming.

Walker rolled a half-turn toward me.

"This just gets better and better," he murmured. "I want to make love to you right now."

I whispered to him that's what I wanted, too, but maybe we ought to wait at least until we were off the boat.

The Li Galli are actually three rocks out there where the gulf meets the Tyrrhenian Sea. Supposedly, Rudolph Nureyev owned one of them. The captain, or whatever, steered the outboard boat into a protected spot in the middle of the three little islands.

We'd been told that there would be swimming, but the rocks seemed to go straight down forever. We wondered where the beach was.

The other Italian lowered a rope ladder into the water and made a flourish.

"*Il bagno*," he said.

We didn't go in right away. There was more wine on the boat, and I was still enjoying the sensation of no-fault afternoon drinking: no headache, no driving, no kids. It didn't even seem to make me drunk. Walker was chugging it pretty good, too.

One of the other passengers was a twenty-something man-boy from California with jet-black hair and what appeared to be an all-over tan, who seemed to take this paradise as his natural right. He'd brought a snorkel along, and he and his blonde girlfriend, both wearing as little as the law would allow, were cavorting around in the water, which felt cold to me as I dangled my hand over the side of the little boat.

It suited me to just sit there with the other couple, retirees from Massachusetts, drinking wine and trying to commit this day and this place to memory. But Walker's blood was up, I guess. He wanted to dive in the water, he said, and play with the fishes. "And with you," he whispered in my ear, but loudly enough so that I'm sure the other couple must have heard.

It seemed a crime not to encourage him. When he dove off the bow of the boat, I gingerly lowered myself down the rope ladder. I'd worn a bikini under my shorts, too bold for St. Andrews, but demure by the standards of the blonde bombshell. I slipped into the cold, clear water. It looked as deep as the Grand Canyon; you could see all the way to the bottom.

I had never been a good swimmer. Don't ask me why. Lord knows, Momma and Daddy paid for enough lessons; it was expected at the club. Every child who was toilet-trained was on some kind of swim team. The best I could figure, the landed gentry felt that the lessons learned from spending cold winter mornings drinking chlorine water and flailing away in an indoor pool would be good for us later in life. Sport as Work Ethic.

But it took me a summer to get so I could stay afloat, and after another half-summer of near-fruitless lessons, my parents gave up and let me play tennis.

Water always made me feel so helpless. The concept that you were somehow supposed to be able to ride along on the surface of a liquid never really took with me. I don't know; maybe I just never had enough trust. As an adult, I had perfected a lazy sidestroke that would allow me to keep my contacts in and not even really get my hair wet.

Even doing that, though, I didn't feel comfortable more than thirty feet from land.

But this water was different. It held you up. It must have had more salt than any water I'd ever been in, because I wasn't sinking like I usually do. To me, it was almost like the dream everyone has where they can fly.

"This is wonderful; I can float," I told Walker when he swam over to me. Walker is a good swimmer; he doesn't seem capable of sinking. He used to tell me that it was lack of confidence that kept me from staying above water. I'd tense up and drop like a stone.

Walker laughed and then slid his hand underneath my bottom, making me jump and swallow some of that salty water.

"Don't do that!" I told him, but he and I were both laughing, and he led me farther away from the boat, in the direction of the rocks that surrounded one of the three little rock-islands.

I remember thinking to myself that I really shouldn't be doing this, but I was feeling good. Walker was as effervescent as a little boy.

Life was good.

14

WALKER IS ALREADY HALFWAY THROUGH BREAKFAST WHEN HIS FATHER COMES IN. BIG WALKER SEEMS SURPRISED, CHECKS HIS watch to see if he's running late.

"Well," he says, "Mr. Bright Eyes." It's a nickname from Walker's childhood, and its usage makes his father seem very old for some reason. "What gets you up so early?"

The night before, Big Walker was already in bed when his son came home after a two-beer detour to Charley's.

"I thought we might ride in together," Walker says.

His father gives him a quick, sharp look.

"Certainly. I'd love to do that every day."

Ginger and Mac come down as Big Walker is gulping down his coffee.

"Where'd you go last night, Dad?" Ginger asks him.

"I had to see somebody."

"Carneal's dad?" Mac says, not even looking up from his pancakes.

Walker has no idea why his son should have guessed that. He feels himself flushing.

"As a matter of fact, yes," he says, including his father and mother in the look he gives his children. "We had some business to discuss. I'd have taken you along, but I wanted you to do your homework."

"Didn't work," Ginger says. "I didn't do it anyhow."

Walker can feel his father's unasked question filling up the room.

"Come on," he tells Big Walker. "We're going to be late."

His father follows him out the door, shaking his head.

Walker turns south rather than north out of the driveway.

"Thought we might talk on the way in," he says. It's always been easier for Walker to talk with his father driving along in a car, looking straight ahead, than sitting across a desk from him.

"About the slavery museum," Big Walker says, no question in his voice.

"Yeah, about the slavery museum. We gave it a pretty good lick this morning. I want to present the other side." There, he thinks to himself. It's out.

In Monday's *Standard*, Ry Tucker has excoriated the idea of a museum that "drags up all of the worst in St. Andrews's past, sullies her fine name." On occasion, it is the *Standard*'s practice to run editorials down the left side on the front page, and this was what Big Walker had instructed Ed McLaurin, the managing editor, to do in today's paper. The plan is to do the same on Tuesday, when Walker is due to write the "official" *Standard* editorial exhorting the citizens to vote against the museum.

Big Walker doesn't say a word for what seems like five minutes. They go silently past Walker and Mattie's former home, past Sycamore Baptist Church, past neighbors out walking or jogging who get a brief wave from Walker and a stony stare from his father.

"Look," Walker says finally, "I've been giving this a lot of thought. I've heard Harold Neely's side, and I've heard Rasheed Aziz's side. I'll bet I didn't sleep two hours last night thinking about the damn slavery museum. I think I'm more capable than anyone in St. Andrews of giving an informed opinion."

Big Walker grunts, then shifts a quarter-turn to the left, toward his son.

"'Informed opinion.' You make it sound like this is a debate or something, son. If we were sitting in some ivy-covered tower somewhere, looking down there at all those poor lost souls needing our guidance, maybe you might want to side with Rasheed Aziz and Raymond Justus and every sorehead that ever got a bad break.

"But here's how it is, in the real world, St. Andrews, North Carolina, in the year of our Lord nineteen hundred and ninety-four. I'm only gonna tell you this one more time."

Big Walker holds out his left hand, the motion so abrupt and full of anger that Walker thinks for a half-second that his father is going to hit him in the face, the way he did one time and one time only when Walker was a child.

"On this hand, you've got the people who think they've been wronged, who think St. Andrews owes it to 'em to build a monument to everything bad that ever happened to their great-great-grandparents. And if we side with them, we're still going to be the enemy; they'll just have a little more ammunition to shoot us with."

Big Walker throws out his right hand, bumping it hard against the side window.

"And on this hand, you've got the people who actually buy the advertising that keeps us from having to sell ourselves to the highest bidder. You've got the people whose parents and grandparents built St. Andrews, gave it everything including its name. You've got your neighbors and friends all along this road. And they don't have any desire to be from a town that's famous for its quaint Old Market, now home of the St. Andrews Museum of Slavery.

"If you go with the left, you aid your enemies. If you go with the right, you aid your friends."

Big Walker turns a bit farther, looking directly at his son, who returns the gaze as they pull into the *Standard* parking lot.

"Son," he says, "it doesn't sound like a hard choice to me, especially with Harold Neely's anchor store hanging in the balance, at least in his mind."

He opens the door and starts to get out, then stops.

"But like I told you the other day, it's your call. I reckon there'll be enough there to keep me and Dottie from eatin' cat food. You answer to your children and their children."

Walker almost lets him go.

"Big Man," he says, coming up behind his father as the old man reaches for the handle to the building's back entrance, "I don't see it that way. If we don't work together, if we don't do something to show half this town's population that somebody, somewhere regrets something, we won't ever get together."

Big Walker gives a thin smile.

"Don't tell me, son. Tell Harold Neely. And then tell all the people who have been your friends for forty-two years and will be, if you'll let 'em, for another forty-two. Tell them." And he goes inside, leaving Walker standing in the parking lot, alone.

Walker knew people, in high school and college, who had defied their parents, who had braved the outer darkness of disapproval that seemed untenable to him. He wonders now if a few rebellions back then would have saved him this agony, this pain he feels at the thought of committing what his father, and probably even his mother, will view as nothing less than treason.

And he knows Big Walker could be right. What black person in Cottondale, other than maybe R.J. or Philly, would

sympathize with the scion of one of River Road's most affluent white families just because he's defied the will of his
parents and friends?

Last night, he ran into Glen Murphy at Charley's. Walker
broached the subject of the slavery museum, wanting to
sound out his old friend, someone his own age, someone
who had gone with him many years ago to Cottondale and
broken bread with Philly and Raymond Justus.

Murphy summed up his stand in considerably fewer
words than Big Walker needed: "Too much water over the
dam, bubba."

Worry about the showdown with his father was only one
reason Walker slept so poorly last night. The other was
Mattie.

This time, he dreamed they were back in St. Andrews, in
their old home. He had awakened and known instantly that
she was there. He can even remember, now, her smell, the
same in the dream as it was in reality, something deeper
than perfumes, just the sweetness of her skin.

He'd rolled over like he used to, sliding his right arm
under her pillow, throwing his left arm around her from
behind, sliding like a shadow up against her curved body,
pressing against her knees and bottom, smelling her hair,
looking at the perfection of her left ear.

He was just stretching forward to nibble her lobe when
she spoke, not groggily like someone just waking up, but
clearly.

"Walker," she had said, from lips he couldn't see, "don't
do anything I wouldn't do."

Whenever he would have to go on a short business trip
or to a newspaper convention, she'd kiss him and tell him
that, and he'd respond, "But you'd do about anything." And
she'd say, "With you."

In the dream, though, he can't think of what he's supposed to say. By the time he does, he's awake, alone at 3 A.M.

Walker is religious, but in a formal, pragmatic way. Even as a child, he wondered, to himself, how all the things he learned in Sunday school could be taken at face value.

Last night was the closest Walker has ever come to believing, really believing, in something beyond the literal. He was wavering even before then on the slavery museum, seriously considering doing the one thing that might earn his father's wrath forever, despite Big Walker's declaration that "It's your call."

Now, he knows for sure what he should do. What Mattie would do.

The morning passes slowly. Big Walker skips the daily editors' meeting, and Walker tells McLaurin to expect his column by 4 P.M. He doesn't tell him what he's writing, but Walker is sure that all the editors take it for granted that he will come out against the museum. Walking through the newsroom, he can feel the disapproval that they dare not verbalize. Easy for you, he thinks to himself. After the paper is sold and they lay off half the newsroom, you all can get $25,000-a-year jobs somewhere else. You don't have to live here.

It is a source of irritation to Walker that almost no one on the *Standard* staff is actually from the town itself, which doesn't seem to turn out very many journalists.

At 11:45, back in his own office, he hears Big Walker's door slam. He had hoped that his father would come in so that they could talk, but he knows he could have made the effort just as easily. Five years ago, Big Walker would have told his son what to write, and if he hadn't written it, he would have simply passed the assignment on to Ry Tucker. Walker isn't sure whether his father has more confidence in him now or is just getting old.

Fifteen minutes later, Walker emerges. He always eats at noon, usually at one of the barbecue or burger places off Route 30, and he thinks that perhaps he can find Big Walker and talk. According to Becky, his father left on foot, probably headed for one of the same fast-food places—not, Walker is thinking, where Big Walker and his aging and long-suspect heart need to be having lunch. He has a set of keys to his son's car; he could have either taken it or asked Walker to join him. It's obvious to Walker that he wants to be alone, or at least away from him.

Walker sighs and tells Becky he'll be back in an hour. He hasn't written a satisfactory word yet toward the editorial, putting it off all morning with mail and phone calls and anything else that availed itself. This is not unusual; Walker feels he works best when he has some kind of deadline, even one he's invented through procrastination. Today, though, he wonders if something more is blocking him. What else do you need? he asks himself. A sign from God?

He steps into the bright September noon, everything in front of him in silhouette. He's still fumbling with his sunglasses when he hears the familiar voice.

"Hello, Walker. I believe we need to talk."

Walker tries to conceal the adrenaline jolt that almost made him crush his glasses. Where, he wonders, did Harold Neely come from?

As his eyes adjust to the light, he sees that Neely, leaning against a car parked next to the backdoor, is not alone. The other man is wearing a police uniform, and he looks familiar.

"I'm going to lunch, Harold," Walker says, angry over what he is sure was an ambush. He wonders if Neely was outside when his father left.

"This won't take but a couple of minutes, Walker." Neely moves in front of him. "Officer West has something I think you ought to see. It won't cut into your busy day much at all."

Walker recognizes the patrolman as the one who helped apprehend Carneal Justus four days earlier. Officer West gives Walker a curt nod.

"You see," Neely says. "We have a little problem here. Officer West is a good friend of mine, and he came to me when this little problem came up, because he was sure, us being such good friends, that I'd want to save you from any grief."

"What in the hell are you talking about?" Walker says. His jaw aches. He wants to hit Harold Neely hard and repeatedly.

"I'm talking about this, asshole," Neely says, dropping any pretense of manners. "Officer West, tell Mr. Fann what you told me."

Officer West looks extremely uncomfortable, caught between two of the most powerful men in the only town he ever plans to live in. But he obviously owes Neely.

"At about three o'clock on Friday afternoon, July 15," he begins, sounding as if he's reciting, "I received an anonymous complaint about drug use in a wooded area behind Rich Valley Mall. Arriving on the scene, I surprised four male youths. They had in their possession approximately one-half ounce of marijuana."

Walker can see from the smirk on Harold Neely's pinched face where this is heading, but he just nods for Officer West to continue.

"Three of the youths escaped, but I managed to apprehend the fourth perpetrator."

Walker wonders where cops learned to talk like this.

"The apprehendee . . ."

"Goddammit, man; talk in English," Neely says, kicking his foot sideways against the tire nearest him.

"The boy had been smoking marijuana. I took him back to the patrol car and asked him where he got the illegal sub . . . the dope from."

"Go ahead," Walker says in a voice just above a whisper.

"He said he bought it from one of the other boys present, a Mac Fann, who is, I believe, Walker McNeill Fann the fourth, your son."

"Yes. That's my son. But my son does not sell dope. Anybody who says he does is lying." Even as he says it, Walker knows it could be true.

"Be careful there, Walker," Neely says. "You don't want to make Officer West here mad. He owes me a favor or two, and he could still throw that kid of yours in jail, give him a criminal record. Might do him good.

"Some of these boys have been selling crack. No telling what the one that was caught might say when he starts facing the prospect of a felony conviction. Officer West says he seems real chatty already."

Walker moves toward his older, smaller nemesis. The policeman intervenes.

"Here's the deal, Walker," Neely says. "You look tired, like you might need an afternoon off. Why don't you just go home and take a nap, maybe go have a talk with that boy of yours? I'm sure that whatever work you have left to do at the paper this afternoon could be handled by somebody else, like maybe Ry Tucker? And you know what? I bet, if you do that, things will look a whole lot better in the morning. I bet you anything that Officer West here, under those circumstances, will come down with a bad case of amnesia. Won't anything bad happen to anybody except maybe a good talking-to, father to son, if you know what I mean."

Neely winks, and in that wink is the knowledge that he has won.

Walker just stands there as Neely and the patrolman

leave in Neely's car. He doesn't know which way to turn first, whether to wait for his father or go to his son to get the truth. He feels sick.

Walker has little trouble getting Mac out of class. He directs his son to the front steps of the high school. St. Andrews High sits on part of the same ridge that, farther south, slopes down to the river from their backyard. The main building predates Walker, and he can remember sitting on these same steps with Mattie their senior year. It has always pleased Walker to know that his children would attend the same high school as he did and not some prep school. He believes that the best town in the world for raising children is one that is just small enough so that everyone attends the same high school.

From here, at the top of the steps, they can see Cottondale. It hasn't rained in days, and the air is getting hot and hazy again, summer's last stand. The houses across the river, even the big mill building, have a softer appearance than reality gives them.

Mac is nervous. Walker just looks at him for a couple of minutes. The boy is finally forced to face him.

"What?" he says finally. "What do you want?"

Walker knows he would have asked already, would have shown more surprise about being taken from class in the middle of the day, if he hadn't known what his father wanted.

"A policeman came by today," he says. "He says they caught a boy smoking dope, back in July, that he bought it from you."

Mac looks up, genuinely surprised.

"He bought it from me? He said I sold it to him?"

Walker nods his head.

"No way! Dad, I'm sorry. I screwed up. I told them we never should have been smoking there behind the mall."

"Or anywhere else," Walker adds forcefully.

"You and Mom used it."

Walker resists the urge to say what he's thinking. That was different. Smoking marijuana back then only led to smoking more marijuana. Weight gain was about your biggest problem. Now, God knows what comes next: crack, pills, something you take with a dirty, AIDS-infected needle.

"We were stupid," he says instead. "We didn't know any better."

"Dad, we smoked dope, O.K.? Like everybody else at St. Andrews High. We all knew that Danny Bass would tell after he got caught. I've just been waiting for it. I was scared to tell you, but I heard last week that he had made some kind of deal. . . .

"But he said I sold it to him? Dad, we bought it together, me and Danny . . . and the other two."

Danny Bass, Walker figures, is one of the Basses who live down in Shootersville, over by the mill, part of the dwindling white population east of the river. He remembers several of them from his teenage years, each with black, oily hair, ruddy complexion, a single eyebrow meeting over the nose, always in trouble. He wonders how his son has come to associate with Basses.

"Who'd you buy it from?"

"I—I don't know. Some black kid."

"Carneal?"

"Nah. Some friend of his, I think. I'm not sure what his name was. Danny Bass knows him. Why did he say I sold it to him?"

Walker sighs. He knows, as surely as he knows his own name, what happened. He's heard stories of power plays like this by Harold Neely, always second- or third-hand before. If you're on Neely's list, he's got the longest arms in town. He can hold a trump card for two months if he has to.

Hell, a lot longer than that. If four kids get caught, and your kid's one of them, guess which one gets fingered? He wonders if Neely himself paid Danny Bass a visit to convince him of the wisdom of naming Mac Fann. He wonders if a Bass, even one of teenage years, might be a tool of Neely's.

He wonders what his son is doing hanging out with people like this, and he wonders what else has happened in the last year that he doesn't know about.

Walker is sure this wasn't Mac's first time smoking marijuana in some semipublic place. Even Neely's luck isn't that good.

But he also believes—knows—that his son is not a drug dealer, although he would like to shake him right now for giving Harold Neely so much satisfaction. He supposes that, if it came to trial, he could at least plea-bargain down to simple possession. It is not something he wants on his son's record, though. He is not sure how far he would go to protect his children from their mistakes. This far, at least.

So Walker stands slowly, ready to give Officer West a case of amnesia.

<u>15</u>

WALKER DOESN'T GO BACK TO THE *STANDARD*, OR EVEN CALL. HE KNOWS THAT, AT SOME POINT, BIG WALKER WILL SIMPLY turn the Page 1 editorial assignment over to Ry Tucker, may already have done so, as a matter of fact.

He decides, at least for the present, not to tell Mac the consequences of his getting caught. He tells his son to go back to class, that they will talk later, that maybe, just maybe, he can keep him out of jail.

Then Walker heads for Charley's and starts drinking.

He didn't drink a drop for most of the past year, terrified of what he might do if something cracked that veneer of control, of what might take Mattie's place if he let it.

Today, though, he tries very hard to get drunk. By the third beer, he knows that in some secret shameful place he's relieved that he has been spared the hard task by Harold Neely, that Neely actually has saved him in some perverted way, forced him to act in a manner that will let him remain within the circle that has bounded his world since birth.

He wonders if some people aren't predestined to be cowards.

By the fifth beer, he's developed a teeth-grinding anger

toward Big Walker. He can imagine his father making a call to Harold Neely as soon as they got to work, Neely telling him not to worry, that he'll have a talk with "the boy." Nothing ever would have been revealed about Mac's being involved with drugs; Big Walker never would let himself know the messy details. In his mind, he was just letting somebody he respected talk some sense into his hardheaded son.

Walker remembers a reporter, a boy named Nance two years out of journalism school, who was too much of a firebrand. It was at least fifteen years ago. Nance wrote a couple of stories that suggested Neely and some of his associates had conspired with city officials to keep downtown Cottondale from getting state and federal funds that would have helped revitalize the area around the Old Market. He quoted black leaders as saying that Neely was trying to strangle downtown to benefit his mall. There were allegations that the *Standard* was in on it.

Neely had no comment. By the end of the month, though, Nance had been accused of statutory rape. The girl was fifteen. Nance swore he was set up, but Big Walker had the managing editor fire him anyhow. Charges were eventually dropped, but Nance soon left town. Walker heard that he had to swear he'd never write anything, anywhere about Cottondale again. To Walker's knowledge, he never has.

Big Walker denied ever saying a harsh word to Nance, but when it was essential for Nance to be gone, Nance was gone.

By the seventh beer, Walker realizes he is drawing attention to himself, sitting alone at the bar and carefully peeling the labels off the sides of the longneck Millers Charley Lampros keeps serving up. There is a pile of soggy paper in front of him. He gets up to go to the bathroom and nearly falls.

"Been a long time since I was this drunk," he says, grinning at Charley, who merely frowns and shakes his head.

In the tiny bathroom, Walker looks at himself in the cracked mirror that is inexplicably, cruelly set directly behind the urinal, so that drunken middle-aged men can see how far they have sunk. He becomes so absorbed with his flushed, out-of-focus face that he urinates on his foot. In the small space, it takes him several minutes to clean up. Someone knocks on the bathroom door, and Walker opens it to see a fat construction worker scowling outside.

"Gonna take all day?" the construction worker demands. Walker slides out the door past him, mortified halfway sober.

He has one more beer, then drifts back to the pay phone. He dials Big Walker's number. Becky answers.

"This's Walker. Let me speak to the Big Man."

"Walker? Where are you? He's been looking for you."

"Yeah, right. Listen. Becky. Tell him to have his butt outside in five minutes if he wants a ride home."

She's still talking when he hangs up.

He pays his tab and looks at his watch. Quarter to five. Big Walker doesn't usually leave this early, but he'll have to make an exception today.

Walker doesn't know how long he's been waiting in the *Standard*'s parking lot when his father opens the passenger door. He doesn't even remember the trip from Charley's.

"You able to drive?" Big Walker asks cautiously as he eases himself in.

"Yeah, Big Man. I can drive like a sonofabitch."

"Why don't you let me . . . "

The sentence is left hanging as Walker slams the Lexus into reverse and they go backward forty feet. He shifts into first and peels rubber.

Big Walker realizes his protests are in vain. He grabs the strap above the door and hangs on.

Walker turns right leaving the lot, then right again on Route 30. By the time he crosses the bridge, his father knows where they're going.

Walker parks on the square, on the southwest side of the Old Market. He turns off the ignition, turns and faces his father. The ride, with the window rolled down and the breeze hitting him in the face, has sobered him slightly.

"I had a visitor today," he tells his father softly. Big Walker is silent.

"How do you suppose that my good friend, my lifelong friend Harold Neely, knew I wasn't going along with the plan? How is that, Big Man? Huh?"

Big Walker clears his throat and looks ahead, where a group of young boys loiter around the base of the market. The bricks are blood-red now in the late-afternoon sun.

"Well, I reckon he knows because I told him," he says. "Hell, I made a promise. He made me swear I'd at least let him know if we weren't going to support him on this."

"And you walked right by him in the parking lot, just sitting there waiting for me with that cop like a couple of hawks waiting for a chicken."

Big Walker's face is flushed. He's sweating.

"I didn't know he would come over to the paper. I figured he'd call up and scream and raise hell like he always does. I figured he'd just pull his advertising and be done with it.

"And I didn't tell him to bring any damn policeman with him."

Walker presses on, wanting to hurt.

"You probably don't even know what the cop was about, do you, Big Man?"

His father shakes his head.

"And you don't want to know, either, do you?"

Big Walker is silent. He is staring straight ahead and seems to be humming softly to himself, as if he would like to muffle any other voices.

Walker wants to tell him, wants to share his pain with the old man, but he pulls up short.

"So, tell me," he says, his voice softening, "what did you do this afternoon? What time did Harold Neely call and tell you to have Ry Tucker start writing that editorial?"

Big Walker is quiet for a few seconds. Finally he says, "About one-thirty. He called about one-thirty."

"Well, tell me this, Big Man. Were you relieved? Did it ease your mind that you'd dodged the bullet again?"

Big Walker rallies.

"You're damn right!" he says. "You're damn right. I don't know what Neely said to you, and I don't want to know. . . ."

"I know you don't."

". . . but whatever it was, it just might have saved this newspaper for your children and their children."

Walker can't resist the urge to push the old man a step farther.

"But you must wonder, Big Man. You've got to wonder how Harold Neely could get me to bend to his all-powerful will. Or maybe you think it was just the strength of his silver tongue that persuaded me."

Big Walker turns away. Walker can see something he's almost never seen in his father's face: real fear. They are silent for several minutes.

Finally, Walker starts the car.

"I have one more errand to run before we go home," he tells his father. "I guess you can tag along."

Big Walker doesn't even bother to protest.

There are children playing all along Second Street as they near the Justuses' homes. Walker stops the car alongside R.J.'s house and tells his father to wait.

He knocks on the door. Finally, Carneal answers. Half-scared and half-sullen, he tells Walker that his father is "lay-ing down." Walker finally gets him to let him in and to wake R.J., who comes out presently, wiping sleep from his eyes.

He offers Walker a beer.

"I can't, R.J.; I can't stay that long."

The black man looks at Walker for a few long seconds, then looks away.

"You're not going to help us, are you?"

Walker would rather have been screamed at by Rasheed Aziz. He feels physically ill, between the beer and his shame.

"No" is all he says. He can't bring himself to offer weak excuses, and even if he did, R.J. is already turning and going back toward the bedroom. He comes back half a minute later, stuffing his wallet in his pocket.

"You go on over to your grandmomma's," he tells Carneal, pointing his finger for emphasis. He has no words for Walker. In another few seconds, he is gone, and Walker hears the red Buick start up.

He and Carneal look at each other for a few seconds.

"I reckon you'll have to leave," the boy says finally, quietly.

Walker has no other words. Carneal follows him out.

Back in the car, he sees that his father has his eyes closed, that he is humming to himself again.

"Well, that's done," Walker says, starting the Lexus again. "These people must be the biggest saps in the world. They actually thought I was going to help them."

"Son . . ."

"No! I mean it! This'll be good for 'em. They'll know not to trust a Fann again. We've knocked that nonsense right out of their nappy little heads."

Big Walker is quiet as his son takes two lefts and heads north on Third Street.

They are almost to the bridge when the old man speaks.

"Did you know," he says, almost inaudibly, "that your grandfather was part of it?"

"Part of what?" Walker says after a long pause.

Big Walker sighs, then answers.

"The Cottondale Massacre."

Walker pulls the car off onto the dirt shoulder just short of the river, beside a fruit-and-vegetable stand that has just closed for the season. They can hear the metallic rumble of cars crossing the bridge.

Walker sits silent, waiting for the rest.

"I wasn't born until 1922," Big Walker says. "It was when I was twelve or thirteen. We used to have this old colored man, Babe Turner, that would help us with yard work. He was over one day, him and this other man, planting some magnolias for Momma, and she had me bring them some water.

"I came up on 'em from behind, after they were just finished burying the root ball of this magnolia tree. And they were arguing. The other colored fella told Babe, 'You can't shush me, old man. I seen what I seen. And I seen your Mister Fann throw that boy off the bridge.'

"Babe wasn't denying it, just trying to keep the other man quiet. 'Shut up, fool,' he said. 'You want me to lose this sweet job? I don't care what he did back then. He's been good to me.'

"They kept at it, and I slipped back around the corner. When I came back, I made sure they heard me 'way ahead of time."

It was four years later, he says, before he got Babe Turner to confirm it. By then, almost a man, he felt as if he could demand the truth, and Babe finally gave it to him.

"You know what he told me? He said, 'You got to remember, Mr. Walker, all the white folks was there.'"

Big Walker never confronted his father with this testimony, he says now; he just went out of his way to cross him on race issues from then on.

"He called me a nigger lover one time," Big Walker says. "I was probably thirty then, I think it was the year you were born, and I wanted us to come out in favor of a ward system so the blacks would have more representation in the city government.

"I just looked at him and told him it was better to love 'em than to throw 'em off the bridge. He gave me such a stare, and he never said anything about it again."

Walker twists around in the driver's seat.

"Why are you telling me this?" he asks.

"I don't know. I don't know. . . . Maybe so you don't think I've always been an SOB. I was in favor of a lot of stuff before the rest of 'em were, you know. We didn't have much trouble with integration down here, after the first year or so. But then they started burning stores, and acting like the world owed 'em a living."

Walker doesn't say anything, just sits there squinting into the late-afternoon sun that turns east-bound cars crossing the bridge into silhouettes. His memory of the *Standard*'s approach to integration differs drastically from his father's.

"Maybe I just wanted you to know something," his father continues. "Maybe I just wanted you to know how hopeless it is. I mean, my daddy did a lot for this town; he started the fund to build the high school, and the library. He tithed every Sunday.

"But how would you see him now? Like some kind of monster is how. But he wasn't, dammit! He was as fine a man as I have ever known. He just got caught up in something wrong.

"And how about me? Am I a monster, too? I did some good things.

"But there came a time when I had to decide," Big Walker says, clenching his fists, getting his second wind. "Sure, there were terrible things done to black people back then, and I wish I could get in some time machine and change all that. But I can't, and you can't, either. All you can do is play the hand that's dealt you. And the hand that's been dealt us is *The St. Andrews Standard.* You think some damn penny-pinching chain from Ohio is going to make things better if we have to sell?"

Walker starts to tell his father that no one's calling him a monster, but Big Walker talks right through him.

"Here's the thing, though. You keep on, you do what you think is right, you be there every day doing all you can for your family and your community, and eventually, I promise you, you'll be a monster, too. 'Cause you know what? If you're a winner, you're fair game."

Walker is afraid he's being told the rules of something that started long before he was born and won't ever end.

He thinks back to something Mattie said to him once, at the end of an argument over busing students. Walker had told her pretty much what Big Walker has just told him, that the Fanns were envied because they were winners.

"Honey," she'd told him, "it would do you more good than you know to lose once in a while."

Maybe she was right, he thinks now. Maybe a little losing is good for anybody now and then.

16

WALKER LOOKS OUT FROM HIS BEDROOM WINDOW AT A HEAVY FOG THAT HE KNOWS PROBABLY WILL BURN OFF BEFORE TEN. He wishes that the day would stay dark and overcast, a day in which a person could hide.

He wanders out, wearing jeans and an old shirt, after he's sure Big Walker has left for work and the children are off to school. Dottie fixes him a large breakfast of sausage and pancakes, despite his protestations, and he barely touches it.

He can't resist turning Tuesday morning's *Standard* to the editorial page, where he sees what he already knows Ry Tucker has written—"a blemish on St. Andrews's fine name," "needless attempt to dredge up a best-forgotten past," "duty of all who want what is best for our future." Walker has seen all the phrases, in different combinations, before.

"Aren't you going to vote, honey?" Dottie asks him, a worried look in her eyes.

"I already did, yesterday," he snaps, walking away from the table, feeling a little worse because she meant him no harm.

"Thanks for breakfast," he throws over his shoulder as he retreats to the bedroom. He feels the way he did as a boy, when he'd have a rare sick day and Dottie would fuss over him as he lay in his big bedroom alone.

He lies on his back, his mind wandering, now playing back the humiliation of the previous day, now thinking of Mattie, as much as he can stand. For a long time, he couldn't do it, just blocked her out of his mind entirely. Then, on a cold February morning five months after it happened, he gave Mac a ride to school at the junior high after the boy had missed the bus. On the way out of the semicircular parking lot, he saw an older boy and girl walking toward the high school next door, hand in hand, and they looked so much like him and Mattie at that age that he had to jerk the car off the side of the road. He cried for half an hour, not even caring who saw him; it was the first time he had let go. He felt better, and he let himself remember her from time to time after that, gradually building up his endurance.

He knows it would have been smarter to get some kind of counseling, probably for the kids, too. At the time, though, he didn't have the will to fight Big Walker, who thought outside help was a sign of weakness. He wonders, lying in bed, if he has ever successfully crossed his father on anything of substance.

By three o'clock, Walker is out of bed. He showers, feeling stiff and useless. He wishes he'd postponed the shower and gone for a jog first, then decides to go running anyhow, shower or not.

He runs through his usual trouble spot and is feeling good walking back home when an older car with two black men in it meets him on River Road. Normally, Walker holds his hand up to wave at anyone he meets; it is considered proper etiquette in St. Andrews. You wave to people you would never consider inviting to your house or your club; they wave back, even if they envy or hate you.

Today, he can't do it. He lowers his head and the car whizzes past.

Walker stands in the driveway. The day has turned out to be beautiful, with a bright blue sky, temperature in the low eighties. He holds out hope that the fine weather will bring out Cottondale voters, who are more easily discouraged by rain than their richer neighbors, having less faith in the democratic process. But he knows, from the posters and bumper stickers, from the line he saw at the community center as he jogged by, from the amount of traffic leading to the voting station, that every registered vote in Cottondale probably won't be enough to carry the day.

He looks across the backyard. It is less hazy than yesterday, and he can see individual houses beyond the river. He is sure that the burst of red he sees is the roof of Philly's store.

He walks back into the house long enough to exchange his running outfit for long pants and shirt.

"Where are you off to now?" Dottie asks him, but he doesn't answer.

As he opens the front door, Mac is walking up the steps.

"Where're you going?" he asks his father.

Walker starts to tell him that he's just going to the store, but he senses that Mac ought to be part of this.

"Raymond Justus's house. Want to come along?"

"Sure." Mac throws his books on the coffee table nearest the door.

"We might not be too welcome," Walker tells him. The boy shrugs and follows his father back out.

By the time they get in the car, Ginger is walking up the driveway, and she insists on going, too.

Walker drives slowly to the curb beside R.J.'s house. He cut the radio off a block away, as if he hopes to sneak up on someone.

"What are we doing?" Ginger asks, almost in a whisper.

"Trying to make something right," Walker says. "You two stay in the car. And lock the doors."

Neither of them argues with him.

The house seems deserted. It's four-fifteen, so Walker knows Carneal should be home from school, but when he peers through the front window, there is no sign of life.

He sees movement out of the corner of his eye and turns in time to see Philly Justus walk inside her house and close the front door.

He walks back to the street, down it sixty feet, and then up to the same door he just heard slam. He wonders that Cracker hasn't already made a run for him; he can see the dog lying flat to the ground in a shady corner of the yard, but he seems to have lost interest in biting him.

"Missus Justus," he calls through the closed door. "It's Walker Fann. Can you please tell me where R.J. went? I need to find him. I need to explain."

He is aware that a couple of the neighborhood kids, neither of them Carneal, are now standing at the corner of the lot, their arms crossed, watching the strange white man talking to a closed door. They probably think I'm a bill collector, Walker figures.

He talks for five minutes before he hears Philly's voice on the other side:

"There ain't nothing to explain. You did what you thought you was supposed to do. Go on now."

"I didn't write that editorial, Missus Justus. I wanted to support the museum, but I couldn't."

Walker knows how lame he sounds, how totally unbelievable. He wonders if he shouldn't just take Glen Murphy's advice. Maybe it is too much water over the dam.

But Philly cracks the door a couple of inches. Walker can see her right eye, baleful and streaked with red.

"It's your paper," she says, her voice a low growl. "Your daddy won't let you write what you want in your own paper? What's the use in owning a newspaper if you can't write what you want in it?"

Walker just shakes his head. He can't bring himself to tell Philly about Harold Neely and Officer West.

"I just want to talk to R.J.," he says at last. "Can't you tell me where he's gone?"

"Don't nobody here know where he's gone," Philly says. "He come back this morning, but now he's gone again. On top of that, Carneal's gone. Didn't come home from school today."

Walker is sure this isn't the first time Carneal hasn't come home, but he can see the anxiety in Philly's face.

Walker has a few ideas of where he might find Raymond Justus.

"If he comes back before I find him," Walker says to Philly, "tell him it isn't like he thinks it is. Will you tell him that? Please?"

"It don't matter anymore how it is," Philly says, opening the door a little more. "'How it is' is like this: Those people over here Sunday night thought something might be different this time—at least some of 'em did. Rasheed Aziz, he told us right after you left that this was going to happen, but we didn't believe him.

"But the rest, they went back and told their people, got the word out, that we might just be gettin' a break from the great *St. Andrews Standard*. People was led to believe we might win this one.

"People saw that editorial that you didn't write, some of 'em just gave up. Reverend Tabor said they weren't getting near the turnout they hoped they'd get in the Fourth Ward. People down here don't need much reason to quit."

They stare at each other for several seconds before Philly shuts the door.

Walker turns and walks back to the car.

"Where to now, Dad?" Ginger asks him.

"We're trying to find R.J.," he tells her.

Walker wonders at the wisdom of taking his children to some of the places where he might find Raymond Justus, but he figures that they don't have to get out of the car. He doesn't even know why he brought them along, really, except perhaps to further their education.

He's told Mac that he thinks he can keep him from going to jail, but that he isn't sure just yet. He wants his son to sweat a little, partly for his own good, partly out of malice, he suspects. Most of his reservoir of compassion has been used up in not telling Mac the consequences of his indiscretion.

He has a feeling, though, that Mac somehow knows he is involved in Walker's betrayal and R.J.'s disappearance. Someday, he'll tell him the whole story.

He drives along Main Street, past the Old Market, with Mac beside him in the front seat and Ginger in the back. Then he starts working his way through the grid of streets and alleys north of Main, the neighborhood of cheap bars and crack houses. He doesn't find R.J., but as they head back south toward Main, Mac spies a small, solitary figure walking purposefully in the same direction.

"Dad. It's Carneal."

Walker pulls alongside him and stops.

"Carneal," he says. "Get in. I can take you home."

"I ain't going home," the boy says, and keeps walking.

Walker rolls along beside him.

"Well, wherever, then. Have you seen your father?"

Carneal looks at him balefully and shakes his head.

"Carneal, come on," Mac says. "Get in. We'll take you wherever you want to go."

"Come on, Carneal," Ginger pleads. "Get in."

The boy does get in the backseat, finally.

"Where to, then?" Walker asks.

"The mall."

Walker thinks about taking him back to Philly's anyhow, but he figures he'll just leave again.

"O.K. Mall it is."

They are pulling into the parking lot near the Sears entrance when Walker has an idea.

He turns to Carneal.

"Do you still need a baseball glove?" he asks the boy.

Carneal stares at him.

"Well, I was going to get myself another one, since my old one seems to have drowned, and I thought you might like one, too."

Mac shakes his head at the obtuseness of grownups, but Carneal doesn't refuse right away, and Walker knows he's reeling him in.

"Come on," he says, and opens his door.

The four of them walk through Sears to Hackett's Sporting Goods.

Walker chooses a first baseman's mitt for himself that he could use either at first or as a pitcher. For the first time, he thinks he might play again next season. Carneal looks carefully among the outfielders' gloves, picking up several and squeezing them as if catching fly balls. Walker can see a salesman, a boy barely out of high school, eying Carneal, and he knows R.J.'s son would probably already have been intimidated out of the store if he weren't with the Fanns.

Finally, he settles on a Ken Griffey, Jr., model, left-handed like Walker's. Walker also has to buy a new tennis racket for Ginger, despite the fact that she has barely used the last one he bought her, hoping it would encourage her to exercise. Mac doesn't ask for anything.

"Can Carneal have dinner with us?" Ginger asks as they

walk back toward the mall entrance. Walker doesn't mind, and he'd like to see Big Walker have the nerve to deny their guest on this day, but Carneal says he has to get back.

"Let me give you a ride," Walker says.

"No. Uh, I got to see somebody first," the boy says, looking across the mall walkway.

Carneal starts to walk away, then stops and looks back.

"Thanks for the glove," he says, and Walker nods. Carneal disappears into the music store two doors down.

When they pull into the driveway, shortly before seven, Walker stays in the car.

"You all go inside," he tells Mac and Ginger. "I'm going to look one last place for R.J."

They both protest, but he insists.

Walker has no idea where Raymond Justus might be. He knows, though, that he has no desire to be around his father right now, that he had rather spend the rest of the evening somewhere dark.

17

WE COULD HAVE AVOIDED WHAT HAPPENED.

WE COULD HAVE NOT DRIFTED SO FAR FROM THE BOAT.

We could have not drunk so much.

We could have used the life jackets that stayed on board, high and dry.

We could have seen that storm coming.

But we didn't.

Storms have their own personalities, I suppose, in different parts of the world. In St. Andrews, they come out of the west, over the hills, presaged by rumbling thunder, gusting winds, and streaks of lightning, then a light sprinkle of rain and a whiff of ozone just ahead of the deluge. Even the fastest-moving ones never catch anyone except golfers out in the open.

This one, though, came out of nowhere.

Maybe it was because the rock islands shielded us from seeing the horizon there in our little lagoon. Maybe it came from a different direction than what we were expecting. Maybe we just weren't paying attention.

I was a couple of feet from what turned out to be a rather merciless rock when suddenly a wave washed all the way over my head. Walker was no more than ten feet away, and I think he saw it a split second before I did; my last memory of him is this wide-eyed look of surprise. I was turning to see what had scared him when it hit.

I remember surfacing, facing in a totally different direction, coughing up the saltiest water I'd ever tasted. I saw a sky that had changed instantly, it seemed, and now appeared to be even darker than the water.

Then the second wave hit, lifting me. Almost instantly, I felt something break in the back of my head.

Once, when my parents were still trying to make me a swimmer, I'd been doing the backstroke and forgot where I was. I smacked my head against the side of the pool, drawing blood and causing no small commotion. They took me to the hospital and said I'd had a concussion.

This was something else, though. The pain subverted any effort at trying to save myself for a few seconds. I might have blacked out. But there was this feeling that something was broken that couldn't be fixed. No one willingly sinks in water and just lets herself drown, but the adrenaline required to drag myself, lungs half full of salt water, up from the bottom of a strange, stormy sea just wasn't there.

It was as if I had already computed the odds and figured I was a goner. Instant fatalism.

God, I didn't want to be a goner.

Once, I must have gotten near the surface, even with my fractured skull, because I could hear Walker's voice up there, somewhere.

Once, I looked up and thought I could see something above the waterline.

Once, the image passed through my broken head of Mac and Ginger without a mother. When you have two kids and you're about to drown, it's their lives that pass before you.

Either my will or Mother Nature failed me.

It wasn't pleasant, that last bit of panic and flailing about, like a shark attack without a shark. By then, I was too far down to ever come back up again, lungs bursting, spurred on not by hope but by a manic desire to be free of pain, one way or the other. I actually had time to think of that Jerry Clower routine, where a hunter climbs a tree to get a bobcat down, and the bobcat attacks him, and he yells down to his friend to "just shoot up here amongst us, because one of us has got to have some relief."

There was a time, though, and it could have been a minute or a second—by then, time had ceased to mean much—when I felt that peace that the old church hymn says passeth understanding, the letting go when you finally turn to see what's ahead of you instead of trying to hang on to what still floats above you, trying to bring you back.

My heart aches, seeing Walker's spirit just dwindle, although I have more hope now than I did a week ago, even though he still can't quite get it right. Those dreams he has? They aren't me; it doesn't work like that. No Voices from the Grave. But in a way I guess they are me. He's not dreaming of the Now Me, but he is pulling in the Me That Was frequency, the one that nagged him about my own little idea of "doing right." Given another chance, I could have probably done a better, more persuasive job.

But it doesn't work like that, either.

18

WALKER IS AFRAID TO REMEMBER.

WHATEVER HE LETS HIMSELF REMEMBER, HE KNOWS THAT he will never forget.

Now, sitting in a booth at Charley's, working on his third Miller and the greasy remnants of a large order of fries that was dinner, more comes back than he would have allowed if his guard weren't down.

As bad as it is to dream of Mattie and wake to find her still gone, it would be even worse to dream of that last day.

He finds he can remember the way her face looked, the instant she turned away from him in the water, the "What?" that was her last coherent word.

He finds that he can remember the sound her head made, against the rock.

He finds that he can remember most of the dives he made, even the color of the sand fifty feet down.

Worst, he finds that he still has, in his treacherous, sadistic memory bank, her face, when he was no more than ten feet away, the look of agony and fear and hopeless hope, just at the point where he could come no farther and neither could she. This one he is able to shunt aside, for another day when he is, he hopes, stronger.

He remembers the way he kept diving back, until they dragged him from the water, physically restraining him until they could get back to land. He remembers, finally, what a coward he was, how he did not have the nerve to follow her all the way, to a point where either both of them survived or neither of them did. Zero or two. No odd numbers.

He knows he was not thinking of the children, or his parents. He was thinking of his own, sorry life, one that seems not to be in danger of making the world a better place.

"'Scuse me. You ready for another one?"

Walker realizes that the waitress, some country girl trying to stay ahead of prostitution or poverty, has asked him this question at least twice, and that he's squeezing the empty bottle's long neck as if it were his own.

"Yes. Please. I'm sorry."

She gives him a sympathetic look.

"You look like you had a hard day."

Walker nods.

"Well," she says, "at least something went right today. They voted down the nigger museum."

Walker has been so sure it would fail that he hasn't even bothered to watch the news.

Now he realizes that the local TV station's news team has cut into whatever sitcom was on to announce the final results: the referendum failed by almost a twenty percent margin.

Walker sits facing the bar's front door and plate-glass window. He chose this seat because he wanted to be as alone as possible. From this side, if he sits in the middle of a space normally allotted for two, he can see people coming and going, but they can only discern his outline in the darkness of Charley's dark-wood, high-backed booths.

He wonders why the defeat of the slavery-museum referendum would mean that much to a white, country-girl waitress, but he supposes her competition for whatever tips are available in a working-class bar like this would likely come from some black girl carrying the same baggage as she, only more of it.

It occurs to Walker that he and everyone else on River Road should hope that nothing happens to disturb the mechanism that makes poor whites align themselves according to race rather than economics.

The waitress has brought his fourth Miller when he sees a car pull off the road, just for an instant, and stop on the shoulder, underneath the streetlight that sits next to Charley's neon sign. He sees two black men inside, talking with each other, and he is almost sure that he is watching Rasheed Aziz and Raymond Justus. Before he can even leave his booth, though, the car has pulled back onto the highway, headed east.

The rest of the nightmare in Italy is something of a blur to Walker.

After the police were able to calm him enough to get a statement, they took him back to his hotel. Divers found Mattie's body the next day, so distorted by the drowning that Walker barely recognized it, thought at first they had brought him the wrong body.

He had spent the night before alone in his hotel room, calling no one and telling no one what had happened, not eating, not sleeping, not calling, subsisting on the bottle of mineral water in the minibar. No one at the hotel knew of the accident until he came back from identifying Mattie late in the afternoon. The concierge was most sympathetic, helping Walker get in touch with his parents.

Dottie answered the phone, and Walker realized that it was sometime after eleven in the morning in St. Andrews.

"Momma," he said, and he had to pause for a second to compose himself.

"My Lord, honey," Dottie said, her voice amazingly clear across an ocean, "what's happened? What's the matter?"

He was afraid to tell Dottie, who really did have a bad heart, but she took charge immediately, told Walker that she would inform everyone who needed to know. He was to tell them when he had made "the arrangements," meaning getting Mattie's body transported back to North Carolina from Italy. Dottie said that either she or Big Walker or both should come over, but Walker said no, they should stay there and look after Mac and Ginger. When he thought back on it later, it seemed so cold and bloodless, like they were shipping furniture, but it seemed the only course to stave off insanity.

It took a week, and it would have been much easier to have had her buried in Italy, but it was not negotiable. Walker wouldn't leave Positano, and then the Naples airport, until he was on the plane that was transporting Mattie's body.

In that week, he had tried once to talk with his children. Dottie put Ginger on the phone downstairs and Mac got on the extension, but when Walker heard them, wanting him to tell them it was all a joke, a misunderstanding, he couldn't do a damn thing to make their lives one bit better. "We'll be O.K.," he kept saying. "We'll be O.K." And they kept saying they knew. Then he told them he had to go, and he put them in Dottie's hands. Whatever explanation Mac and Ginger got for their mother's death in that first week they got from their grandmother. Big Walker was noticeably absent.

And, by the time he returned to St. Andrews with Mattie's body, Walker was on the verge of collapse. He spent five days in the hospital, depressed and dehydrated. By the time he was released, to follow his already-moved clothes and children to Big Walker's house, there was little to explain, just a funeral and a year of grief and silence.

All the memories that are bubbling up now he has not shared with his children, and he doesn't know if he ever can. He wonders if Mac and Ginger ever cry together. He hopes so. He does know that he must find a way to share this grief that they suffer separately now, if he's ever going to do anything for them more lasting than buy them new tennis rackets.

Walker starts nursing his beers, trying to time things so he can still drive home late enough to miss his father altogether. He has lost count by the time the Budweiser clock over the bar shows eleven-thirty.

For the last forty-five minutes, a voice has been worrying him, forcing him to search deep into his memory bank for its owner.

The voice comes from the other side of his booth's partition. Its owner must be leaning against the side facing the street, because when Walker reels back from the bathroom, he can only see the gap-toothed old man facing The Voice from across the adjoining booth.

But Walker knows he's heard that voice before, somewhere long ago. He is fixated on it the way only a drunk can be fixated. He can't even get the drift of the two men's conversation, but something about the cadence and pitch is familiar, and he can't let it go.

Finally, as Walker is getting ready to leave, having knocked over his last, half-empty beer, the man slides out of his booth and turns to walk unsteadily to the restroom.

Walker only gets a glimpse of him. The man is old, probably past retirement age. His hair, slicked back the way it was twenty-eight years ago, is gray and mostly gone, and his face and hands bear the weathered look of a laborer.

The man sees him staring and locks eyes, as if he's

about to ask Walker what the hell he's looking at. Ten years ago, he might have been ready to fight. Now, though, he continues on.

Walker knows that look; he's seen it from time to time over the years, passing on the sidewalk or standing in line for a movie. In a minute, he has put a name to it. It's the look Purvis Freeman employed to frighten his ninth-grade shop students.

Memory begets memory, and Walker sits stone still for several more seconds, as the tumblers click into place. He's still there when the old man comes back to his booth, not giving him a second glance as he passes. Walker has had a premonition all day; recently, he has been much more inclined than ever in his life to be what he used to laugh off as superstitious. He blames age and loss.

Sitting nine sheets in the wind in a honky-tonk bar just a bridge away from Cottondale, Walker Fann believes he knows where Raymond Justus is, and what his plans are.

19

IT SEEMS LESS OF A CERTAINTY AFTER HE GOES OUTSIDE AND THE CHILL NIGHT AIR TAKES THE EDGE OFF HIS DRUNKENNESS. STILL, HE has to find out.

He drives across the river, its dark water illuminated by the streetlights along the bridge. At a little alleyway between Cotton Creek and the river, he sees a patrol car backed in, waiting to pounce, and thinks of Harold Neely and Officer West. He concentrates very hard on keeping his car on the right side of the street.

When he reaches the Old Market, there are no cars parked anywhere on the streets facing it. The clock on the dash shows five minutes after midnight.

Walker stops near the market and considers going home; excessive drinking has always made him want to sleep. But he can't let it go, feels that quitting now would be some kind of permanent surrender. He goes east one block farther and then drives one block south, two west, two north, two east, then another south, back to the intersection of Fourth and Main. The only cars he sees parked look unfamiliar.

He fans out another block and begins another circle. As he slowly passes Third Street on Adams, he looks right, then left. He almost misses it. He circles back at the next intersection, comes back to Third and heads slowly toward the market, three blocks away.

A quarter of the way between Friend and Adams, there is an alleyway off to the left. Backed into it, just enough sticking out to be glimpsed at the next intersection, is the red Buick.

Walker doesn't see anyone around the car. He does a U-turn and parks halfway down the next block to the south, then walks north. Checking the car as he goes by, he sees that it is locked. He feels the hood; it is faintly warm.

He walks east a block, then north, so that he comes up on the Old Market from the east.

He finds a place out of the suddenly chilly wind in the doorway of an abandoned shoe store, its entrance long boarded up but its plate-glass front inexplicably intact. From here, Walker can see the Old Market through the glass.

Once, a very old-looking black man comes up on him from the east. Walker smells him before he hears him, not five feet away. He stifles a yelp and stays in the shadows. The old man looks neither right nor left, just stumbles past, carrying on a dialogue either with himself or an invisible companion. When Walker looks down the street a few seconds later, the man is as gone as if he'd never been there. Walker feels strangely sober.

He stays next to the glass, his eyes pressed against it, his head leaning on it. He is about to doze off standing up when he thinks he sees something moving in the shadows. He checks his watch: 12:45.

Suddenly, a figure darts across the street from a building on the next corner, disappearing into the darkness surrounding the Old Market's one first-floor room.

Walker comes out of his hiding place, his hunch justified. He crosses the street as silently as he can, but he has no way of knowing whether he's being watched from the open area underneath the second story.

He stands by one of the street-side pillars for a few seconds, waiting for his eyes to adjust to the new level of darkness. Nothing is moving. Finally, he tiptoes the few feet to the one first-floor room. He slides along the cool brick exterior, stopping at the corner to peer around it. He slips out and is most of the way to the next corner when a small sound, like a shoe sole sliding on brick, stops him.

"What the hell are you doing here, man?" Raymond Justus says in an urgent whisper, right behind him. Walker expends the rest of his night's supply of adrenaline; he fears he is perilously close to having a bowel movement.

"I know what you're going to do," he tells R.J. after he catches his breath.

"And what's that?"

"Ninth-grade shop, all over again."

Walker is suddenly aware that he can smell gasoline somewhere nearby.

R.J. says nothing at first.

"I don't know what the hell you're talking about," he says, "then or now."

A car goes past them on a north-south route and they back against the bricks.

Walker isn't sure exactly what brought him out here, other than too many beers. What's it to him if Raymond Justus burns down the Old Market. Who could blame him? Screw the Old Market. He certainly doesn't want to do anything to cause him to get caught.

Now, with the wind whipping up out of the west, the two of them pressed side by side against the market's bottom room, Walker knows what he wants to do, what he needs to do.

"I'm going to help you," he says.

R.J. looks at him sharply. It has been Walker's experience that it takes something truly inexplicable to make amazement climb all the way to Raymond Justus's face, but it has now.

"Get the fuck out of here," he says in a fierce whisper. "In the first place, it don't take but one person to burn this piss-ant building down. In the second place, it ain't any of your business."

Walker has no argument, only the trump card.

"Either I help you, or I drive right back up to the bridge and tell that deputy there's a black man down here with a gas can trying to burn down the Old Market."

R.J.'s look says it all: Why didn't you help us when you could do some good?

Walker holds his hands out from his sides, palms up.

"It's all I can do, man. You've got to let me do this."

R.J. stares straight ahead.

"We ain't here to get caught," he says. "I ain't buying into no martyr game."

"I'm not here to get caught, either. I just want to see the son of a bitch on fire."

"Well," R.J. says, sighing, "we do have that in common."

He makes a small hand motion and Walker follows him. At the next turn, there is an old wooden door. R.J. twists the handle, and it opens. The smell of gasoline is overpowering inside. They go in, and R.J. quickly closes the door three-quarters of the way, so that they are almost in total darkness.

"O.K.," he says. "You want in, you are in. You say a word, and I've got people will swear they saw a white man up here after midnight, by himself. That's what they'll want to believe, anyhow."

R.J. reaches down into the darkness. He produces a couple of rags. He takes the gas can, the kind Walker uses to get fuel for the lawn mower, and opens the lid. He tips the can slightly, soaking the rags.

"Here," he whispers, and Walker feels something cool touch his right hand. "See if you can punch a hole in that ceiling there. Might make things go faster."

Walker is holding a metal pipe; it seems to be at least five feet long. He takes it and reaches upward, making contact with the ceiling. He punches violently at it four times before he feels it break through. He hits it several more times, and plaster falls down around them. He can detect some illumination where streetlights shine into the second-floor room above.

"That's enough," R.J. says softly. "Set it down and come on."

Then he splashes most of the rest of the gas over the walls and floor of the little room. He reaches down again and produces several sheets of newsprint.

"The *Standard*. Good for something at last." Walker could swear that his old teammate is smiling.

They leave a paper trail ten feet long, the newsprint crumpled slightly.

"That's enough," R.J. says, and Walker stops and stands up.

"Now, listen. I don't know where you're parked. . . ."

"Half a block the other side of you."

R.J. looks at him.

"You're just a regular little James Bond, Mister Secret Agent Man, ain't you? O.K. Here's the deal. We make sure nobody's coming, anywhere, and we just hope that wino isn't around here and sober enough to remember anything.

"Then we light the paper and run like hell. I figure I can run at least two blocks before it burns back to the gas, and I ought to be able to get the rest of the way to the car before anybody notices anything."

He looks at Walker. "I hope you can run a little, too."

"As goddamn fast as you," Walker says. He realizes he is grinning like an idiot.

R.J. looks around one more time. They are far enough away from the little room in the middle of the bottom floor that they are almost exposed by the light from the deserted street. "Here goes, then."

R.J. takes a pack of matches from his pocket, lights one, throws the rest on the nearest sheet of paper, then lights the paper.

Walker stands transfixed for an instant.

"Run, dammit!" R.J. says, already moving.

They are sprinting down the sidewalk, headed south on Third Street. Walker has the brief feeling that they are kids again, perhaps competing in some long-forgotten hundred-yard dash. His bad knee doesn't even hurt. R.J. is two steps ahead of him as they cross the intersection of Third and Adams.

That's when the gasoline catches.

Walker can see the flash reflect off a shop window to his right, half a second before he hears a muffled roar from within the Old Market. He imagines that he can feel the heat, two blocks away. He almost turns around.

R.J. peels off into the alley where his car is parked. Walker runs through the intersection at Friend and, after fumbling seemingly forever for his keys, gets in his Lexus. As he starts the engine, R.J.'s Buick goes past him, headed south at a moderate rate of speed.

The two men have not discussed Walker's getaway, but he realizes that he should go left on Friend, then head north on First Street, along the river and away from the fire. He realizes what a spur-of-the-moment thing this must have been, not just on his part but on R.J.'s as well.

As Walker turns left, he realizes that he still has not seen another living soul since they lit the newsprint and started running. The fire, which he can now see out of the corner of his eye as he turns the corner, is still, for a few more seconds, his and R.J.'s, even if his contribution was mostly symbolic. He almost stops, for a second time, to admire their handiwork.

By the time Walker stops at the intersection of First and Main, he can look right and see flames shooting out even the upstairs windows, and he knows they have succeeded. He turns left, toward home, as he hears the first distant wail of fire engines. As he crosses the bridge, the first truck passes him; he sees its lights blend with those of the fire in his rearview mirror.

Back home, he parks the Lexus and goes inside. It's after two in the morning, and he realizes how dog-tired he is. Before he collapses, though, he knows he must go out in Big Walker's backyard and see what the Old Market's demise looks like from this vantage point.

He steps onto the back porch and walks over next to the screen, finding a spot where he can see the bright glow from across the river through an opening in the trees. Far off, a million miles away, fire engines howl their disapproval in ever-growing numbers.

"Move. You're blocking my light."

Walker jumps. His father is sitting on the chaise longue directly behind him, hidden in the dark.

"Where've you been?" Big Walker asks, casually.

"Out drinking."

"Well, somebody's decided to put the Old Market out of our misery, it seems. That McLaurin boy, your managing editor, woke me up not ten minutes ago."

"Yeah, I heard about it," Walker says, transfixed by the man-made light that dominates the horizon. He puts his hands in his pockets to keep them from trembling and to hide the smell of arson.

"Walker," his father says, and there is something different in his voice, maybe fear, "if anybody were to ask me, I'd say you were here all night, watching the election returns and then reading. If anybody were to ask me, I'd say I never smelled any gasoline or anything like that. Now get inside and wash your hands."

Walker turns and starts to do just that, then pauses.

"I don't care anymore," he tells his father, in a quiet, firm voice. "I'm sorry. I just don't."

Big Walker is silent for a couple of seconds. As Walker walks inside, his father says, "If you didn't care, you'd of done it in broad daylight."

Walker knows he's right, but he also knows his father realizes just how close he is to truly not caring, just how far over the edge he's gone, and he knows that something as basic to their world as air or gravity has changed.

Inside, in his bathroom, Walker finally washes his hands, but he can't seem to get the smell of gasoline off him. It's in his hair, his clothes, his memory. He takes all his clothes off and climbs into bed.

He is just about to fall asleep when the phone rings. He picks it up, hearing Big Walker do the same on his extension.

"Oh. Hello, Walker," McLaurin says when he realizes who is on the phone.

"I'm here, too," Big Walker says.

"I'm sorry to keep waking you all up," the managing editor says, "but all hell's breaking loose at the Old Market. Somebody started shooting at the cops, and they shot back. I don't know all the details, but Jenkins, the cop reporter, says there are several bodies on the street. Says it's a bloodbath."

"Good God," Big Walker says softly.

"Jenkins says apparently some of the kids from Cottondale marched down there, and then somebody heard a shot, and then it just turned into a war. The firemen aren't even trying to save the building."

Big Walker tells the managing editor to wake up every reporter and photographer he can find, right now, and get them working.

"If you can wake me up," he says, "you can damn sure wake everybody else up, too."

Walker puts down the phone without saying another word. He has the same feeling, the same electricity along the back of his neck, he had earlier when he saw Purvis Freeman in the bar. His mind has become more open than he'd ever have imagined to the black humor of fate.

He grabs an old pair of pants and a shirt and puts his shoes back on, not even bothering with socks and underwear. He's out the door before Big Walker can either try to stop him or come along.

20

CARNEAL MEANS TO GO HOME, EVENTUALLY, BUT HE RUNS INTO TWO OF HIS FRIENDS, LAFONSA PETTY AND ALBERT MEANS, AT Orange Julius in the mall's food court. Knowing that his father won't be there waiting for him makes him feel reckless, like he did the night he got arrested. He's still carrying the new glove that Mac's daddy bought for him, and he slumps into a seat at the table where his friends are slurping away at sodas.

"You better hide that glove," Lafonsa says, talking with the straw still in his mouth. Lafonsa believes he's stolen it, and Carneal realizes every white person in the mall will, too. Any time he buys anything in a store, he knows he'd better hang on tight to the receipt. Even then, the white people act like they don't believe him.

"I didn't steal it. It was bought," Carneal says.

"By who? You?" Albert says, incredulous.

"Never mind by who. Let's get on out of here."

"Yeah," Lafonsa says, "I expect we'd better, before we get our asses hauled in as accomplices to glove theft. Everybody knows Carneal's bad to steal a baseball glove."

The other two boys laugh, loud and raucous. When he and his friends start having a good time, Carneal notices, it makes white people uneasy, and sometimes a security guard will come over and tell them to either buy something else or leave. He sees white kids raising hell all the time and nobody says anything. He hates the mall, but it's where you hang out.

Lafonsa is from Fifth Street, three blocks away from Carneal's house; they've been together since first grade, playing ball and raising hell and now chasing girls. Sometimes, Lafonsa comes over to Philly's—he calls her Aunt Philly like every other kid for five blocks—because that's where everybody seems to congregate.

Carneal doesn't know Albert Means quite so well, although they are both starters on the junior high football team; Albert is almost as fast as Carneal and a little stronger. He's from north of Main, and to Carneal it seems like Albert has a tough time at home, tougher than Carneal does.

Once, Carneal and a cousin went to Albert's house because there was supposed to be a tag football game there. There wasn't anybody around old enough to be Albert's mother or father, but there were a lot of older guys, guys that would have already graduated from high school if they had stayed in, hanging around.

The football game turned into a fight when one of the older guys got tackled and went to his car to get a gun. Carneal has seen people pull guns in fights and arguments probably a dozen times, but the closest thing he's seen to what the people in Cottondale call a dirt nap is when Rodney Watkins shot Jackie Carter in the arm over what they said was a drug debt.

Carneal is proud that he doesn't deal drugs or smoke crack, just a little marijuana now and then; it was plain bad luck that he got caught the one time and got kicked out of school for a week. Philly and his father are always lecturing him about drugs, and he knows enough about his mother's and father's history to know how bad things can get. He has a picture of his mother that he has pressed into the pages of the Bible Philly gave him, and the only time he prays, he asks God to please let her and his sister come home. Philly has told him that it doesn't work that way, that you can't make deals with God, but Carneal tries anyhow.

Carneal and his friends do sometimes get in a little trouble, though, skipping school or lifting this and that, little stuff like candy bars mostly, although never from Philly's store. Anybody that steals from there is in for a whipping from any of a number of young men who have enjoyed free meals at Philly's when they needed one.

The night he stole Walker Fann's glove, he was just plain mad. He had wandered over to the ball fields, just to watch. He was leaning against a Ford Taurus, not bothering anybody, when these three white boys, older than him, came up from behind.

"What the hell are you doin'?" one of them said, almost on top of Carneal before he knew he was there. "Get your black ass off my car."

The other two were coming around the other side, so that Carneal was surrounded, with the fence in front of him.

"I ain't hurting nothin'," he had said, putting his hands in his pockets.

"Look out!" one of the other boys said, and all three of them backed away a long step. You put your hands in your pockets, Carneal knows, and the white folks think you're packing. You leave 'em outside, and they think you want to fight. About all that's left is The Position: legs spread, hands flat against the fence in front of you. White folks felt so threatened, were so sure Carneal was going to pull out an Uzi and just start shooting, that he sometimes fantasizes doing just that.

His father tells him that he has to learn to make it in the white world, that all white people aren't bad, that it used to be a lot worse than it is now, but Carneal wonders how in the world he's ever going to live with people like this.

He doesn't know what would have happened if the preacher from the white Baptist church hadn't come up.

"What are you all doing?" he asked the white boys, who had moved two steps forward, sure now that Carneal wasn't armed, angry at him for making them think he was.

The boy who owned the car stared hard at Carneal for a long five seconds.

"Nothing, Reverend Graham," he said at last. "Nothing. Just trying to take care of what's mine."

Like your rich daddy didn't buy that car for you on your sixteenth birthday, Carneal thought but didn't say. He hears his white classmates talk about when their older brothers and sisters turn sixteen, about what kind of cars they got. Some of them already know what they're going to get when they're sixteen. What Carneal knows is that you aren't really a man where he lives until you've stolen some white boy's car and trashed it good.

Mac and Ginger are nice to him, but Carneal knows they'll both be driving whatever they want when they're sixteen, just like the rest. Hill kids get their wishes just by making them, it seems to him. The only sixteen-year-olds driving good-looking cars in his neighborhood risked their freedom and their lives for the privilege, and already Carneal knows a lot of them don't get to be twenty.

The preacher told the three to let "the boy" go, that nobody was going to steal a car right there against the fence at the city softball tournament. Carneal took that to mean sufficient light and an audience were all that kept him from stealing. By now, there was an audience, lots of kids, almost all white, gathered around them, taking in the night's entertainment.

Carneal is usually more careful, making sure he doesn't wander into a mostly white crowd without some friends along, even if the softball field is smack in the middle of Cottondale.

The white boys finally backed off, and Carneal was allowed to escape. He was furious, choking on all the things he knew he would have to say sometime or explode. He didn't realize the game was over until the old white guy, who turned out to be Mac's daddy, started throwing a fit over losing.

When Carneal saw the glove, thrown down in disgust, he didn't even think. He wanted to let somebody know he was not just going to take shit forever. He was sure that on his bicycle he could outrun anybody at some white-ass softball game, and he couldn't believe it when he got caught.

Sitting in the back of the patrol car later, with two old pissed-off white guys in the front seat, he was half terrified about going to jail, half saying to himself, "Hell, why not just get it over with? You're going sometime. Might as well be now."

"Hey," Albert says, "let's go see *The Air Up There*. Last show starts in thirty minutes. It's about basketball and all."

"Yeah," Lafonsa says, laughing, "maybe we can trade Carneal's glove in for three tickets."

"Don't have to do that." Albert reaches into his pocket and produces a twenty-dollar bill. The other two boys are impressed but not surprised. It is not uncommon for a boy their age to suddenly whip out some serious money; there are many favors to be done for the older guys, the ones who hang out at the places north of Main where Carneal is not supposed to go, the ones with the cars. Usually, the money is produced late in the evening, as a way of impressing less-solvent friends, but Carneal knows that sometime soon it will be his turn to produce that twenty.

They go to the movie, where Albert's largess continues; he treats them to sodas and popcorn. The crowd is mostly black and young, so they can relax and not worry about laughing and talking if they feel like it.

By the time they leave, it's after eleven.

"Come on," Albert Means says. "Let's go on over to my place. Might even get you some pussy."

Lafonsa and Carneal would rather go home, but they feel indebted to Albert for treating them, and the last thing any boy in their neighborhood needs is for people to start thinking he's scared to be a little wild, scared to come home late once in a while.

So the three of them walk the two miles to Albert's house on North Fourth. Albert keeps seeing cars that he says he bets he could steal, but to the other two boys' relief, he doesn't try.

The streetlights north of Main are half shot out, and it seems scary to Carneal. The unpainted one-story house Albert leads them into is the only one on the block that is definitely lived in.

Inside, there are several young men and women watching cable television. Some of them are passing around a joint. Once in a while, one will leave the room and come back humming from some newfound electricity. Or a boy and girl will leave the room and not return for a while. One of the older girls winks at Carneal, but he knows she's just playing with him. He knows what's going on, is pretty sure what his options are.

An older woman, who could be Albert's mother, wanders out to tell them to "shut the fuck up," but then retreats to a back room when she gets only insults and threats for her trouble.

Carneal takes a short toke when the joint comes his way. He knows he shouldn't even do that, but he wants to belong, too. He knows a couple of the older boys from the neighborhood, and they know him.

They are watching some raggedy old John Wayne movie, making obscene comments about the Duke's manhood, when a boy comes running in the front door.

"The market is burnin' down! They blew up the market!" he shouts.

The place explodes in disbelief and indignation.

People go running out the front door to look. The sky to the southwest is so red that the flames must be just below the treetops.

"Ain't enough to vote against it," somebody mutters. "Now they got to burn it down!"

"We oughta do something."

One of the older teenagers, who looks as if he might be Albert Means's brother, takes one long last toke and throws the remnants of a joint into the yard. The air is filled with the screaming of sirens.

"It sure would be a good night for some target practice," he says.

"Amen to that," somebody else chimes in. The one who looks like Albert's brother goes back in the house and comes back out putting a pistol into the inside of his jacket. Several of the others also seem to be armed.

An older boy from Carneal's neighborhood, Michael Stubbs, who seems to be the leader, starts walking toward the Old Market, whose flames they can see now. The others fall in behind him.

Lafonsa and Carneal look at each other. Lafonsa shrugs and follows the crowd, and Carneal feels he must follow, too. Maybe later he can slip away and go home to face Philly's wrath. He hopes his father didn't come home yet.

The crowd picks up numbers and steam in the five-block walk to the market. It is joined by old men and women, little children awakened from their sleep and rubbing their eyes, workers who have to get up in less than three hours, all awakened by the noise and then galvanized by the report, now accepted as fact, that a white mob has burned down the Old Market. To Carneal, it looks like at least one hundred people, growing with every house they pass.

When the crowd turns the last corner, now almost at a run, flames are shooting out all the second-floor windows. Each street approaching the market is blocked off by fire trucks and police cars.

"Come on," Michael Stubbs says, and he leads them back half a block and then into a side alley. Carneal has somehow moved to near the front of the pack, which now must move single file through a narrow opening. Somewhere in the interior of the block they turn left, toward the noise and the fire.

The opening widens as they near Main Street, and when they look out, they are half a block inside police lines, half a block from the largest fire any of them has ever seen.

Carneal looks back and is surprised to see that there are only about twenty people at the alley entrance. He doesn't see Lafonsa or Albert Means, just older boys.

"They just burnt it down, goddammit," Stubbs says. "They think they can come over here and do whatever the fuck they want."

He steps out of the alley and shoots at the copper roof. There is a fireman working a water hose from the end of a ladder, above the conflagration, and Carneal can't tell if Stubbs is aiming for the roof or the fireman.

The boy who looks like Albert Means's brother starts

shooting as well. In all the noise, smoke, and general confusion, it takes the firemen a while to realize that they are being shot at.

Carneal is in the middle of the crowd that is now bunched together at the alley's entrance. Two or three of the others have moved out to storefronts closer to the fire.

Suddenly, they see policemen moving along the sidewalk, one at a time, running from one store entrance to the next, looking for cover. Some are on the same side of the street as the crowd, some are on the other. They don't seem to know yet where the shooting's coming from.

One tall white policeman is just edging out to the sidewalk across from them, stepping out of the darkness of a shut-down department store, when he suddenly goes to one knee, then topples over. Carneal looks at Stubbs, whose gun is pointed not at the burning building but at the storefront. For a second, Stubbs looks scared. Then he sees Carneal looking at him and recovers.

"Got him!" he exclaims. "Got the motherfucker."

"Shit," a couple of people behind them say in unison.

Carneal turns to run, but a man he doesn't recognize catches him by the arm.

"Ain't no runnin' now, Junior," he says. "If you ain't got a gun, throw rocks."

Carneal is trying to get away when the lead policeman on the near side of the street pops out of the entrance of another abandoned store and the one who looks like Albert steps out and shoots him several times with a semiautomatic pistol. The policeman does almost a 360-degree spin before falling to the sidewalk. Part of his face has been shot away.

Even with the smoke, Carneal can see that the policeman is black.

By now, everyone is shooting. Carneal, trapped from

the rear, is down on his knees, protected by the stone front beneath the plate-glass window. He peers out the alley and across the street. A gust of wind clears the smoke for a few seconds, and he sees that there is a similar alley across the way.

He estimates that it is about forty yards across Main Street. Just a forty-yard dash. He's the fastest boy in junior high in the forty. Surely he can make it across. And then he only has to run out the back side of the alley and keep running until he gets home. He doesn't care if Philly and his father beat him till the sun comes up.

Carneal finds something else to pray for. Opening his eyes, he waits for the smoke to roll in again.

Then he makes his move. Coming out of his crouch like a sprinter leaving the blocks, like pictures he's seen of his father winning the state hundred-yard dash back in high school, he explodes into the open. The crowd behind him, which has now shrunk to only ten, sounds to him like the fans at a football game, urging him on as he slips a tackle, then leaves another defender in the dust, headed for pay-dirt.

He knows he can run the forty-yard dash in a little over four and a half seconds, but he feels like he's been out here forever. The smoke is choking him; it's worse than no air at all. He sees the yellow center line of Main Street go past, but for some reason he can't seem to go anywhere. It sounds like Christmas, when all the kids on Second Street set off firecrackers and bottle rockets. Pop-pop-pop. It's like the dreams he has, in which the white boys are chasing him and he can't run, can't lift his legs. So tired.

He can actually see the opening across the street now. It can't be more than feet away. Then it's like somebody yanks him back; he thinks of old Cracker, when they used to chain him up. Somebody'd walk by on the street, and he'd run at them just as fast as he could until he ran out of chain, and all four feet would leave the ground as he was jerked back.

Lying flat on his back, with the pain on him all of sudden like a sack of cement from a second-floor window, Carneal feels the wetness on his shirt and wonders if he's fallen into a puddle. But when he puts his hand over his chest, he knows it's not water.

He prays, very hard, for it all to be a dream, for his mother, for anything but what he knows is happening. When he looks up, though, all he sees, far above him and fading fast in the smoke, is Officer J. D. West, his rifle still at the ready.

21

WHEN WALKER CROSSES THE RIVER BRIDGE THIS TIME, HE FEELS AS IF HE'S ENTERING SOME OTHER COTTONDALE, BARELY related to the one he's known all his life.

The Old Market is still burning in the distance, and from the size of the fire, he guesses correctly that several of the buildings facing it also are ablaze. There is a barricade at the intersection of First and Main, with three city police cars and one belonging to a state trooper blocking the road. He's already heard on the radio that the local National Guard unit has been called out. He's tired, he figures he could still blow a .10 on the Breathalyzer, and he's returning to the scene of the crime, hoping he doesn't smell of gasoline. He has had dreams that seem more real than this.

Walker parks his car twenty feet from the barricade and gets out. He recognizes the chief of police, Barry Traylor, a man he went to high school with. Traylor recognizes him and lets him walk up to the barricade.

"What's going on?" Walker asks. "How bad is it?"

"It's about two policemen bad. And at least two snipers."

"Dead?"

"One policeman is dead: Sutter Jakes, got a wife and two kids. And I don't think Ronnie Wells is going to make it, either. You know what's unbelievable? Jakes is black. They shot one of their own. We still haven't finished searching, but there were two civilians killed, a couple more wounded. God, it's awful."

Walker sees that the man has tears in his eyes.

"I'd like to bring tanks in there and clean the whole mess out," the chief says, banging his fist against the hood of his car, actually creating a discernible dent. "Why in hell would anybody start shooting at firemen?"

"Do you have any names?"

Traylor looks at him coldly.

"I can't give you the names until we notify the next of kin."

"No, I don't mean for the paper. I need to know for me. I think one of 'em might have been somebody I know."

Traylor takes out a notebook.

"One was a Michael Lee Stubbs, of 312 Knowles Street. The other one—let's see—the other one was Troy Carneal Justus, of 802 South Second Street. Good Lord, he wasn't but thirteen years old."

Walker sinks to the ground beside the chief's car.

"You O.K.?" Traylor asks. "Did you know one of those boys?"

"You remember Raymond Justus?"

"R.J.? Sure." Traylor had been a scrub on the state championship team. Then he makes the connection.

"Oh, my God. R.J.'s kid?"

Walker says nothing.

"I'd heard the boy had been in some trouble, some little thing . . . "

"Stolen baseball glove."

The chief looks at him.

"Yeah, that's it. But I didn't think he'd be involved in anything like this."

Walker gets up off the pavement.

"I need to get through there, Barry."

"It ain't safe in there, Walker. I can't be responsible for letting you in Cottondale tonight."

Walker is so close to telling him exactly why he has to get behind police lines, why he has to be at Raymond Justus's house at 802 South Second Street, that it scares him.

Finally, he just says, "I'm not going in there as a reporter, Barry, and I don't hold you responsible. Hell, I'll sign a release if you want."

Traylor looks at Walker, then goes over and talks with the two state troopers. Finally, he comes back.

"Go on through," he says with a jerk of his head. "But you're a fool."

Walker nods his thanks, gets in his car and waits for one of the policemen to remove a couple of barricades.

Then he's in Cottondale again.

He turns right, going down by the mill. Men and women are standing around in the parking lot, although it is not time for shifts to change. He can see them in the distance, partially shrouded by the smoke that has settled along the river bottom, looking like ghosts.

At Franklin Street, just beyond the mill, a seventies vintage boat of a car comes squealing around the corner, barely slowing down, right in front of him, its occupants yelling something unintelligible. Its taillights, like two glowing cigarettes, soon fade into the haze.

Walker feels that he is in a foreign country, behind enemy lines.

He parks at the corner of Simmons and First, a block behind R.J.'s and Philly's houses. He would rather come up on them walking than to announce his presence by parking out front.

He sits in his car for at least ten minutes, trying to work

up the nerve to see R.J. When he finally gets out, he has no more idea what he's going to say than he did when he parked. He only knows that he has to be there.

A dog scares him by starting an incessant barking that follows him all the way up Simmons Street and around the corner, where he can see that the news has already reached here. There are cars parked on both sides of the street, men and women standing in the front yard at Philly's. R.J.'s house is lit up, but no one appears to be inside, and the front door is wide open.

Walker has been spotted. Neighbors on the side street have probably called ahead to announce his presence. As his feet bring him closer to Philly's, he recognizes two men from his meeting on Sunday. They only stare at his nod.

Finally, it is up to Rasheed Aziz to actually confront him. Aziz comes storming out the front door, finally coming to a stop inches from Walker's face.

"What in the hell are you doin' here, man?" he says in his booming voice. "Don't you think these people have suffered enough without you coming around here bearing more bullshit?"

"I want to see R.J."

"You want to see R.J. Man wants to see R.J.," Aziz says, turning to the crowd as if he's just heard the most amazing news. "What? You want to tell R.J. how sorry you are, how you wish you could've supported the slavery museum, but your mean ol' daddy wouldn't let you? Philly told me that sorry-ass story."

"I just need to see R.J."

"Get on out of here," someone in the crowd mutters.

"Go on," others shout. "Get out of Cottondale."

Something makes Walker look toward the house. In the southernmost front window, he sees R.J.'s face. He looks ten years older than he did a few hours earlier, when they were racing down Third Street like two schoolboys who've just pulled a Halloween prank. Walker is standing under a streetlight, and he knows he can be seen. R.J. stares at him for a few seconds, no more than four or five, and then the window explodes and R.J.'s head is sticking out of the hole where the glass was, blood already trickling down his face. He is laughing, out of control.

The crowd is silenced and halted momentarily, an "Oh my Lord" escaping from one of the women.

Walker, transfixed, becomes aware that the crowd has again turned to him. A boy, no older than Carneal was, starts chanting something. The crowd slowly joins in; there is a sort of rhythm to it. Finally Walker understands. It's a variation of an old high school cheer, one he and Raymond Justus performed to many times. The words, though, are different.

> *"Go back, go back, go back up on the hill.*
> *Go back, go back, go back before we kill you."*

It gets louder, and the crowd starts moving toward him.

Rasheed Aziz, shaken by the image of Raymond Justus's head sticking out a shattered windowpane, looks back at the approaching mob. He seems to have at least momentarily lost the anger that Walker has seldom seen him without.

"You better run, man," he says softly, almost as if he cares for Walker's safety.

"Let the cracker go," Aziz says, turning back to the men and women who are approaching slowly but surely, like some human tide. They ignore him, and from somewhere in the back ranks, a rock flies past Walker's head. Another strikes him in the ribs, almost bringing him to his knees.

Walker turns and runs.

He first thinks he can beat the mob to his car, but as he rounds the corner, he can see that he has no chance. He runs past it, almost stumbling as a hen's egg of a rock glances off his shoulder blade.

There is nothing in front of him except the river.

He runs past First Street and onto the dirt lane that stops three houses down at a small embankment. He looks back and sees that the mob has traded quantity for quality; six or seven young black men are behind him, and they seem to know that they have him trapped.

He keeps running, and when he comes to the embankment, not even knowing how close the river is, he leaps.

He lands, feet first, in five feet of water, just enough to break his fall. He knows only one way out: swim. He was once the city age-group freestyle champion, as a nine-year-old. He hopes no one behind him is carrying a loaded gun.

Two strong strokes and he's in a current that is carrying him away from land. Splashes ahead of him tell him that they're throwing rocks, but in a long ten seconds he's out of reach of anything but a lucky toss, probably out of sight in the darkness of the water.

A gunshot scares him badly, but he doesn't hear another, and he'll never know whether the shooter meant to hit him or not.

By this time, Walker has somehow shed his shirt. He doesn't even remember losing his shoes. The Rich River here is one hundred yards across, and it is not without some current. The bottom, once dredged for river boats, is still more than six feet deep for almost the full width.

Perhaps forty yards out, Walker turns and does the backstroke for a few seconds. He can see the figures on the shore, silhouetted by something brighter than a streetlight. He realizes that it is his Lexus, glowing brightly just beyond the shacks along the river.

He is forced by the current to do a zigzag pattern across the water, and somewhere in the middle third he becomes snagged on a mass of stumps that have wrecked on a submerged rock. In his panic, he almost goes under. Finally, it seems easier to slide out of his pants than to untangle them from the spidery limbs that seem to catch every thread.

Breaking free of his last piece of clothing, he turns back to his task. He has no idea where his tacking will land him, only that it will be on the safe, familiar western shore.

After twice seeking bottom and failing, Walker tries a third time and feels river mud beneath his feet. He is still ten yards from the shore, up to his chest in the Rich River, and he almost drowns right there, too weak to fight the current carrying him toward the middle again, almost too weak to resume swimming.

At last, he regains his stroke. This time, he doesn't stop until his arm, on the downstroke, grazes solid earth.

Walker Fann stumbles out of the river, more tired than he has been in a year, feeling the cold seep in as the wind hits him, suffering from cuts inflicted by man and nature. He looks up and is amazed to see, high above him, the back porch where he was standing not so many hours ago.

He starts climbing, but he feels as if he is carrying dead weight on his naked back.

He is driven onward by the fear that all those angry people, and R.J. in particular, are still chasing him, will catch him if he doesn't keep climbing. He struggles past crepe myrtles and weeping willows, azaleas and ornamental pears, a lifetime of Dottie's strategic planting. He realizes, toward the end, that he is actually plowing through the damp earth with his chin, unable to rise any higher.

He awakens to the feel of someone tugging on his arm, saying something he can't understand.

He rolls over with a start, his right arm raised over his face, sure that he has been caught by the mob. But then he sees, in the early light, his father and his son. Big Walker is trying to rouse him; Mac is looking away, across the river, as if he is embarrassed to see his father naked.

"Come on in the house, son," Big Walker says. He looks pale and frightened. He has a blanket with him, which he hands down.

Walker Fann wraps it around his body. Only then does he begin to shiver.

He puts his head down between his knees and begins to cry.

"Come on," Big Walker says, then murmurs to his grandson, "He'll be O.K. Just give him a minute."

After less time than that, he and Mac help Walker to his knees and, finally, to his feet. They climb the rest of the way up.

22

WALKER. OH, WALKER.

IT NEVER TURNS OUT THE WAY WE THINK IT WILL, DOES IT? It never seems as if there is a plan that you can follow without fear of getting tripped up.

You're down there just plugging away. You think maybe you can change things and still make everybody happy, but sometimes it isn't that easy.

Sometimes, it's just not in the stars.

We always told each other life wasn't fair. It was a kind of emotional insurance when friends would break up, or when Daddy died too young for a good man, or when some innocent child would get run over by a cement truck while chasing a red ball across the street.

Well, we were right, but we were wrong.

Life isn't fair. But it is fair in its very unfairness. It's easier to see that now, although I'd like to think I had a clue before all this happened.

Life works everybody over, Walker, if you stay around long enough. The trick is to be good anyhow.

If you have it soft, like we did, it just makes the inevitable harder to deal with.

If you can deal with disaster and keep your sanity, it means you've probably had it pretty tough all along.

You get born a woman—well, I had it better than most.

You don't draw one of the favored colors, that's a sack of bricks to carry around until you die.

Or maybe you just have a crippling disease, or you're not so smart. Maybe your parents are divorced, or they beat you, or worse. Maybe you forget for a couple of minutes that you can't swim so well.

I'm talking to you, Walker, but you can't hear me. All you can do is think of me, dream of me. And it would probably be good, honey, if you could stop doing that.

You can't help the past. Just learn from it.

And here's the thing, and I can see this, too, the way we couldn't have before: However bad it gets, it gets better. However good it gets, it finally gets worse. Find a plan, Walker; do what it is you want to do, and stop worrying about it. It all works out.

The thing I learned, Walker? When I was struggling to get back up to the surface, to get just one sweet lungful of air? I learned you have to let go sometime. There comes a point where, if you just go with what's right, it will turn out O.K. Nobody does that, Walker, or hardly anybody. I can see that, too. And we all carry the weight for not doing what we know is right.

If you take that other road, the one you are thinking about following, the one Big Walker would rather die than see you take, the one that you are afraid will lead you and our children and our children's children to rack and ruin, you will be right, and everyone else will be wrong. And you soon will know that.

Trust me on this, Walker.

Let it go.

23

WALKER STEPS OUT THE FRONT DOOR. THE WEATHER HAS TURNED COLD FINALLY; THE SKY IS TIRED AND GRAY, WITHOUT quite the energy to make Christmas white. His stocking feet are freezing; he wonders if he's bought and cut enough wood.

The front porch creaks from unknown but surely fatal ailments. Walker has been reading a home-repair guide that tells how to replace rotted boards.

He leans against one of the two brick pillars that border the entrance to the porch, a cup of coffee warming his hands.

Cottondale looks different to him, from down here. He doesn't know whether it's him or some real change, wrought by flames. He's seen forests enhanced by fire that clears the underbrush and makes everything grow up new and clean, a fresh start. He's heard it said that no city has any true character until it has been burned once or twice.

In the waning weeks of the Civil War, Cottondale, thus far unscathed, was less than a day from the wrath of Sherman.

The merchants in town, rather than turn their only two corn mills over to the enemy, burned them to the ground.

When Sherman himself rode into town less than twenty-four hours later, he just laughed and thanked them for saving him the trouble.

But it gave the white townspeople some sense of pride, some feeling that they had done what they could, even if it meant hardship and hunger, even if it was a fruitless gesture that cost the Union troops, already bulging with food and other bounty, nothing.

As recently as Walker's childhood, you couldn't sit around a group of old men for long without someone recounting the burning of Warren's and Cotton Creek mills, of how they had another mill up and running within two months, better than either of the ones that burned down.

Walker wonders now if the ghosts of that stubborn white tribe can appreciate the fury that burned this later Cottondale, laying waste to a full block not a quarter-mile from where those mills stood, claiming the old slave market that Sherman and his men spared. He wonders if there is enough ash in Cottondale's dirt now.

Walker has a small color television in the house. One of the few luxuries he has allowed himself is cable, and he catches the news on CNN with more interest than before. He sees Croatians and Serbs plowing up grievances older than America, watches Irish Protestants and Catholics never forgiving, sees rival Africans replay their very own ancient tragedy, and he wonders what will become of St. Andrews, wonders if all the good work they've done since the fire is only temporary.

The days after the Old Market burned were among the strangest in the history of St. Andrews and Cottondale. Newspapers and television crews poured in from around the nation. Old troubles were dug up and new ones picked over. The Cottondale Massacre was presented as a true and rightful ancestor to the killings at the Old Market, as if it were obvious that another tragedy would one day spring from such a place as this.

Walker's car, overturned and burned, was found by the police shortly after they ventured back deep into Cottondale at 8 A.M. on Wednesday. By the time they identified it from the license plate and sent two officers up River Road to check, the ambulance Dottie called had already come and taken her son away.

A few inquiries among those living nearest the Fanns revealed the fact that Walker was passed out cold as a mackerel, naked as a jaybird, when his father found him in the backyard.

On Thursday, when questioning was allowed at the hospital, a fat detective named Grimes and his assistant, a thin, jumpy young man called Cain, visited the room where Walker was being kept for observation.

Walker told them that he heard about the fire when the managing editor of the *Standard* called him and his father at home. He was worried about his old friend Raymond Justus, and when he heard that a boy the age of Justus's son had been killed, he became doubly concerned. He was set upon by a vengeful mob and was forced to run and swim for his life.

Big Walker stood in the corner of the room. Grimes filled the only available chair and Cain sat on the unoccupied bed, his feet barely touching the ground.

"Where were you earlier in the evening?" Grimes asked, looking at his notepad.

"I had a few beers at Charley's."

"You were there how late?"

"He was home by eleven forty-five," Big Walker cut in. "He and I had a couple of drinks, and then we both went to bed. Phone woke us up."

Cain looked at the old man for five long seconds, then they both turned back to Walker.

"That right?" he asked. The bartender had told him already that Walker had had "several" beers before he left, sometime after eleven. The bartender stopped short of admitting that he let him leave dog-drunk.

"That's right," Walker said, hoping he remembered correctly the time he had staggered out of the bar.

"You know, that fire was set," Grimes said. "And not even set real well. Amateurs. We figure a lot of people would have been just as happy to see the Old Market burn down, but we haven't had many show up buck naked in their backyards. It tends to draw attention to yourself."

Walker said as little as possible. When the man asked him about Raymond Justus, he told him that he hadn't seen him until after he had learned that Carneal had been shot, and then only long enough to watch him put his face through a window. He trusted that R.J. had friends to swear to his whereabouts for most of the night.

Grimes and Cain finally left, promising that they would have other questions later, although they never would.

In the silence of the hospital room, Walker looked as his father moved over with arthritic slowness and sat down hard in the now-vacated chair. He stared at Big Walker, who stared back.

"You were home by eleven forty-five," he said. "Dottie was asleep, and so were the children. We had a couple of drinks. Anything beyond that, I don't want to know about it."

Walker closed his eyes. I'm already gone, he's thinking to himself, and Big Walker doesn't even know it.

On Wednesday, Walker had dreamed the same dream twice. It had seemed so real to him, lying face down in his father's fescue grass in the predawn, only to be erased the moment he was awakened. That night, though, in the hum and twi-light of the hospital, Mattie returned.

She was with him, although he knew, even asleep, that she was dead, and she had helped him swim that last ten yards, when he didn't think he had anything left.

He was lying next to her, not on cold earth but in their bed just up the street."You saved my life," he remembered saying to her.

She was smiling, her eyes closed, the way she used to look when he'd try to wake her on a cold Saturday morning when the cuddling was almost as good as the sex.

"I didn't," she murmured. "You saved it yourself."

"You've got all the blankets," he said. She had always done that. He had a bad taste in his mouth and knew he needed to get up and brush his teeth and gargle.

"Walker," she had said, her face hidden from him, "you saved yourself."

"I wanted to save you." He was crying in the dream.

"You couldn't have. Save what you can. Save what's left."

And then she was gone.

That Thursday afternoon, Walker was released. Big Walker came and got him.

For two days, Walker stayed in his room except for meals. On Saturday afternoon, though, he came out dressed and borrowed one of the two remaining cars.

He crossed over into Cottondale, turning right at the barricade a block before the charred remnants of the Old Market. Two blocks up and one block over, less than a block from where R.J. had parked his car Tuesday night, he stopped at the old house where Big Walker had begun his family. Walker knew that it had been abandoned for six months, because his father still owned it and complained bitterly that he couldn't find tenants anymore, that it would "burn down one of these days, as soon as the bums figure out they can break into it."

Walker got out and climbed the steps to the porch. He looked in the front door at peeling paint and scuffed floors. A window in front was broken out, harbinger of the irreversible vandalism to come soon.

He walked around the house. The backyard was littered with kids' cheap abandoned toys. A clothesline rusted between two oak trees, the ragged remnants of a dress still hanging from it, as if the last tenants had fled on a moment's notice.

He nodded to himself.

It would do.

When he got home, he pulled his father into the study. Big Walker went hesitantly, the way his son had done years ago when grades or conduct demanded unpleasant action. Big Walker had called this room "the woodshed." Soon, Dottie could hear her husband's voice rise and fall. Her son's was steady and sure. She turned the volume up on the television, her hand shaky on the remote control.

Afterward, preceding his pale father, Walker went upstairs to pack a few things. The rest could wait.

He took his children outside and told them how it was. He swore by Mattie that he wasn't leaving them for very long. He said there was something he had to do so that things would be better for everyone, including them. He prayed he was right. Big Walker could see his grandchildren nodding, could see Ginger wiping her hand across her face. He felt like crying himself.

Walker moved what he needed in two days. He made four trips over in his car Sunday and Monday, and then the house at the corner of Adams and Third was his, for a modest rent. He had a television, a radio, enough clothes, some books, and a few pieces of furniture, hauled over by him and Glen Murphy, who had a truck, to go with what was left by the last tenants. There was an old refrigerator that still worked. He got the electricity and the gas for the stove turned on, along with the water, and he had the oil tank filled for the big heater that dominated the living room.

The understanding was that Mac and Ginger would stay with their grandparents until Walker could get settled, without anyone really knowing what "settled" meant. With the insurance money, he bought a used Toyota. He put the house, the one with his and Mattie's and the children's names on the mailbox, up for sale.

The old house was broken into the first week Walker moved in, and he was awakened in the middle of the night several times by angry voices and harmless gunfire outside. What neighbors were left on the block, all of them black, avoided him for what seemed like a long time.

Walker wasn't sure what would come next. He had enough money saved to live this new life for a few months, he was sure, until the house was sold. He would still occasionally have dinner at his parents' house and spend a decent amount of time with Mac and Ginger.

The children came over to his house one night a week, and he would get up and take them to school in the morning.

It was at the house at Third and Adams that he and his son and daughter finally talked about Mattie.

One night in early October, the chill gave them an excuse to try out the old fireplace, which had just been cleaned. They managed to get a blaze going with assorted paper, sticks, twigs, and a burn log, and Walker ran to the 7-Eleven around the corner for wieners and marshmallows, which they impaled on coathangers the last renters had left. Anywhere more than ten feet from the oil heater, the house was cold, and would get colder, and the warmth Walker felt sitting on the ancient couch, his children on either side of him, an overachieving fire in front, gave him as much pleasure as any single thing since Mattie. He had enjoyed $50 meals less than those wieners and marshmallows.

"Do you want to talk about her? About your mother?" He said it so easily, just blurted it out, and yet it had taken him more than a year.

Neither of them said anything for a long time, and when he looked to his left, he saw that Mac was trying to keep from crying. To his right, Ginger was weeping silently.

And so the three of them cried a year's worth of tears, and then they talked until so late that Walker let them skip school the next day, when he drove them down to the river to show them the still-blackened spot on the pavement where the Lexus had been burned and the place where he jumped in the river. Walker wondered if he could ever tell them the whole story about the fire that led to Carneal Justus's death.

They drove by Philly's house, slowly, and saw no signs of life. Walker had driven by there twice before; he never had the nerve to stop and go in.

"Dad," Mac said, "what happened to Carneal's father? Somebody at school said he went nuts."

The funeral had been held on Saturday, the same day Walker decided to move to Cottondale. There were three other funerals that weekend, because the second policeman died, too, and there were six others hospitalized for gunshot wounds in the melee that followed the fire.

Eight hundred people packed the Beulah Baptist Church and the grounds around it. People thought it strange that the boy's mother and sister and maternal grandparents weren't there, but nobody mentioned it to Philly. Raymond Justus, with twenty-six stitches in his face, was there, alongside his siblings, nieces and nephews.

Afterward, the family was in Philly's house, surrounded by several months' supply of casseroles and pies, when R.J. got up abruptly and left.

One of his sisters moved to stop him, but Philly shook her head, and her daughter stepped back. They all figured he just wanted to be alone for a while.

When they heard the car start, they just assumed that he was going out in the country somewhere to get away from all the noise and other people's grieving.

He didn't come back that night, and the booming, disembodied voice full of hate and hopelessness that was heard on both sides of the river the next morning, demanding a son for a son, was generally thought to be that of Raymond Justus.

He didn't return the following night, and they notified the police.

Not until Tyron Key called Philly from New York City on Tuesday did they know that he was alive and in the hands of his mother-in-law and father-in-law. He had driven nonstop ten hours from Cottondale, then had somehow managed to find what he craved and ended eight years of sobriety by going on a crack run that cost him every cent he had on him. He had sense enough, in the fleeting instant between a high and a crash, to give an old drug acquaintance Tyron Key's address, and that's where the closest thing he had to a friend in the vicinity dropped him Tuesday night, so strung out that he could barely say his name.

The Keys were taking care of their granddaughter. Tyron told Philly that R.J. was in such a state, with his eyes on fire and his face stitched like a baseball, that he knew he had to either let him in or shoot him. He apologized for missing the funeral, filling her in on his wife's failing heart and his daughter's troubles.

Philly talked with her son briefly and told him she would pray for him.

The St. Andrews police would come to New York in October to question Raymond Justus about the fire, but they wouldn't find out anything very helpful, then or ever.

The *Standard* went up for sale in October. Big Walker had hoped that his son would come back to his senses; when six weeks passed, he decided to force his hand.

"It's yours if you want it," he told Walker after a Sunday dinner together. "But if you don't want it, we might as well sell it now."

Walker told him to get rid of it, told him that the only way he would run *The St. Andrews Standard* would get them closed down anyhow.

Walker told his father to put the money in a trust for Mac and Ginger, that he didn't want any of it.

"You might ask them what they want," Big Walker snapped.

"I already have," Walker told him.

By late November, they had a bid from the Creed chain that Walker knew would keep Big Walker and Dottie in their present style forever and ensure a comfortable bequest for his children.

"Look," he told Big Walker over Thanksgiving, when the old man appeared to need cheering up, "you did a great job. You made that a better paper than your daddy did. You didn't just sit on your talents. But I can't make it better. I don't deserve it."

"And Mac and Ginger, I don't suppose they deserve it, either. Nice of you to decide for them that they won't be rich."

"They won't exactly be poor, either. And they'll be better for going their own ways. We were getting diminishing returns, Big Man. Not money. I don't mean money. But I was getting less out of it than you were, and they would have gotten less than I did. I felt that was true for a long time, but I didn't know it for sure until September."

Big Walker stubbed out a cigar on the back-porch ashtray.

"I don't understand you," he said to his son. "I don't suppose I ever understood you the whole way, but what you are doing makes everything this family has been trying to accomplish since Reconstruction mean nothing. It would have been almost better if you'd have quit and become a painter or a banjo picker or something. Why not just get the hell out of newspapering? Who ever heard of a cub reporter your age?"

Walker knew that his father never would understand him. He took it as a sign of progress, though, that he hardly cared what Big Walker thought anymore.

It was easy enough, with his contacts, to get a job at the *News & Observer* in Raleigh, forty miles away, even if it was covering the night police beat. And while Big Walker would never really know what his son saw in such a step backward, the job made Walker feel as good as anything he'd ever done for a newspaper. It reminded him of that summer in Baltimore, though it made him sad to think what he might have done if he'd cared this little for his father's approval twenty years earlier.

Only three major felony convictions came out of what would come to be known as the Cottondale Riot. Shawn Means was convicted of first-degree murder of a policeman; perhaps because he was seventeen, he only received a life sentence. Rodney Watkins got twenty years for attempted murder, malicious wounding, and a variety of other charges. Officer J. D. West, whom several witnesses saw shooting the unarmed Carneal Justus, got twenty years for manslaughter. Some editorials in state newspapers put forth the opinion that a more punitive judicial thrust would have only made things worse. There were other, lesser charges due to the fire and the riots that followed, but the general feeling in St. Andrews was one of fatigue. There seemed to be a longing for peace, if not justice.

Certainly there were those who wanted to go farther. Harold Neely, stinging from the loss of his much-coveted anchor store, which he blamed on the riots and "bad press," demanded that someone be made to pay more dearly, but not even the *Standard* would support him on this. Big Walker, with the paper up for sale, finally got to do something he'd often wanted to do: tell Harold Neely exactly what he thought of him.

"You know," he told Neely the last time they spoke, "the Creed chain is pretty big. I think it's big enough so that they won't feel obligated to kiss the butt of some piss-ant small-town operator like you. If I hadn't thought that, I wouldn't have sold it to them."

And there were many in the black community who saw a twenty-year sentence for killing an unarmed teenager as just another whitewash.

But, in the days following the fire and the killings, the demonstrations receded like a tide, each night's wave failing to quite reach the previous night's standard.

To the surprise of many, Rasheed Aziz was a peacemaker. He had the trust of younger, angrier men in the black community, and he was able to thwart the wishes of some state and national civil rights leaders who advocated a permanent force around city hall and, in general, a "No Peace, No Justice" confrontation, with violence "as is deemed necessary to achieve our goals."

Aziz was able to convince other black leaders in Cottondale that they could turn a tragedy into progress, that he would not allow justice to go unserved, and that it was time to stop rioting and start rebuilding. He advised that they use their anger to, first and foremost, boycott Rich Valley Mall.

Buy anywhere, he told them. Drive to Raleigh. Go over to Dawson or Henryville. Hurt Harold Neely and his kind with your pocketbooks.

By the Christmas season, hundreds of black families, smoldering for years over ill treatment and poor service by the mall's clerks and store owners, angry over a lost downtown business district that was moved, along with their jobs, across the river, were mobilized. Sales in some mall stores were down twenty-five percent from the previous year. Rumor had another anchor store and several smaller ones closing after the holiday rush.

It was Rasheed Aziz's rebuilding project, though, that finally showed Walker Fann why he had moved to Cottondale.

Walker had been in the old house for three weeks when he first heard of it. Aziz's plan was simple. Now that the Old Market was a burned-out hull, it was worthless to the city, which hadn't cared enough about it to have it insured. Aziz went to the black churches and community groups with his plan: Make the city a token offer for the site, and rebuild it ourselves.

Route 30 had already been detoured one block north; it would be simple enough to close off the four streets leading in to the building and go to work.

"If we do it ourselves," he told congregation after congregation, "it will mean more. It will truly be our museum."

Walker was at least partially right about fires' clearing the underbrush and spurring new growth. The burning of the Old Market turned the tide and made white River Road less rigid about the idea of a Museum of Slavery. There was still much opposition, although not as loud and not enough to keep the city council, even with Harold Neely's influence, from selling the charred remains of the Old Market to the New Cottondale Coalition for $5,000.

Volunteers were sought, and the work had begun in late September.

One of the first to come, and the first white person, was Walker Fann.

He did not do it lightly. He was aware that some in that first-day crowd of fifty might have been the ones chasing him a few weeks before.

There was a stony silence as he leaned against a storefront, a few feet from the others, that first morning. Finally, a young black man walked away from his friends and stood in front of him, feet apart, hands spread and ready.

"Why don't you get your white ass on back across the river?" he spat at Walker. "We don't need no help."

"The hell we don't."

Walker turned to see where the voice came from. To his amazement, it was Rasheed Aziz who was now confronting someone half his age on Walker's behalf.

"What you mean we don't need no help?" he said, poking a finger into the younger man's sternum. "We need everybody we can get in the world. Every body. This shit won't work if we start gettin' exclusive. Where you think you're at, young man, the country club? We can't blackball this man 'cause he's white. That would be discrimination."

There was some light laughter in the crowd, and Aziz put his hand on the younger man's shoulder.

"Be cool, brother," he told him softly, almost in a whisper. "We have the cards now. We are almost there. We are taking control of what's ours, and those that want to help us, we want their help."

The young man finally nodded, tight-lipped, and walked back to his friends.

Rasheed Aziz didn't say a word to Walker, just gave him a quick glance before he introduced the foreman who would direct what he called "our labor of love, our monument to our forebears, those who suffered and died in slavery and anonymity, whom we now validate."

They prayed, and then they went to work.

Walker would get up, Tuesday through Saturday, and put in two or three hours of manual labor, mostly hauling and hammering. Sunday and Monday, his days off, he would work an eight-hour day or more.

At first, he was often tempted to give up, to go back to his falling-down house, pack up his scant belongings, and go back to River Road. Certainly, no one, black or white, was encouraging him to stay. Big Walker and Dottie seemed near tears over it, his old friends either disappeared or tried "to talk some sense" into him. It was a good day when the residents of Cottondale merely ignored him.

"Buddy," Glen Murphy had said when he'd tried to get Walker to come to the club for a round of golf on an unusually warm late-October day, "when you come back to Big Walker and Dottie's, there'll be two parades: one to bid you good riddance from Cottondale and one to welcome you home."

But it started to seem less and less like home to Walker. Everything was too big. There was too much.

And things were happening.

The second week after he volunteered, he was taking Mac and Ginger to school after their night with him. He'd already dropped Mac off and was heading for the junior high when his daughter reached over, squeezed his hand, and said, out of nowhere, "We're really proud of you, Dad." It was a shock. He looked at her and thought he saw something there he'd been hoping for: a little bit of Mattie Gray Fann. He realized that there was probably more mutual pride between him and his children than there ever had been, and it meant more to him than money or power ever had.

He had felt little guilt over his parents, even if Big Walker did have to sell the paper, but he would lie awake nights worrying about his children, who had been reduced from two parents to about half of one, by his reckoning.

He wondered how, on River Road, they had developed so much character.

Then, the week after, a young white woman was waiting at eight one morning with the rest of the laborers. She was the daughter of Jim and Kerri Beard, people Walker knew from high school. She was going to the community college and wanted to help. The next day, she brought a friend, a boy who seemed uneasy but was big and strong and knew bricklaying.

There were even reports that a convenience-store chain and a shoe-repair shop were going to relocate on the square.

Perhaps the biggest thing that happened, though, was Rasheed Aziz. The fire seemed to have changed Rasheed, to have burned away something inside him and left room for new growth there, too.

At first, he'd nod to Walker, then say hello. One week in late October, he said a whole sentence, not sarcastic or hateful, just one human being talking to another.

"It looks like we might make it," he had said, standing next to Walker and looking up at men on scaffolds laboring over new windows. The sun caught his hair, and Walker could see the gray and the wrinkles. Rasheed Aziz hadn't just gotten small; he'd gotten old.

Walker had been too shocked to respond to this kindness, and then the lawyer was gone.

A week before Thanksgiving, Aziz did something even more startling.

On Monday, at the end of the work day, he walked up to his old teammate and suggested they have a beer together.

"Sure," Walker told him, then asked hesitantly, "You can drink beer?"

Aziz looked at him, slightly amused. "If you can have lapsed Baptists and lapsed Catholics, I demand the right to be an occasionally lapsed Muslim."

By this time, Walker had become, if not beloved, at least accepted by his neighbors, and it wasn't uncommon to see him in one of the stores, or in conversation with those who lived nearby. He'd even raked some leaves and cleaned gutters for Mrs. Hardy next door. But he had stayed away from the hardscrabble bars, where men with red-and-yellow eyes sometimes vented a month's rage in one slash of a knife blade.

With Rasheed, though, he felt safe. They walked inside a combination grocery and pool hall two blocks east of the Old Market. People turned to watch, out of curiosity. The only whites who ever entered The Billy Club were lost tourists and salesmen, who usually were back outside as soon as their eyes adjusted to the darkness.

They sat on two old brown stools. Rasheed turned to greet two friends and watch a game of nine-ball. Everyone went back to what he was doing before.

They talked a little bit, mostly about R.J. Rasheed said Philly had heard from him two days earlier. He was back in a recovery program, going to Cocaine Anonymous, and working for his father-in-law.

"What about his wife?" Walker asked.

Rasheed shook his head.

"She's passed the test," he said.

"What test?"

"The AIDS test, man. HIV positive. She won't have to worry about getting old or fat, either one. That's why none of 'em came to the funeral. Just figured it would be grief on grief, I guess." Rasheed sighed and put a cold Budweiser to his forehead.

In the stillness, with nothing breaking the peace except old men's murmurs and the click of ball against ball, Walker thought about how some people on the hill supposedly thought the Fanns were unlucky, cursed.

"How about R.J.?" he asked at last.

"I don't think so, although he didn't say. It's probably something she picked up after she left him."

"I don't guess we'll ever see R.J. back here again," Walker said. "I don't see how he could bear it."

Rasheed Aziz gave him a long look.

"Sometime," he said, "I'll tell you a sad, sad story."

And then he finished his beer and left, Walker right behind him.

"Sometime" came two weeks later, on a Monday night when Mac and Ginger were staying over.

Nowadays, they stayed from Saturday morning until Tuesday morning. It almost worried Big Walker and Dottie to death that they sometimes were alone in the old house on Saturday nights, but this was what the children wanted. Sometimes, their grandparents would come over and stay; sometimes Mrs. Hardy would keep them. Sometimes, Walker would take them with him on Saturdays to Raleigh, where they would take in a movie and then stay with a woman who worked in the Lifestyles department and had weekends off, and who would occasionally make dinner for Walker.

More and more of their clothes and other belongings were finding their way to the house at Third and Adams. They even joined the small but growing group of whites helping to rebuild the Old Market.

On this Monday, they were listening to music. Walker's rule was that they'd listen to one of Mac's or Ginger's tapes, then one of his, on the old tape deck. They were playing Scrabble in front of the fire.

Shortly after ten o'clock, over the sounds of Fleetwood Mac, there was a knock at the front door.

When Walker answered, it was Rasheed Aziz.

"We have to talk" was all he said. Walker told Mac and Ginger he'd be back soon.

Oak leaves made scratching noises as they tumbled down the street in front of them. Rasheed had a fifth of Jim Beam. He took a swallow; he'd already emptied about one-third of the bottle. He handed it to Walker, who took a deep draft.

"I am going to tell you something," he said. "It is something that you must never ever tell another living soul. I don't know why I am telling you, except that I am getting drunk and I have to tell someone. Maybe it's because I care so little about what you think."

Walker thought to himself that, if drink brought out the true nature of people, the Rasheed Aziz who talked the talk of the day laborers was the contrivance of a black man straining to stay true to himself and his old neighborhood. One on one, and drunk, Rasheed Aziz enunciated clearly and spoke with a purity of grammar that would have made any English teacher proud.

"Go on," Walker said.

So Aziz told him about Raymond Justus.

He talked about how R.J. had always been his friend and idol, about how it hurt him to see how badly it went over the years, how guilty he felt that everything seemed to fall into place in his world while everything turned to dust in R.J.'s.

"You know," he said, passing the bottle back to Walker, "Raymond Justus was just as smart as anybody I ever knew, even if he didn't make all As in school. And he was twice as principled. He had a kind of inner core to him that you just couldn't crack. Whatever happened to him when he went down to Southeastern to play football, it changed him. It hurt him."

They were stopped by an old man wearing someone's hand-me-down jacket with the zipper stuck halfway up. Rasheed gave the man five dollars. Walker couldn't swear it wasn't the same old man who passed him the night of the fire. He shivered as a cold wind from the north hit them head on.

Aziz told Walker how he had envisioned the two of them leading Cottondale back.

"R.J. didn't say much about it; that wasn't him. I'd run my mouth for half an hour about how we were going to show those white crackers who really ran Cottondale—no offense; that's just how it was—and R.J. would just sit there, staring off into space. But he wanted it, no doubt about that. He wouldn't have come to you if he hadn't. R.J. didn't come to anybody asking for anything. You know that."

Walker nodded.

The day of the election, Aziz went on, R.J. had come by to see him, in the afternoon.

"He was upset, which wasn't like R.J. at all. And you know I was upset. So mad I couldn't see straight. And we got to talking."

Rasheed Aziz lowered his voice a little, even though there was no one else on the street. They were standing at the corner of Third and Main, with the Old Market, bracketed by scaffolds, in front of them.

"I said it would serve 'em all right if somebody just burned the place down. If the white folks are going to do this to us, then let's make sure nobody can have it. We'll leave a monument of scorched earth."

Aziz took another drink and passed the bottle. He lowered himself down to street level, and Walker did the same.

"I know it doesn't make any sense, man. I know what you're thinking: Dumb niggers burn their own damn side of town down. But you get so you have to do something, you want to just lash out.

"But I was just talking, the way I do sometimes. And we talk about how it wouldn't take anything but a couple of gallons of gasoline. And I told him about how I bet a ten-year-old boy could pick one of the locks on the door there, and how easy it would be to get that old firetrap going."

Aziz sighed.

"At some point, R.J. just looks at me, shrugs, and says, 'Well, let's do it, then.' Hell, I was for it. We agreed that we were going to meet at midnight there under the eaves. He said he'd bring the gasoline.

"But I didn't go. I got to thinking about it all, and I convinced myself that we were just yapping, that we were drunk and we'd both get up and laugh about it in the morning. But I knew that wasn't so. I knew that Raymond Justus never said a thing in his life that he didn't mean.

"When I heard those sirens, I was already half asleep, but I knew what they were. Didn't even have to think about it. R.J. had done it."

"And you feel guilty because you talked him into it or because you didn't help him?" Walker asks quietly.

"Both. It seems to me sometimes that it is going to take me all my sorry life to walk the walk. Sometimes, it seems like I am never going to get there, that all I'm good for is fucking up the people I care about."

Walker was quiet for a couple of seconds. Then he took a leap.

"Like the other fire?"

Aziz stared at him and said nothing.

"The one in ninth-grade shop."

Aziz laughed, short and harsh.

"My God, I forgot all about that," he said. "Yeah. I talked him into that one, too. Except that one didn't cause anybody any trouble except that cracker-ass peckerwood Purvis Freeman.

"You know, when I'd be busting on you back then, he'd kind of defend you, like 'Oh, he ain't so bad. Leave him alone.'

"And one day I asked him what the hell he was doing defending some white boy that took his position away from him. And he just looked at me and said, 'Dexter, he knows about the fire. He didn't tell.' And that's all he ever said about it. Didn't cut much ice with me, but R.J. thought you were O.K., and that was something."

By now, they had almost emptied the fifth. Walker was giddy. He knew he shouldn't feel that way, but it was good to know that there was one person in the world at least that he could tell about the Old Market fire, about that second car that someone thought he recalled seeing parked in the downtown area that night but couldn't begin to identify.

He had found somebody as guilty as he was.

"How would you have felt," he began, "if you had helped him?"

Now it is Wednesday, the first day of winter. Christmas is Sunday. Walker has taken time off to buy presents; with his lack of seniority, he will have to work the police beat Christmas Eve and the day itself. He and his children spent Tuesday shopping in Raleigh. This evening, they will have dinner at Big Walker and Dottie's.

Ginger and Mac are still sleeping inside. They stay here more than they do on River Road now. His parents miss them, all three of them, but Walker and Big Walker can't yet be in the same room for long before the lost *Standard* slips into the conversation like a cockroach and ruins it.

Walker steps out into the yard and looks up Third Street. The Old Museum appears almost finished, although it will take much of the spring to make it presentable inside. A black artist who left Cottondale after high school and then came back ten years later has contributed several paintings depicting the slave auctions. They are building up a small library on the African-American experience. From farms and antique sales, they are starting to gather examples of the kind of tools the slaves used. A large map, covering half of one wall on the second floor, will show where the slaves came from, where they landed.

There will be, in one second-floor room, photographs and narrative on the Cottondale Massacre.

Two white families, old River Road stock, have donated photographs from just before and after the Civil War, perhaps the only ones in thirty miles showing African-Americans of that era. A federal grant looks likely; a state grant is possible. There is hope for a summer opening. Rasheed Aziz thinks he can persuade the nation's poet laureate, an African-American woman, to come.

Much of River Road has turned its back on the project, but some of it has not. There is a new coalition, St. Andrews–Cottondale Cooperative (SACC) to seek political and social answers to the problems in the bottom. When some of the black community showed a reluctance to work with the several dozen whites, Rasheed Aziz told them, "We are almost half of St. Andrews. Black folks and a few good white folks are the majority. We can move mountains instead of cursing them."

Walker looks to his right, to the south. A car passes; Walker waves at two men who have been working with him on the rebuilding. They wave back. One of them even smiles.

A dot of red catches his eye from two blocks away. There must be a thousand red cars in Cottondale, he thinks to himself, but by the time it's half a block away, he sees that this one is driven by Raymond Justus.

The car looks as if it has suffered with R.J. It is dented; it is rusting near the back bumper. The muffler hangs low, giving one last rumble as R.J. glides to a stop, pulls up the emergency brake and eases out.

He seems to have aged five years since Walker last saw him. He moves like a man wrestling with arthritis and middle age. It is hard for Walker to believe that they raced down this same street just a season ago.

He doesn't notice Sonya, who must have been slouched down in the front seat, until he sees the passenger-side door open. She has the look of a child who would rather be doing anything than riding around this hick southern town with her father.

Walker and R.J. stand for a moment, three feet apart, not sure how it all works now. They start to shake hands, then hug awkwardly, Walker spilling part of his coffee on the sidewalk.

"I didn't know if I'd ever see you around here again," he says.

"I didn't think you would."

R.J. introduces him to Sonya, who is now eleven. The three of them hear a door slam; Mac is standing on the porch, wiping the sleep from his eyes.

Walker takes them both inside, where he gets a fire and more coffee going. Sonya is persuaded to go into the next room to watch television with his children.

R.J. is only visiting. He says he wanted to show Sonya where he came from, and to give Philly a chance to see her granddaughter again.

"We might come back," he tells Walker, "someday."

Janette is already starting to show signs of drifting over the gray line between HIV positive and AIDS. R.J. figures she must have contracted it not long after she went back North; he tests negative. He is helping her parents take care of her and Sonya.

"It isn't a good time," R.J. says. "On top of everything else, she's still on crack. I thought this year would kill me for sure, but it looks like not." He shakes his head.

He says he believes all the disaster around him has helped him stay straight.

"It's funny. All the experts say that stress is what brings on the relapse, and losing Carneal is sure what did it. I will never get over that. But I've got to stay right for her," and he nods toward Sonya. "She gives me the strength to stay right."

Walker looks at Raymond Justus's face and realizes that the scars are part of what make him look so much older. Neither of the men broaches the subject that binds and separates them, until Walker blurts out, "I'm sorry, R.J."

Raymond Justus looks away.

"Who can ever figure out what's going to happen?" he says finally. "If you thought about it, you'd just go hide under the bed and do nothing, I expect."

And that's all either of them says about it.

Soon, there is little else to say, and R.J. tells Sonya to get her jacket; they have to leave. He tells Walker to go see Philly, that she wants to see him. Walker says he will, but he isn't sure.

On the way out, R.J.'s daughter looks up the street and asks her father about the building they seem to be constructing in the middle of the street two blocks ahead.

"I'll tell you about that building sometime," he says. He turns to wink at Walker, but he can't pull it off; he has to look away.

Walker stands and watches as the old red car turns left onto Adams and disappears around the corner of the house. He remembers, too late, to wave.

He turns to go back inside. Oak leaves scrabble past him on the sidewalk, headed south. For an instant, he imagines a new century and a different world, one in which he and Raymond Justus can sit and rock on a summertime screened porch, sipping beer and murmuring the murmurs of men in the gray neutrality of old age, comparing their scars.

Now and then they will smile about something or other, and shake their heads.